PRAISE FOR SEISHI YOKOMIZO'S MYSTERIES

'Readers will delight in the blind turns, red herrings and dubious alibis... Ingenious and compelling'   *ECONOMIST*

'At once familiar and tantalisingly strange... It's an absolute pleasure to see his work translated at last in these beautifully produced English editions'   *SUNDAY TIMES*

'The perfect read for this time of year. Short and compelling, it will appeal to fans of Agatha Christie looking for a new case to break'   *IRISH TIMES*

'This is Golden Age crime at its best, complete with red herrings, blind alleys and twists and turns galore... A testament to the power of the simple murder mystery and its enduring appeal'   *SPECTATOR*

'The diabolically twisted plotting is top-notch'   *NEW YORK TIMES*

'A stellar whodunit set in 1940s Japan... The solution is a perfect match for the baffling puzzle. Fair-play fans will hope for more translations of this master storyteller'   *PUBLISHERS WEEKLY*, STARRED REVIEW

'With a reputation in Japan to rival Agatha Christie's, the master of ingenious plotting is finally on the case for anglophone readers'   *GUARDIAN*

'A delightfully entertaining locked room murder mystery... An ideal book to curl up with on a winter's night'   *NB MAGAZINE*

'Never anything less than fun from beginning to end... Truly engrossing'
BOOKS AND BAO

'A classic murder mystery... Comparisons with Holmes are justified, both in the character of Kindaichi and Yokomizo's approach to storytelling—mixing clues, red herrings and fascinating social insight before drawing back the curtain to reveal the truth'
JAPAN TIMES

'The perfect gift for any fan of classic crime fiction or locked room mysteries'
MRS PEABODY INVESTIGATES

SEISHI YOKOMIZO (1902–81) was one of Japan's most famous and best-loved mystery writers. He was born in Kobe and spent his childhood reading detective stories, before beginning to write stories of his own, the first of which was published in 1921. He went on to become an extremely prolific and popular author, best known for his Kosuke Kindaichi series, which ran to 77 books, many of which were adapted for stage and television in Japan. *The Honjin Murders*, *The Inugami Curse*, *The Village of Eight Graves*, *Death on Gokumon Island* and *The Devil's Flute Murders* are also available from Pushkin Vertigo.

BRYAN KARETNYK is a translator of Japanese and Russian literature. His recent translations for Pushkin Press include Seishi Yokomizo's *The Village of Eight Graves*, Fūtarō Yamada's *The Meiji Guillotine Murders* and Ryūnosuke Akutagawa's *Murder in the Age of Enlightenment*.

THE LITTLE SPARROW MURDERS

PUSHKIN
VERTIGO

Seishi Yokomizo

Translated from the Japanese by Bryan Karetnyk

Pushkin Press
Somerset House, Strand
London WC2R 1LA

AKUMA NO TEMARIUTA

Original text © Seishi Yokomizo 1971, 1996
English translation © Bryan Karetnyk 2024

First published in Japan in 1971 by KADOKAWA CORPORATION, Tokyo.
English translation rights arranged with KADOKAWA
CORPORATION, Tokyo through
JAPAN UNI AGENCY, INC., Tokyo.
First published by Pushkin Press in 2024

1 3 5 7 9 8 6 4 2

ISBN 13: 978-1-78227-887-0

Map hand-drawn by Neil Gower
Designed and typeset by Tetragon, London
Printed and bound in the United Kingdom by Clays Ltd, Elcograf S.p.A.

www.pushkinpress.com

CONTENTS

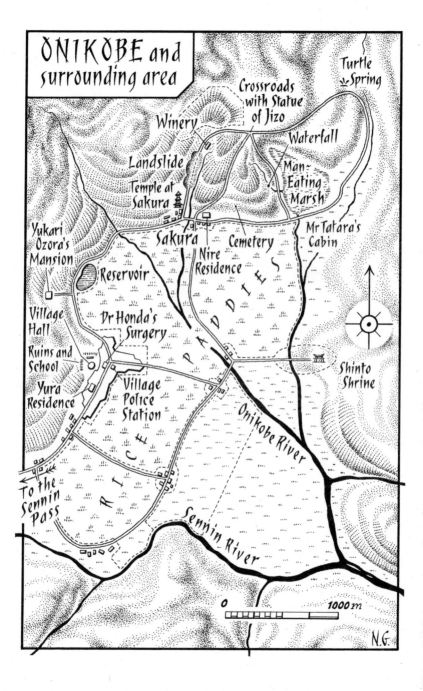

LIST OF CHARACTERS

THE YURA FAMILY

Ioko YURA	the matriarch of the family
Utaro YURA	her son
Atsuko YURA	the wife of Utaro
Toshio YURA	their son
Yasuko YURA	their daughter
Eiko YURA	Toshio's wife

THE NIRE FAMILY

Jinpei NIRE	the former head of the family, now deceased
Kahei NIRE	Jinpei's son and the current head of the family
Naohei NIRE	his elder son
Shohei NIRE	his younger son
Fumiko NIRE	his youngest child, daughter
Michiko NIRE	Naohei's wife
Sakie NIRE	Kahei's sister

THE AOIKE FAMILY

Rika AOIKE	a friend of Inspector Isokawa's
Genjiro AOIKE	her late husband, also known as Shiro AOYAGI

Kanao AOIKE	their eldest son
Satoko AOIKE	their daughter
O-Miki	their maid

THE TATARA FAMILY

| Hoan TATARA | the village chieftain |
| O-Rin | his fifth wife |

THE BESSHO FAMILY

Ryota BESSHO	the head of the family
Harue BESSHO	his daughter
Chieko BESSHO	Harue's daughter, also known as Yukari OZORA
Tatsuzo BESSHO	Harue's older brother
Goro BESSHO	Tatsuzo's son

OTHER CHARACTERS

Ikuzo ONDA	a travelling salesman
Koreya KUSAKABE	Yukari's manager
O-Ito	the owner of the Izutsu Inn

Kosuke KINDAICHI
Inspector ISOKAWA
Deputy Inspector TACHIBANA

Prologue

An acquaintance of mine publishes a little magazine called *Folk Traditions*. It's an altogether modest affair: only sixty-four pages in octavo with a tiny circulation limited to subscribers. Nevertheless, it makes for some interesting reading.

As the title suggests, the magazine is devoted to folklore and local customs collected from all over Japan. With the exception of a few well-known writers, the contributors are mostly ordinary members of the public who have sent in an article to the magazine. So, even if the writing can be somewhat naive at times, the articles, owing to their novelty and curiosity, are full of genuine interest, and you can learn a thing or two from them as well.

I collect copies of this publication, and, whenever I'm bored and have some spare time, I enjoy taking them out and flicking through their pages. Recently, I came across one particularly interesting article that had previously escaped my attention. Published in the September 1953 issue and titled "On One of Onikobe's *Temari* Songs", it was a study of a practically forgotten example of the genre. The article was signed by a certain Hoan Tatara, but the magazine does not make clear who exactly this man was. Perhaps he was one of those people who just happened to write to the editor.

Since this *temari* song plays such a crucial role in the dreadful story that I am, with Kosuke Kindaichi's permission, about to unfold, I believe the reader would benefit from seeing a reproduction of Mr Tatara's offering, before I add a few reflections of my own.

A *Temari* Song of Onikobe Village

In the trees in the garden behind our house,
Three little sparrows came to stay.
The first little birdie said to me:
In the faraway land where I come from,
Many are the pleasures of the shogun's man—
Women, wine and hunting all day long,
But most of all, he likes the women,
Oh yes, it's the women he likes.
A good little woman was the cooper's girl,
A pretty little thing, but she liked a drink,
All day long, she would guzzle it down,
She would measure by the barrel and drink through a funnel,
But before she'd had her fill, she was sent away,
They were all of them sent away...

The second little birdie said to me:
In the faraway land where I come from,
Many are the pleasures of the shogun's man—
Women, wine and hunting all day long,
But most of all, he likes the women,
Oh yes, it's the women he likes.
A good little woman was the weigher's girl,
A very pretty thing, but rather mean,
She lived for money, weighing up her coins
Both great and small, all day and night,
But before she'd time to rest, she was sent away,
They were all of them sent away...

The third little birdie said to me:
In the faraway land where I come from,
Many are the pleasures of the shogun's man—
Women, wine and hunting all day long,
But most of all, he likes the women,
Oh yes, it's the women he likes.
A good little woman was the locksmith's girl,
As pretty as they come, but rather stiff,
Then one fine day her lock did break,
And when a lock breaks, the key won't fit,
And since his key didn't fit, she was sent away,
They were all of them sent away…

The song appears to have had additional verses, too, but these three are all that the author provides.

According to Mr Tatara, *temari* songs—that is, the nursery rhymes that children traditionally sing while bouncing those brightly coloured *temari* balls—are mostly counting songs by nature, but there are also many that are based on wordplay. At any rate, these songs tend to have very little internal consistency and sooner flit from one idea to the next by word association alone. This one from Onikobe, however, seems to be much more consistent. In Mr Tatara's view, this likely stems from the fact that, back in the old days of the shogunate, the farmers of that region liked to use these ditties as an indirect means to criticize the feudal lords who ruled them.

Let's now turn to place the village on the map.

Onikobe is situated right on the border between Hyogo and Okayama prefectures, around seventeen miles from the coast of the Seto Inland Sea. Surrounded on all four sides by mountains, the village is in a valley that's cut off from all major transport networks. Looking at its position and the few roads leading in and out of the village, one would think that Onikobe ought to have been incorporated into Hyogo Prefecture, but, oddly enough, probably because of its historical ties, it now finds itself in Okayama Prefecture.

This peculiar setting has forever caused problems, and nowhere more so than in the case of criminal investigations. Because of its geography, the local Okayama prefectural police treat the village as an unwanted stepchild, while the police in Hyogo, despite its better transport links, have a distinct tendency to turn a blind eye to anything going on there, since it is outside their jurisdiction. It will come as no surprise to learn that this has a significant bearing on the case that I am about to impart.

Historically, this region was the domain of a certain Ito, the Intendant of Shinano. Now, if you were to look at the historical records for the first year of the Meiji era, you would see in the ledgers for Ito a paltry fief of only 10,343 *koku*. His domicile is listed as Onikobe, so he must have lived there, although the size of his fief was the bare minimum to qualify for the rank of daimyo—possibly explaining why he is recorded as having had a "residence" rather than a "palace" or a "castle".

It stands to reason, then, that "the shogun's man" mentioned in the song was one of Ito's relatives, and indeed, according to Mr Tatara's research, there was in the eighteenth century a certain feudal lord by the name of Sukeyuki Ito, a tyrant of great lust and depravity who would tour his fiefdom on the pretext of hunting and, whenever he came across a great beauty, be she a maiden or a married woman, would callously abduct her and force her to attend his bedchamber. Then, once he had wearied of her pleasures, he would kill her for the most trifling of misdemeanours. Apparently, this Sukeyuki died suddenly, around the end of the Tenmei era, probably having been poisoned by one of his entourage.

Consequently, Mr Tatara believes that the refrain at the end of each verse—"They were all of them sent away"—is in fact a euphemism for the killing of those women. As for the professions listed in the song, these likely refer to the common people, who under the laws of the time were not permitted to have family names and distinguished themselves by their trades alone. Though these people officially received the right to bear surnames later, in the Meiji era, there are still those old-fashioned types who call each other by their family's historical professions even today.

Such is the background to this section of the Onikobe *temari* song, as it was presented in the magazine *Folk Traditions*. Now, with this knowledge, it's time to lift the curtain on the dreadful murders of which those three little sparrows told.

PART I

What the First Little Sparrow Said

A Con Artist in the Village

It was late July, in 1955, when Kosuke Kindaichi, accompanied by a letter of introduction from Inspector Isokawa, took a rickshaw over the Sennin Pass—astonishingly, this mode of transport was still in use in those parts—and set foot for the very first time in the village of Onikobe. Of course, never in his wildest dreams could he have known about the *temari* song.

He had come to the village not because a case awaited him there—after all, he is a human being, too, and does not always go chasing after cases—but rather because, like anybody else, there are times when he longs for some peace and quiet and a chance to rest his body and mind.

He had pondered where to go for a retreat for some time, until eventually he alighted on the idea of somewhere in Okayama Prefecture. He'd had a connection to the area ever since the Honjin Murder Case, one that had only grown with other cases such as those on Gokumon Island and in the Village of Eight Graves—and at one point or another, he seemed to have developed a fondness for the local people and their ways. He especially liked this welcoming region for the warmth shown to him by its inhabitants.

And so, having made up his mind, and with the freedom that comes from being a bachelor, one fine day he slung his travelling bag over his shoulder and headed out west from Tokyo.

His first port of call was Inspector Isokawa at the prefectural police headquarters in Okayama.

As ever, Kindaichi hadn't sent a letter or even a postcard in advance, so when Inspector Isokawa saw him sitting in the spartan waiting area, he could scarcely believe his eyes.

"To what do I owe the pleasure, Kindaichi? When did you get here?"

So delighted was the detective inspector to see his old friend that he immediately bombarded him with questions.

"I've only just arrived," the famous detective replied. "I'm so tired, though. For some reason, I never seem to be able to sleep on trains."

He yawned extravagantly as he said this, as if to show the inspector that he really hadn't managed to get any sleep on the overnight train.

"You've just arrived, eh? Are you here on a case?"

"Oh, come, Inspector! You take one look at me and think I must be on a case?... Couldn't I just have wanted to pay an old friend a visit after all this time?"

"That'll be the day!" said the inspector, laughing.

"No, I really mean it!"

"Well, then, I'm honoured."

The inspector had aged considerably since they last met, but his whole face beamed as he stroked his chin with the palm of his hand.

The hair on his closely cropped head was now almost completely white, and it was so thin that you could see his dark scalp beneath it. His eyebrows had turned white, too, and his forehead had grown wrinkled; yet his robust physique still projected a tough fearlessness, and the ruddy bronze tan of his skin contrasted pleasingly with this dazzlingly white hair. For decades, day in, day out, he had been a police detective—and in recent years, he had also become a widower.

"So then, Kindaichi, what are your plans?"

"Well, that's just it, Inspector…"

Kindaichi told his old friend that he was looking for a quiet spot where he could go and rest for a month without being troubled by anyone or anything.

"Do you happen to know any nice spots around here? Somewhere remote. You know, a little village up in the mountains perhaps, totally cut off from the outside world?"

"Hmm, I'm sure I can think of somewhere…"

Inspector Isokawa looked at his friend, who, as usual, appeared dishevelled in his tired white-and-indigo kimono, which he wore with a pair of threadbare summer hakama.

"You never change, do you?" the inspector laughed, a warm crease forming in the corner of his eye. "Very well, let's leave that discussion for this evening. Seeing as you're so tired, I'll give you the address of a nice inn where you can take a bath and rest until then. I'll come and meet you there after work."

That evening, after they'd enjoyed a couple of beers together, Inspector Isokawa extracted a letter from the breast of his yukata.

"I have, as per your request, brought you a letter of introduction. Though I feel duty-bound to warn you: it's impossible to cut yourself off entirely from the outside world. The winds of the world blow even in this little village."

On the envelope was written:

Rika Aoike, Onikobe Village

"Who is this Rika Aoike?" asked Kosuke Kindaichi. "It looks like a woman's name…"

"Yes, indeed. And the lady's had her fair share of sorrows, I'm afraid to say," said the inspector, looking strangely moved as he stroked his chin. "Her husband was murdered, and to this day they don't know who did it."

Holding the letter in his hand, Kosuke Kindaichi fixed the other man with a serious look.

"No, this will never do, Inspector! As I told you just this afternoon, I'm looking for somewhere to rest, a place where nothing and no one will—"

"I know, I know!" said Inspector Isokawa, interrupting the detective with a dismissive wave of the hand. "You may rest assured, though: the murder took place more than twenty years ago. It didn't happen just yesterday! All I'm saying is that finding somewhere that's *entirely* cut off from the world is a bit of an impossible task nowadays. Twenty-odd years ago, Onikobe was far more isolated than it is today. But even then, there was a murder that's remained unsolved."

Inspector Isokawa was keen for Kosuke Kindaichi to hear the story, but, given the latter's wish to get away from all that sort of thing, he was reluctant to broach the subject any further with him. Kindaichi, however, reasoned that, if he was going to be a guest of this Rika Aoike, it would be no bad thing to know a little about her circumstances. Quite the opposite, in fact: it was vital that he know, so he raised his eyes from the letter lying in his lap.

"It sounds rather interesting," he said with a broad smile, intended to encourage the inspector to divulge more of the tale.

"Well, yes, you could say that…" the other said, seeming a little tentative. In his eyes, there was the look of a child pleading for something. "Would you care to hear the story?"

"By all means! I could never resist the chance to hear about an unsolved case from twenty years ago," Kindaichi said with a laugh. "It's a terrible habit of mine."

"Very well, then. But there's something you should know first…"

Touched by his friend's show of consideration, Inspector Isokawa suddenly relaxed and began to talk with great enthusiasm.

"As you know only too well, Kindaichi, in any village, no matter where you go, there's always one family that wields power, just as there's always a dangerous rival family."

"You're not wrong there, Inspector. So, what you're saying is that there are two powerful families in the village of Onikobe?" asked Kindaichi, coaxing him on.

"Exactly!" cried the inspector, fidgeting in his chair. "Or rather, let's say that there *were* two powerful families there. Because, you see, the balance of power in Onikobe shifted in more recent years. It all started back in 1932, the year after Japan invaded Manchuria. I need hardly remind you, Kindaichi, that, at the time, our farming villages were suffering in the depths of economic depression."

"Yes, I remember… If I'm not mistaken, it was that very fact, in large part, that led to the Mukden Incident, which began it all."

"Quite so… At any rate, back in those days, the Yuras and the Nires were the two families that wielded power in Onikobe. There was also the Tatara family, whose members had held the title of village chieftain since the days of the shogun and ought to have been the most powerful there; however, the leader at the time, and likewise his predecessor, had both given themselves over to debauchery, and so the house had fallen into ruin. It was then that the Yuras and the Nires seized power. And so, everyone in the village was forced to declare their support for one family or the other. Neutrality was not permitted."

"It sounds a lot like the situation with the Americans and the Soviets these days."

"Exactly! But, you see, the Yuras had for a long time been the richer of the two families because they owned a lot of farming land—not just in Onikobe, but in the surrounding areas, too. And, to think, so much of that land fell into their hands because of the profligacy of those two generations of the Tatara family! The Nire family, which was an emerging power at the time, owned a lot of land too, but theirs was mainly in the mountains. But back in those days, the mountains weren't profitable at all, and the simple fact of having land there wasn't enough to allow them to compete with the Yuras. Yet the head of the family, a certain Jinpei Nire, was a man of great foresight, and at some point in the mid-twenties he began cultivating grapes on his mountains—well, I call them mountains, but I suppose they're more like hills. In any case, by the early thirties the grapes had begun to give a crop, and that's how the Nire family became the richest and most powerful in the village."

"And they still grow these grapes?"

"Of course! They've become Onikobe's greatest resource."

"I see. Then the Nires must still be the most powerful, seeing as they're the source of the village's prosperity?"

"That's right, yes… He was a remarkable man, this Jinpei Nire. He realized that the basin where Onikobe is situated is practically identical in terms of climate, humidity and hours of sunlight to the Koshu Basin, which is renowned as a grape-producing area. He checked everything with the greatest care. Then, he set to work in the mid-twenties and, a couple of years later, his efforts paid off. Well, you know how people are. It's in their nature to flock to success. So old Jinpei found himself surrounded by people fawning over him, and, before he knew it, he'd been elevated to the level of 'the boss'. You can imagine how it was: he let it all go to his head."

"I see… So, when that happened, I suppose the Yuras were none too pleased by their reduced status and decided they'd have to do something about it?"

"A very good deduction, Kindaichi! That's exactly what happened. The Yura family wanted to retaliate, and that's how this terrible tragedy all began… The head of the House of Yura was a man called Utaro, and he must have been around forty at the time. In the eyes of old Jinpei, however, he was still a young whippersnapper—and besides, he'd been spoilt since childhood and knew little of the world. To make matters worse, he was desperate not to be outdone by the old man. That's when they were taken advantage of…"

"Taken advantage of by whom?"

"By a con artist… A trickster who went round gulling those poor people in the villages. And it wasn't just the Yura family that was thrown into disarray by this, but the whole of Onikobe."

"A con artist?… Fancy that!"

Kosuke Kindaichi was astonished to see the story take such a bizarre turn.

"I know… But he ended up killing a man before absconding and plunging the whole village into turmoil." Inspector Isokawa's face clouded over. "He called himself Ikuzo Onda, but of course that probably wasn't his real name. He turned up on Utaro's doorstep towards the end of 1931, bearing a letter of introduction from somebody. He was a handsome fellow of around thirty-five, and he wore a pair of gold-rimmed spectacles and had a little moustache. Well, he said he'd come to bring a new sideline business to the village, and that business was making tinsel. You know, for Christmas trees?… Obviously, it was intended for export."

"Yes, I see… Obviously…"

As the story was no longer merely about a power struggle in the village, Kosuke Kindaichi's interest had been piqued all of a sudden. Without realizing it himself, he leant in, rapt with interest, while the inspector really got into his stride.

"Anyway, Utaro thought the pitch sounded interesting, and so he decided to go for it. He planned to give the extra work to the impoverished farmers and benefit from their obligation of gratitude to him. When the farmers heard about all this, they jumped at the chance. It all seemed simple enough: Onda would lease the machines—they were quite simple affairs—to those farmers who wanted them, and also supply them with the raw materials. Then, the farmers would make the tinsel, and Onda would buy it back from them at a reasonable price. Eventually, the farmers would have enough to buy the machines outright. Such was the arrangement. And while the farmers were saving up the means with which to buy the machines, the rent on them would be covered by Utaro. It all seemed to go well at first. The farmers, who had profited from this unexpected source of income, were grateful to Utaro, who himself seemed to grow in prestige. After about a year, by the autumn of 1932, most of the farmers had bought their machines outright. But it was around then that one of the farmers began to have suspicions about Onda's methods. This man was called Genjiro, and he was the husband of the woman I've promised to introduce you to, Rika Aoike…"

The Femme Fatale

"Apropos of which, I should tell you a little about the Aoike family," said Inspector Isokawa, taking a long drag of his cigarette. "For generations, they've run a sort of spa resort called the Turtle Spring, which is in a little hamlet just outside Onikobe."

"Ah, so there's an *onsen* there?" asked Kindaichi, leaning forward again out of curiosity.

"Well, I wouldn't exactly call it an *onsen*. The water only ever reaches twenty degrees, so it's really a cold mineral spring. You have to heat up the water in order to bathe in it, but, during their off-season, farmers come from the surrounding areas to take the cure. Those farmers are a strange lot, you know. The rice farmers are the only ones who enjoy any respect, and they have a tendency to look down on anybody even a rung below that. In extreme cases, those who make their living by growing anything other than rice—vegetables, for example—are scorned as 'lower farmers' by the others. Even old Jinpei Nire, who made his fortune growing grapes, wasn't held to be on the same level as Utaro. But to return to the topic in hand…"

Inspector Isokawa gently tapped the ash off his cigarette.

"It was much the same story with the Aoikes and the Turtle Spring. The farmers looked down on them for running a spa resort. The Aoikes' younger son was called Genjiro, and he would have been twenty-eight at the time. In his youth, he'd gone to Kobe and Osaka and travelled around quite a bit, and so he knew something of the world. Then one day in the autumn in 1932, he returned to the village along with his wife and son… or rather, he returned to the Turtle Spring. Apparently, he took one look at what Onda was up to and immediately had his doubts. And not only did he have them, but he voiced them to Jinpei Nire. He told the old man that he thought Onda was a con artist, and, delighted by this, the old man apparently gave him some money to investigate. Jinpei denied it all later, of course. But still, one way or another Genjiro managed to catch Onda by the tail. He went to pay Onda a visit at the village chieftain's cottage, but when Genjiro took him to task for it…"

"… he ended up getting killed?" Kindaichi asked.

"Precisely."

"How exactly was he killed? Strangled? Stabbed?…"

"He was struck down… It was late autumn, so a fire had been laid in the *irori* sunken hearth, and, beside it, there was some firewood and an axe. He was killed with a single blow to the back of the head," said the inspector, frowning. "It was on the 25th of November."

"Were there any witnesses?"

"No. If there had been, they'd have intervened and prevented it."

"So, how was the body discovered?"

"Well, it was like this, you see. Rika knew that her husband had gone to have it out with Onda. In fact, when he left, she'd apparently tried to stop him, saying that it was none of his business. But then an hour went by, and then another, and still her husband hadn't come home. Genjiro had left a little after six o'clock in the evening, but when there was no sign of him by nine, Rika began to worry and went to look for him where Onda was staying."

"And where exactly was he staying?"

"Ah, yes, I haven't told you that, have I? You see, he didn't live in Onikobe. He would come once every month or so and stay for a couple of nights while he was seeing to matters of business before going home again. At first, he stayed with the Yuras, but that became a little cramped, and so, later on, he rented a little cottage on Hoan Tatara's estate."

"The same one whose family has been the village chieftains?"

"The very same. His real name is the very solemn-sounding Kazuyoshi, but he calls himself Hoan and is the sort of man who essentially just suits himself. For two generations, that family had been profligate, and things had already gone downhill, but Hoan still had the house left to him by his father, and that was where he eked out his frugal existence with his fifth wife, O-Rin."

"His *fifth* wife, you say?" said Kindaichi in astonishment.

The inspector had a mischievous look in his eye.

"That's nothing!" he said. "Mr Tatara's in fine fettle even now and has had a succession of other wives since then. I believe he's had eight, all told."

"Well, I never! And you say I'll be able to meet this singularly vigorous man in Onikobe?"

"Yes, he's quite an amusing old boy! He's always done just as he pleased ever since he was a boy... Oh, and there's another extraordinary character you can meet if you go to Onikobe!"

"That being...?"

"I'll leave that surprise for later," said Inspector Isokawa with another mischievous twinkle in his eye. "For now, let's get back to the story. Since her husband still hadn't returned by nine o'clock, Rika decided to find out what was going on at Onda's. That evening, however, there had been a disturbance at the Tatara residence. After an argument, O-Rin had up and left him. Frantic, Mr Tatara had been looking for her everywhere all evening, but she was nowhere to be found. Certain that she'd run off for good,

29

he was drowning his sorrows when Rika arrived. And that was when they went to check at the cottage."

"… and found Genjiro already dead?"

"Yes, exactly. His face was buried in the *irori*…"

"In the *irori*?!…"

Kosuke Kindaichi looked at Inspector Isokawa in astonishment, then suddenly burst out laughing:

"That's a good one, Inspector. You really had me for a moment there!"

"No, you've got it wrong, Kindaichi!" said the inspector, waving his hands. "I'm serious. That's really what happened…"

"All right… So, what you're saying is that the body was difficult to identify?"

"It wasn't impossible to make the identification, but there was considerable damage to the face."

"But you're sure that it was Genjiro?"

"Yes. It wasn't just Rika—his parents as well as his older brother and his wife also identified the body as Genjiro's."

Kosuke Kindaichi felt a growing sense of impatience. He had the distinct impression that Inspector Isokawa was holding something back.

"Were there any signs of a struggle?" he asked.

"No, but it was clear that somebody had turned the place over in a hurry."

"And I presume the murderer was never found?"

"That's right. Ikuzo Onda seemed to disappear off the face of the earth."

"So, what makes you say he was a con artist?"

"Ah, yes, that… It's hard to prove anything, of course, but when you look at it all in retrospect, it's clear that he was one. The farmers were conned into buying this rather expensive machinery, and then the work dried up. At the time, though, you couldn't have said that he was a crook for sure. He paid the workers well enough for the goods they produced. We even found the tinsel concern that he represented. It was based in Kobe, and it folded a short while before the tragedy took place. You see, it had been affected by the Great Depression in America."

"And the company had no idea about Onda's whereabouts either?"

"None whatsoever. The company hadn't even done the proper background checks on him. You know how it is: so long as they receive their guarantee... So, we don't know for certain whether he was a con artist and set out to swindle the villagers to begin with, or whether things really did fail because of events in the United States. Either way, the fact remains that the murder took place shortly afterwards, and this Onda, if that was his real name, simply vanished... It was just after the Mukden Incident, so it was the perfect time to disappear. He could easily have absconded with the money he took from the farmers and fled to China..."

Inspector Isokawa's voice did not betray any particular emotion, but Kosuke Kindaichi knew well what he must have been feeling. It was the regret of an officer of the law who had let a suspect slip through his fingers.

"So, what happened in the village after that?" Kindaichi asked.

"It was Utaro's reputation that suffered most of all. He'd never had much backbone, nor any common sense—so, although he tried to compensate the farmers for part of the money they'd lost, they still resented him. He became a laughing stock in the village. Before long, he sank into a deep depression, and three years later, in 1935, he died."

"You mentioned that the Yuras owned a lot of land. What happened to them after the war?"

"Like so many others, they lost practically everything in the land reforms. Luckily for them, though, these reforms didn't extend to the mountains, and so they were able to hang on to the small area of mountainous farming land they owned. Utaro's widow Atsuko is made of strong stuff, and, after her husband's death, she swallowed her pride and asked old Jinpei Nire to teach her how to begin growing grapes. And so they managed to survive after the war, but the influence they had in the old days is long gone. These days, it's the Nire family that holds the power in Onikobe."

"Is Mr Nire still alive?"

"No, Jinpei died a while back. But his heir, Kahei, is a chip off the old block. When Utaro passed away, there were all kinds of rumours about him and Atsuko. Now he's king of Onikobe."

"You said that Genjiro was the younger son. Did Rika stay on in the village afterwards?"

"Ah, that poor woman… She was pregnant when it all happened. You can imagine the shock it must have been to see her husband killed like that…"

"You mean she had a miscarriage?"

"No, she had the baby, sure enough. But the child, that little girl…"

The inspector grimaced.

"Well, you'll see for yourself if you go… It was a tragedy, of course, but you could also say that Rika was lucky. The elder brother and his wife had no children of their own, so it's Kanao, Rika and Genjiro's son, who's taken over the Turtle Spring. They say he does an awful lot to help his mother."

Kosuke Kindaichi scrutinized his old friend's face.

"Do you visit Onikobe often, Inspector?"

"I occasionally go to take the waters at the Turtle Spring. And Rika keeps in touch. She sends cards at the O-Bon festival and at New Year's, so I'm pretty well abreast of what goes on in the village."

They both fell silent.

"Well, Inspector," said Kosuke Kindaichi after a few moments, "you've certainly piqued my curiosity, but I know you're still hiding an ace up your sleeve. You mentioned that I'd meet another extraordinary character in Onikobe. Who could it be, I wonder?"

"Ah, yes, that…" said the inspector, gazing intently at his friend. Then, with his eyes fixed firmly on Kindaichi's dishevelled hair, he said something strange. "You go to the cinema from time to time, don't you, Kindaichi? And you listen to popular songs on the radio and on television?"

This apparent non sequitur took Kosuke Kindaichi by surprise, so much that he blinked when he heard it.

"Why, yes… now and then… Only, why do you ask?"

"Well, it's like this, you see. While Ikuzo Onda was staying in the village, he was very good to the blacksmith's daughter, Harue Bessho. Only, in 1933 she had a child… a little girl… out of wedlock. The father was clearly this Onda fellow. She would have been stigmatized for giving birth to a bastard child anyway, but since she'd had the child of a con artist and murderer, she incurred the wrath of the villagers, who made her into a pariah. But this Harue was made of strong stuff. She placed the daughter—her name is Chieko—in the care of her father, Ryota, who, together with his wife, officially adopted the girl. And so, having entrusted little Chieko to her parents, Harue left the village and went to Kobe, where she became a waitress or something like that. She soon came back to take Chieko with her to Kobe, but then the

33

pair of them were forced to return to the village late in the war, to live with Harue's parents. Then, in 1948, they left the village a second time. Chieko would have been fifteen at the time. Since then, the girl has grown up to become quite the celebrity."

"A celebrity, you say…?"

"You'll have heard of Yukari Ozora? She's phenomenally popular these days. They say she rakes in several hundred thousand just from a single performance… In films, she always plays the beautiful and mysterious femme fatale…"

Kosuke Kindaichi clenched his fists instinctively.

"And you're saying that she's come back to Onikobe again?"

"Well, last year, she had a beautiful, almost palatial house built for her grandparents… Well, strictly speaking, I should say her parents, since they adopted her… She's due to go back there any day now, so all the newspapers in the prefecture have been making a big fuss over it, needless to say."

And true enough: this was exactly how Kosuke Kindaichi found the village of Onikobe when, after a bone-shaking journey by rickshaw across the Sennin Pass, he arrived there, wearing a crumpled old panama hat, a similarly tired-looking white-and-indigo kimono, and his threadbare summer hakama.

The Turtle Spring

For fourteen days already Kosuke Kindaichi had been resting at the Turtle Spring on the outskirts of Onikobe, and it was now the month of August.

As is often the case in these rural spa resorts, the building itself was a dilapidated two-storey wooden affair, and its dreary appearance was more reminiscent of a boarding house or a hostel than a proper *ryokan* inn. You wouldn't even dream of mentioning it in the same breath as the renowned hot-spring resorts at Hakone and Izu.

People from nearby areas flocked there during the farmers' off-season and even brought provisions so that they could cook for themselves—from pots and pans to rice, salt, miso and soy sauce. They would get together in groups of four or five and lodge together, with the Turtle Spring charging them a pittance for accommodation and use of the bathing facilities.

From time to time, however, the resort would also receive ordinary visitors like Kosuke Kindaichi. For these guests, they had a separate single-storey building, which was a little rustic but looked more or less like a typical *ryokan*. It had a half-dozen guest rooms and a bathing room. This was also where the owner's family lived. There were four of them in all: the proprietress Rika, her son, Kanao, her daughter, Satoko, and the maid, O-Miki. During the busy season, though, another maid would be taken on temporarily.

According to Inspector Isokawa, Rika's husband had been killed in 1932, aged twenty-eight. Given the three-year gap between them, Rika must now have been forty-seven or -eight, but she looked as though she were in her fifties. She didn't carry herself like an old woman, though. On the contrary, despite her slight and delicate-looking frame, she was tall and projected a certain strength.

As it was summer, she wore simple, light clothing, but that isn't to say that she didn't take care over her appearance. Her hair was always neatly combed, and she would never go to see Kosuke Kindaichi without first changing into a kimono. Everything about her, from her refined features to her elegant and sophisticated manners, made one think that she had been a great beauty in her youth.

However, the terrible tragedy that she'd experienced in those days had left its mark. There was a certain darkness about her, and a trace of sadness; she spoke rarely. This must have been why she seemed older than her years.

Her son, Kanao, had piqued Kosuke Kindaichi's interest. He was twenty-five and had attended high school in one of the nearby towns, which was a rarity among the children of the village in those days. He was tall and had once been a pitcher on his high-school baseball team, and, like his mother, he was good-looking, with fine, chiselled features. Besides the family business, he also cultivated several rice paddies and grew grapes on a nearby mountain, all of which had given him a dark tan and strong muscles. He was cheerful and had a lovely, mellow voice, and so you could always hear him singing songs while he worked in the vineyards.

Needless to say, he was popular with the village daughters and enjoyed a reputation as something of a Don Juan—a fact that seemed to give his mother sleepless nights.

Kanao's younger sister Satoko was born in 1933, the year after her father died, and so she would be twenty-two now. However, as she kept herself hidden away in an annex at the far end of the wing where the family lived, Kosuke Kindaichi had yet to set eyes on her.

Then, one evening, as he was returning from a stroll, the detective entered not through the main door as usual, but via the rear gate. Seeing Kindaichi, the young woman, who was in the garden at the time, rushed back to the annex, so he caught only a glimpse of her from behind.

Inspector Isokawa had not dwelt on the subject of the girl, but, having now seen the way she fled from another's gaze, Kindaichi understood that something terrible must have happened after the tragedy, while she was still in her mother's womb, and he wondered what this could have been.

Later that evening, Kindaichi discreetly enquired of the maid O-Miki as she was serving his dinner:

"Earlier on, I came across a young lady in the garden. Would that have been the owner's daughter, Satoko, I wonder?"

"Yes, sir, that's very likely."

"Strictly speaking, I didn't really see her. I just caught a glimpse of her from behind. Does she always live in that annex?"

"Yes, sir," the maid replied hesitantly, as she balanced the tray on her knee.

O-Miki must have been in her late twenties. She had married a farmer in one of the neighbouring villages, but since she had a bad relationship with her mother-in-law, she'd run away and come back to Onikobe. Upon her return to her parents' house, however, she found that her brother would soon be marrying and bringing his wife to live with them, and so, unable to stay there, she had relied on Rika's kindness and been taken on as a live-in maid at the Turtle Spring. Despite Rika's strict discipline, O-Miki still had a natural tendency to talk, but today for some reason she wasn't quite so forthcoming. Perhaps this subject was strictly off-limits.

"But how can the young lady bear being cooped up like that and not let out?"

"Her health is poor, sir," replied O-Miki, still reluctant to say anything.

"What's the matter with her?"

"It's her heart, sir. Even a little walking makes her breathless."

She could well have had a heart murmur—such cases are known to happen when the mother has a severe shock during pregnancy—yet that still didn't explain why she was so afraid of meeting people.

"So, what does she do with herself all day in the annex?"

"She reads, sir," O-Miki said with a strange look on her face. "She likes to read an awful lot."

"She reads, eh? What sort of books does she read?"

An ambiguous smile appeared on her lips.

Kosuke Kindaichi realized that there was no point pursuing this line of enquiry with the maid. Very likely it was of no concern to her what other people read. He decided to change tack, but just as he was trying to think of another question, O-Miki asked him:

"It's very good of you to concern yourself with Satoko's welfare, sir, but perhaps you're finding it a little dull here in the countryside?"

"No, that's precisely what I came for! They do say that dullness extends one's lifespan, do they not?"

"Ah, to be without a care in the world!... How the other half live."

But Kindaichi, of course, was not "the other half". Indeed, if he were, he wouldn't have come to such an out-of-the-way place as this. Thankfully, he just managed to stop himself before saying so.

Realizing that, no matter how much he asked about Satoko, he would get nothing further out of this woman, he gave up.

"By the way," he said, changing the subject, "Yukari Ozora hasn't arrived yet, has she? I hear there's a lot of excitement about her upcoming performance…"

With this question, he had of course intended to ingratiate himself, but O-Miki's face suddenly clouded over.

"Ugh, her!" she said, screwing up her plump little face with its button nose. "I really can't understand why people make such a fuss over a woman like that."

"Have you ever met her?" Kosuke Kindaichi asked with a degree of trepidation.

"A long time ago, when she was evacuated here during the war," she said, scowling. "She was a dark, dirty-looking thing."

"So, you haven't seen her since she became famous?"

"How could I? The woman's never come back! I see her photos in magazines and the like often enough, though. Always showing herself off half-naked… It's shameless, it is!… And to think, she's nothing more than the locksmith's bastard daughter!"

"The locksmith's daughter?!" exclaimed Kosuke Kindaichi. "I'd heard that her mother was the daughter of a blacksmith…"

"Locksmith's a family name of sorts. In these parts, people have always been known by the old 'guild names'—professions their families used to work in. Take me, for example—mine is basket-weaver."

Naturally, at that time, Kosuke Kindaichi attached no particular importance to the name "locksmith" that was attributed to Yukari Ozora's family. But later on, by the time he realized its grave significance, three people were already dead.

"But what do you think, sir?" asked O-Miki.

"Think about what?"

"About women like that, going around half-naked, making a show of themselves…"

"Well, I've no real objection to it. But then, I am a man," Kindaichi laughed.

That he could be so off-handedly in favour of the woman elicited a cry of horror from the maid.

"Oh, you men are all the same," she said. "Even Kanao's crazy about her. He's already kicking up a fuss about throwing a welcoming party for her and organizing some singing contest… Oh, it's just awful! Just awful!"

O-Miki began to clear away the empty plates from Kindaichi's meal.

"If you need anything, sir, just ring the bell," she said, before shuffling out of the room, her shoulders slumped.

Kosuke Kindaichi watched her go in silence. He no longer had the heart to ask her any more questions.

For the moment, Kindaichi was the only guest staying at the Turtle Spring, and so he sprawled out in the tatami room, being lulled to sleep against a backdrop of rolling hills and amber-coloured grapes. With the smell of fruit wafting through the air, he could quite happily give himself over to idleness without being disturbed by anybody.

He hadn't gone there in order to drag up events that had taken place more than two decades ago. Nor did he feel any particular sense of obligation towards Inspector Isokawa. Instead, he contented himself by opening his eyes and ears, little inclined to seek out every last detail of what had become of the Houses of Yura and Nire since the tragedy. Instead, he spent most of his time holed up in his room at the Turtle Spring, occasionally reading a book or organizing his case notes, but mostly dozing all day long. Truly, there were few things he enjoyed more than lazing around idly like a cat. It was for this reason that, during his evening walks, he almost never ventured in the direction of the village. Mostly, he limited himself to the vineyards in the mountains.

Nevertheless, he had met several people since arriving at the Turtle Spring and had even become quite close to one of them in particular. You see, even though the resort had no other guests, the two-storey building did have a recreation room that was open to the public and was used as a place for the young people in the village to get together and it also had a large public bath.

The first person Kosuke Kindaichi came across, other than the proprietors of the Turtle Spring, was Hoan Tatara, whom he met by chance rather than by design. The day after his arrival, he had wanted to try out the more spacious public bath, and that was where he had encountered Mr Tatara.

This bath was connected to the two-storey building by a corridor, but it could also be accessed directly from the garden. It was a generously sized wooden affair topped with a gable roof, and it was divided into two spaces: one for men and the other for women. Stacks of draining baskets littered the changing room, and, while there were mirrors fixed to the walls, the mercury was so patchy that they were practically useless. At the back of the changing room, there was a glass door that led to the plaster-walled washroom, at the far end of which was the enormous bath for men overflowing with hot water. The only thing bobbing there in the water was a single bald head.

Kosuke Kindaichi nodded to the man before plunging into the warm bath. He was intrigued by the look of affectation on the man's face and had an idea that it might be Hoan Tatara.

"Excuse me," said the man, as Kindaichi splashed himself with hot water, "but aren't you the gentleman who arrived with a letter of introduction from Inspector Isokawa?"

"Yes, the name's Kosuke Kindaichi. How do you do?"

"Ah! And I'm Hoan Tatara. I'm something of a hermit here… Tell me, Kindaichi-san, how do you know the inspector?"

"He's an acquaintance of mine," said Kindaichi.

Tatara didn't seem to take offence at his evasive answer and, after the usual questions about the reason for his visit and how long he intended to stay, he asked:

"So, what line of work are you in?"

"I suppose you could say I'm a writer of sorts," Kindaichi replied.

He always had this answer at the ready for these kinds of situations.

"Oh, I see," said Tatara, taking Kindaichi's words at face value and not pressing the matter any further.

Then, after a little more idle chat, the bald man stood up and said, "Well, I'll leave you to it… Enjoy your bath."

How old would Hoan Tatara have been? At least seventy, to be sure. Yet, despite his age, he appeared to be in rude health. He had a small but muscular frame. Only, his right hand seemed to be weak, and he handled his towel with some difficulty.

Mr Tatara would come to the Turtle Spring every afternoon, and, after meeting Kindaichi two or three times in the public bath there, they gradually began to warm to one another.

"You must be bored out of your mind here in the countryside!" said Tatara one day. "You should come and visit me one of these days. The house is nothing to write home about, but I live alone, so it suits me just fine."

Rika, the proprietress, didn't like to gossip about other people's business, but O-Miki later explained that Mr Tatara's latest wife had left him in the previous year.

Bluebeard's Fifth Wife

The next character whom Kosuke Kindaichi met was the head of the Nire family, Kahei, who was reputed to be the most powerful man in Onikobe.

It was around eight o'clock on the evening after his arrival, and Kindaichi's ears had pricked up. He was surprised to hear the sound of a shamisen coming from a little room just around the corner from his own. It wasn't especially loud, but, against the gurgling of a nearby mountain stream, the gentle plucking of the strings had the melancholy resonance of falling raindrops.

He got up and went out onto the veranda, but all he could see was the flickering shadow of a lamp through a round window on the far side of the garden. There wasn't a soul in sight. Just as he was wondering who it could be, O-Miki came in with the tea.

"Is there a new guest staying here?"

"There is indeed, sir," O-Miki replied with a knowing smile.

"Who is it? Somebody from out of town?"

"No, sir. It's old Mr Nire."

Kindaichi's eyes widened in surprise. Who could Kahei Nire be entertaining at such a such a busy time for the farmers?

"Do you know Mr Nire?" the maid asked with a probing look.

"No, not especially," Kosuke Kindaichi replied. "I've heard he's the richest man in the village, though… But tell me, who's playing the shamisen? Has he called for a geisha?"

"No, sir, that's the mistress."

"The mistress? Mrs Aoike?" exclaimed Kindaichi. "You mean she's keeping him company?"

"Yes, sir."

"Is anybody else with them?"

"No, it's just the two of them."

"And Mr Nire comes here often, does he?"

"Fairly regularly, sir."

"And when he does, the proprietress keeps him company and plays the shamisen for him?"

"That's right, sir. Mr Nire lost his wife last year, and he's been lonely ever since," said O-Miki, leaving the room with a knowing laugh. She seemed to have come with the tea expressly to tell him all this.

After that evening, Kahei came to the Turtle Spring once every three days or so, and he would always drink sake while Rika played the shamisen for him in that little out-of-the-way tatami room.

One evening when Kahei came, Kosuke Kindaichi met Rika in the corridor and was surprised to see her face positively glowing and looking much younger than she usually did.

Yet again, it was in the bath that Kindaichi first spoke to Kahei. This was on the eighth evening of his stay at the Turtle Spring. After dinner, Kindaichi had gone to take a bath, and, as he was listening to the sound of the mountain stream outside, the door to the changing room opened and in came a man. Kindaichi took one look through the glass door and knew immediately that it was Kahei. He took off his clean yukata and lumbered over towards the bath, smiling amiably.

"Good evening," Kahei said, seeming almost to have anticipated finding Kindaichi there.

Kahei must have been around sixty. He was exceedingly tall and well-built, but, with his fair skin, he looked nothing like a farmer. His salt-and-pepper hair was cropped short, and he had the relaxed and easy manner of a true gentleman.

44

"G-good evening…" Kindaichi replied hastily.

As soon as Kahei joined the detective in the bath, he began spouting off all manner of inanities while he splashed himself with the warm water. Suddenly, though, he turned to Kindaichi with a roguish look in his eye.

"Incidentally, Kindaichi-san," he said, grinning, "I happened to hear from the owner this evening that you came here with a letter of introduction from Inspector Isokawa…"

"That's correct."

"And you're a writer, I'm told… Are you quite sure about that?"

Kindaichi was so taken aback by this that he accidentally splashed water. He had been found out.

"W-well… I *do* write a little…"

"Detective stories, is it?" said Kahei, laughing. "Forgive me, Kindaichi-san, but Inspector Isokawa's certainly persistent, I'll give him that. It shows just how seriously he takes his duties."

"How do you mean?"

"Well, I dare say he'll have told you about the affair with the con artist that took place here twenty-odd years ago?"

"He might have mentioned some of the details, yes…"

"Back then, you see, the inspector had his doubts. I'm sure he must have told you that Genjiro, the husband of this establishment's proprietress, was murdered."

"Yes, he did tell me that."

"Then he'll have told you that Genjiro's corpse was found face down in the *irori*. Only, the face was so badly burnt that he couldn't really be identified—who can say whether it was Genjiro or not! The inspector certainly had misgivings about it. What if it was really the con artist?… And, if it was him, then the husband could still be alive somewhere. So, the inspector believes that, if he is alive, there's every chance he could come back. That's why he keeps such a close eye on the Turtle Spring, you know…"

Kahei paused to catch his breath, scrutinizing Kosuke Kindaichi's face all the while.

"Isn't it possible that this is the reason for your visit, and that—"

"I-I'm afraid you've got the wrong end of the stick, sir," said Kindaichi, cutting him off. "I've come here to relax…"

"'Sir'?… So, you know who I am, then. I hear also that you've made Mr Tatara's acquaintance…"

Kindaichi laughed.

"Do you really suppose I've come all this way to solve a murder that took place here more than twenty years ago?"

"Well, haven't you?"

"As I've told you, I've come here for some relaxation, plain and simple," Kindaichi said. "As for the inspector, he just happened to tell me what went on here back then."

"Is that so?" Kahei murmured.

Seeing the shadow of despair that then passed over his face, Kindaichi started. Could it not be this man who wanted the case to be reopened? And if he did, why?…

"What a pity, Kindaichi-san. And here I was thinking you'd come to look for clues because you'd learnt that the con artist's daughter has come back…"

"Pure coincidence!" said Kindaichi. "But seeing as I am here, why don't you tell me all about it?"

"At your service!"

"Why don't you start by telling me what's become of the Yuras ever since the incident?"

"Well, now, let me see… After everything that happened, Utaro

quit this world in 1935. And then there was the war, of course…
But they came out of it not too badly because they started growing grapes."

"And his widow, Atsuko? Is she well?"

"Well, she's an old woman now, but I believe so." As he said this, Kahei had a glint in his eye. "The inspector must have told you that she and I were once…"

"Ah, so the rumours were true then?" said Kindaichi.

"I'm not proud of it… But she threw herself into my arms. What was a man to do?… But when my late father found out, he rebuked me and made me call it off immediately." Kahei laughed. "Ah, the folly of youth… Then again, I was forty-one at the time, and she was thirty-eight…"

Looking somewhat embarrassed, Kahei laughed as he splashed himself with water, but he immediately recovered a more serious look.

"In any case," he said, "come and see me one of these days. We'll talk more about this. In the meantime, your secret is safe with me, Kindaichi-san."

That evening, as was his wont, Kahei had a drink with Rika, although he returned home earlier than usual.

It was a little after that that Kosuke Kindaichi met Hoan Tatara again during his afternoon bath, but he did not visit him at his home until the evening of 7 August, exactly two weeks after he first arrived at the Turtle Spring.

Thinking back on it later, Kosuke Kindaichi realized that on that day, unbeknownst to him, he had in fact stumbled across his first clue in solving this tragic case.

While Tatara's abode was about half an hour's walk from the Turtle Spring, it was still the nearest dwelling. To reach the first scattering of houses in Onikobe took another fifteen minutes' walk from there.

Tatara's little house was perched on the bank of a large marsh-land that stood in the shadow of one of the mountains. When Kindaichi arrived, he found the pond covered entirely with white water-chestnuts in full bloom, the branches of several pine trees spread over the roof like an umbrella, and the evening cicadas making a terrific din.

Really, the house was more of a cabin: there was a single kitchen-cum-living room with an *irori* hearth right in the middle of it, and one other little room off to the side. The roof was untiled, and the rough-coated walls had been left bare, while the woven bamboo that served as the ceiling had taken on a reddish hue that betrayed its age. It was elegant in a way, but it also seemed a little forlorn.

Kosuke Kindaichi sat across from Mr Tatara, on the opposite side of an old mandarin crate that had been covered in scrap paper and served as a table. Luckily, however, the host appeared to be the tidy sort, and the whole place was spotlessly clean.

"Well, Kindaichi-san, what do you think? It's not a bad little place, is it?"

For some reason, Mr Tatara seemed to be in high spirits that evening, and he continued:

"The breeze that blows in across the water is second to none, and nobody in the village can boast of having a place like this!"

He laughed.

It was true enough: the cool breeze felt like a gentle caress on the skin, but it also brought with it the unpleasant stench of the marsh's stale waters. Perhaps with time one grew accustomed to the smell…

"Your timing couldn't be better, Kindaichi-san!"

"Oh, and why's that?…"

"Well, you see, I've been meaning to ask somebody to help me, but I didn't want to be ridiculed, so I've been a little hesitant about it. Take a look at this, if you will…"

Seeming a little out of sorts, Mr Tatara extracted an envelope that was a surprising shade of pink. With a bashful smile, he turned to his guest.

"You've been here for fourteen days now, Kindaichi-san, so I suspect you'll have heard a bit about me already. You must know, for example, that I've had eight wives…"

"Y-yes, I'd heard something to that effect…"

Kosuke Kindaichi stared at this Bluebeard of a host in front of him. He looked calm and refined (nothing at all like the Bluebeard of legend) and, for all the rakishness of the life he must have led, it appeared not to have left its mark on him. Indeed, he seemed altogether young and lively for his age.

"Of my eight wives," said Mr Tatara, stroking his chin, "some of them I chased away because I no longer liked them, while others left because they could no longer stand to be around me. Take it from me, Kindaichi-san, it's best to get rid of them while they're still young. When they're on the wrong side of fifty, then you're in trouble." He laughed. "I have here a letter from O-Rin, my fifth wife. She says she wants to come back to me."

Kosuke Kindaichi's eyes widened in surprise. Wasn't O-Rin the one who had been his wife at the time of the incident back in 1932?

Mr Tatara, however, appeared not to notice the expression on Kindaichi's face.

"Would you mind taking a look at it for me, Kindaichi-san? The letter doesn't contain anything too intimate," he said with a childlike smile.

With seemingly little choice but to acquiesce, Kosuke Kindaichi lowered his eyes to the piece of stationery that Mr Tatara had just thrust into his hands.

Written in a rather fluid hand, the woman's letter bemoaned her advancing years and pitiful lot. She added that she had heard a rumour that her former husband was lonely, just like her, and she asked how he would feel about her returning and living with him. At great length she repeated that they should let bygones be bygones and, now that they were in their twilight years, live out their last days peaceably together.

"I see," said Kosuke Kindaichi, a little moved by this. "Well, it sounds like a perfect solution," he added, returning the letter to his host.

Mr Tatara's eyes lit up.

"Are you thinking what I'm thinking, Kindaichi-san? Back then I resented her, but her words have made me see her in an entirely different light. I'd like to send off a reply at once, but as you can see…"

Mr Tatara showed Kosuke Kindaichi his trembling right hand. Compared to the left one, it looked atrophied, as though he hadn't been able to use it for quite some time.

"You see, Kindaichi-san, you arrived just as I was wondering who I could ask to write the reply for me. I'm sorry to put you to the trouble, but would you mind doing the honours?"

"Of course not! It's no trouble at all. I'm just glad to be of help…"

"I'm in your debt. Well, in that case…"

Mr Tatara took out a fountain pen, some letter paper and an envelope, and cheerfully set them on top of the old mandarin crate.

"In that case, please take down the following…"

Kosuke Kindaichi did as he was bidden and wrote that O-Rin could come back whenever she pleased, that he was also lonely, that this time they would live happily together, that he too had matured with age, that he was no longer so rash and that he would treat her well. He asked her to come as soon as she read the letter, and so on and so forth… The words came gushing out of him, so much that Kosuke Kindaichi felt honour-bound to cut him short.

After reading the letter over, Mr Tatara said:

"I'm very much obliged to you, Kindaichi-san. You've been a real help to me."

"While I'm at it, I may as well write the address for you, too," said Kindaichi, turning O-Rin's letter over. "O-Rin Kuribayashi, c/o Mr Maeda, 2–36 West Yanagiwara, Hyogo Ward, Kobe," he said, reading out the address. "I say, what beautiful handwriting. Is it O-Rin's?"

"Oh, no, Kindaichi-san, she could never have written that well. Like me, she must have got somebody else to write it for her."

Mr Tatara was so delighted at the prospect of the return of his fifth wife that Kosuke Kindaichi hesitated to mention the reason why he had called. And so, in the end, his visit that day consisted solely in writing a letter on Mr Tatara's behalf.

Meanwhile, excitement in the village was growing daily. It had been officially announced that Yukari Ozora would be arriving on the 11th of the month. Almost every evening, the young people of the village would meet in the recreation room at the Turtle Spring to discuss the reception that was to be held in her honour.

The day before Yukari Ozora's arrival was the anniversary of Utaro Yura's death, and so that afternoon Rika had gone to help with the memorial service. That same evening, Kosuke

Kindaichi had an errand to run, and he was going to a little village called Soja on the other side of the Sennin Pass, over in Hyogo Prefecture. Kindaichi had told the people at Turtle Spring that he would stay the night there only if he was detained unexpectedly.

Night was already beginning to fall by the time that he reached the mountain pass, and everything around him was bathed in the reddish light of dusk. In the valleys on either side of the pass, little lights began to flicker.

Just as he reached the highest point of the pass, Kosuke Kindaichi passed an old woman.

She had a *tenugui* towel wrapped around her head, and she was carrying a large *furoshiki* on her back. The burden was so heavy that she was practically bent double as she walked, so Kindaichi couldn't so much as catch a glimpse of her face. All he could see was her white hair poking out from under the *tenugui* and the striped-cotton work trousers she was wearing. On her feet she had on some white *tabi* that were now grey with dirt and a pair of well-worn straw sandals. Perhaps to stop her arms and legs from tanning, she also wore some *kyahan* leggings and a pair of gloves.

As they passed each other, the old woman bowed her head even lower.

"Forgive me," she muttered almost inaudibly. "My name is O-Rin. I'm on my way back to see the village chieftain."

Hearing those words, Kosuke Kindaichi stopped dead in his tracks. But with that, the old woman simply carried on her way down the mountain pass, her sandals tapping against the ground.

Apparently, the old woman met another half-dozen other people along the way after that, and each time she had repeated exactly the same thing, only nobody had seen her face clearly because of the fading light and her stoop.

That fateful evening, the old woman calling herself O-Rin crossed the mountain path and headed down into the village of Onikobe, bringing with her, in her sinister *furoshiki*, all manner of misfortunes, horror and baffling mysteries...

Whenever Kosuke Kindaichi reflected on that meeting afterwards, the little hairs on the back of his neck would always stand on end. At the time, however, never in his wildest dreams could he have imagined all the terrible things to come. Instead, before turning on his heels and hurrying down the Sennin Pass in the opposite direction, he had simply thought to himself, "Ah, so that's Bluebeard's fifth wife, O-Rin..."

The Femme Fatale Returns Home

Kosuke Kindaichi had been determined to return to the Turtle Spring that evening and had even taken a torch with him for that very purpose. In the end, however, a terrific thunderstorm that suddenly swept across the whole region at nine o'clock had forced him to spend the night in Soja.

Kindaichi knew well that the weather in this mountainous country was liable to change suddenly, but the storm that night was more violent than any he had seen in a long while. The awesome claps of thunder reverberated from one mountain to the next, quite literally shaking the earth, and the deluge that accompanied them lasted for two whole hours.

Fortunately, Kindaichi had already foreseen the possibility that he might have to spend the night there and had taken precautions. Rika had recommended to him a travellers' lodge called the Izutsu Inn, which was where he sought refuge. The owner, a certain O-Ito, was originally from Onikobe, but had left the village in order to marry.

As Kindaichi stood on the veranda of his room, where O-Ito was now rushing to put the rain shutters in place, he looked up towards the Sennin Pass. All of a sudden, his eyes were blinded by a flash of lightning that rent the pitch-black sky. In the midst of the incessantly echoing thunder, with its reverberations rumbling right in the pit of his stomach, he watched on as the lightning flashed here and there, seeming to create great fiery columns amid the rain that was coming down in sheets.

Still, mused the detective, this was the night that the reunion between Mr Tatara and his fifth wife was to take place. It just seemed a pity that the weather was so wretched.

And yet, if Kindaichi had known what was happening at that very moment in Mr Tatara's little cabin perched on the bank of the marshland, or had an inkling of what else was coming down the line, he would never have been so carefree…

The storm passed at around midnight, and the following morning the weather was so fair that it seemed as though the night's tumult had been nothing but a dream.

Because of the leaking roof, Kindaichi had had trouble getting to sleep, so when he woke up in his room at around nine the next morning, he was still drowsy. What roused him from his slumber was the curious sound of fireworks in the distance. As he lay there, drifting in and out of sleep in his uncomfortable bed, he listened to their merry explosions and remembered that today was the day when the "femme fatale" was due to return to the village.

Kindaichi blearily recalled that the young people of the village had talked about a day-long fireworks display to celebrate Yukari Ozora's return, but then he suddenly noticed the sunlight streaming in through the gaps between the rain shutters and sat bolt upright.

He groped around for his wristwatch. The hands showed nine-thirty. He hastily opened one of the shutters and was greeted by the dazzling sunlight.

Kindaichi squinted as he looked out, a little disoriented. He had planned to get up as early as possible and walk back to Onikobe while it was still cool, and he had even asked the owner of the inn to wake him. The village lay over three miles from Soja, a journey that would take a good hour and half. He did not much relish the prospect of crossing the pass under the blazing summer sun and had no intention of suffering the humidity beneath the canopy of a rickshaw for a second time.

It was a little after ten o'clock when Kosuke Kindaichi finally went along for his breakfast.

"I'm sorry," said O-Ito, looking slightly sheepish as she set the tray down in front of him. "I came in to wake you earlier, but you were sleeping like a baby…"

"Oh, it's fine, really," said Kindaichi. "I've nothing in particular to do today, so I'll take the opportunity to spend the day here and then head back once there's a cool breeze."

"Yes, please do. I'd hoped the rain last night would make it a little cooler today, but just look how hot it is already!"

O-Ito really did seem to feel the heat. She mopped her brow with the cuff of her hemp kimono. The sound of fireworks rocketing up amid the sweltering heat made it seem even hotter.

"That was some rainfall last night," said Kindaichi. "It didn't cause any damage, did it?"

"I've heard there were a few landslides in the mountains behind Onikobe, but they can't have been all that serious, judging by the fireworks this morning." O-Ito stared at him. "By the way, I hear you're staying at the Turtle Spring. Do you have any connection to Yukari Ozora?"

"No, not really… In fact, I almost feel as though I've picked the wrong time to come here. I believe she's awfully popular these days, isn't she? Do you know her?"

"Not Chieko, no. That's her real name, you see. Although I do know her mother, Harue, a little."

O-Ito looked around fifty, which meant that she would almost certainly have been married by the time the tragedy had taken place. But Kindaichi asked the question all the same:

"I suppose that back in 1932 you must have already been married and settled here?"

"That's right, yes. I'd even had my firstborn by then. Every now and then, Harue would stop by with that man of hers," said O-Ito with a curious laugh.

Kosuke Kindaichi started.

"You mean to say she came here with the con artist Onda?"

"Ah, so you know about all that!"

"Well, I've been in these parts for more than a fortnight. And what with Yukari Ozora's arrival, it came up naturally in conversation... So, did you know this Onda fellow?"

"Yes, it was the village chieftain who introduced him to us. Perhaps you know him? The village chieftain, I mean..."

"You must mean Mr Tatara. I do indeed know him. I've even been to his house."

"Oh yes? So much the better! He was awfully kind to me when I was young, you know. He did so much for me. Why, he even helped to arrange my marriage. He's too kind for his own good, truth be told. He always wants to help people, but then he gets taken advantage of. It's a real shame."

The fact of knowing Mr Tatara seemed to have won Kindaichi the confidence of his host, for her talk suddenly became much more animated.

"That reminds me," said Kindaichi. "Didn't this Onda fellow once rent one of Mr Tatara's cottages?"

"That's right, yes, he did. But it wasn't easy for them to meet over there, you see, so they'd often come here in secret. I seem to recall that Harue was only sixteen at the time. We wanted to warn her father, god rest his soul, but Mr Tatara said to leave things well alone. He said that nothing good would come of standing in the way of young love."

"So, the tragedy must have come as quite a shock to you then?"

"I'll say!"

"Did the police know that they had been using your inn as a meeting place?"

"Well, it was like this, you see," said O-Ito, sidling up to him. "Her late father was a very timid man and fretted about this an awful lot. So, he spoke to the village chieftain, who said not to worry about it. When they—that's to say, the police—came and asked their questions, he said, it wouldn't be necessary to tell them every last detail. He said there was no need to tell them they'd come here, and so the police remained in the dark about it. The village chieftain didn't take much notice of the police, and he just kept on saying to leave things well alone. Well, you can see for yourself what came of 'leaving things well alone'..."

She laughed, and as she spoke of Mr Tatara, there was a glimmer of nostalgia in O-Ito's eyes.

"I don't suppose they ever found out the real identity of the man, did they? Or did you, perhaps, for that matter?"

"I'm afraid not, sir. I never bothered to ask where he came from—all I cared about was that poor girl, Harue. In the months after, she would come here, awash with tears, to find out whether we'd had any word from him. At least the child turned out so well... Fate's a funny old thing, isn't it?"

The memory of it seemed to move O-Ito deeply, but there was something bothering Kosuke Kindaichi.

"Perhaps Mr Tatara knows something about it?"

"Now that I couldn't say. You never can tell with him... At any rate, I still can't believe that Mr Onda would have done a thing like that. I mean, he was no angel when it came to the ladies, but all the same..."

"Do you mean to say," asked Kindaichi, scrutinizing O-Ito, "that Onda had other women besides Yukari's mother?"

"Well, no, what I meant to say was…"

Clearly, O-Ito felt she had said too much. Kosuke Kindaichi's question had caught her off guard and now she seemed flustered.

"You know, it was all so very long ago," she said. "Why don't you relax a little… You did say that you wouldn't be taking lunch today, didn't you?"

With that, and regretting having let her tongue run away with her, O-Ito cleared away the dishes and quickly took her leave.

Kindaichi watched her go, his mind racing.

O-Ito had implied that Onda had had a mistress—or possibly even several. And it seemed that fact had been concealed from Inspector Isokawa, since he hadn't mentioned it, although others in the same business as O-Ito would surely have known about it. At any rate, not having spotted the role of the Izutsu Inn at the time was a serious oversight on the part of the investigating authorities.

But as O-Ito had just said, all that had happened a long, long time ago.

To distract himself, Kindaichi picked up the newspaper that O-Ito had brought him. When he opened it, he saw that the local news page was full of articles about Yukari Ozora.

In addition to the photographs of her, there were also some of the house she had built for her adoptive parents. Despite having been in the village for more than a fortnight now, Kindaichi had yet to see this house, since it lay in a different direction from the Turtle Spring, but it certainly looked like a fine building in the photos. The architectural style was said to have been based chiefly on her adoptive parents' wishes, but carpenters had been brought in from Tokyo and had given it the appearance of a country mansion.

As Kosuke Kindaichi perused the article, two names jumped out at him.

When in March 1945, Chieko and her mother had fled Kobe to escape the air raids, Yukari would have been twelve, and so, naturally, when they came to Onikobe, Yukari spent a year in the village school. Two of her classmates from then—Yasuko Yura and Fumiko Nire—were reminiscing about her. It was these two names that struck Kindaichi.

The girls must have been in their early twenties now, and, judging by this, Kindaichi surmised that Yasuko must be Utaro's daughter, while Fumiko would be Kahei's.

A third girl of a similar age—Satoko—was also mentioned, and this, he assumed, must be Rika Aoike's daughter.

The discovery made a curious impression on the detective.

It was different for the Nire family, of course, but the Yuras and the Aoikes had been bound to Yukari's father by the ties of fate. Yukari's father had killed Satoko's father and was indirectly responsible for Yasuko's father's death, too. In old-fashioned terms, Yukari was the daughter of these girls' fathers' enemy. And now the daughter of this con artist, of this heinous criminal, was returning home, crowned in glory, while the daughter of the Yura family, who ought to have been her sworn enemy, had to welcome her, even if it was only with a few well-chosen words.

The fireworks in Onikobe continued, and that afternoon there was also a firework display in Soja. While Kosuke Kindaichi was pondering the surprising information, O-Ito came in, bearing a glass bowl of white peaches. She seemed to have something on her mind.

"These peaches are lovely and cold. Would you like one?"

"Oh, thank you," replied Kindaichi. "I see that the fireworks have started here, too."

"Yes, they're a bit much, don't you think? It feels as though the emperor's come to pay us a visit," said O-Ito, chuckling as she peeled a peach.

As they talked, Yukari Ozora was on her way, travelling by car along the military road that ran from Kobe to Sakushu, skirting past Soja. The road itself had been built by the army during the war, and now it served as a bus route.

To put his mind at rest, Kindaichi enquired about Yasuko Yura and Fumiko Nire. It was just as he had surmised. According to O-Ito, the Yura family now consisted of five members and was led by an old woman in her eighties by the name of Ioko. Even the imperious Atsuko bowed before her, so she said.

The other three members of the family were Toshio, the heir, his wife, Eiko, and Yasuko, whose name had appeared in the newspaper. Between Toshio and Yasuko, there had been another two siblings, a boy and a girl, but the boy had died in the war and the girl had been married off: now only those five remained in the village. The thirty-four-year-old Toshio had returned from a prisoner-of-war camp in Siberia two years ago, and, since he had married only the previous year, he had no children.

"That poor man," said O-Ito. "Stuck in Siberia all that time, and when he did finally make it back, he found that all his fields and rice paddies had been taken from him... But as the saying goes, ill-gotten gains are short-lived."

"Oh, I see... So, it was the Yura family that was tricked by the village chieftain?"

"As I say, Utaro was a kind and gentle man, but the two generations before him had a reputation for ruthlessness."

Kosuke Kindaichi took the opportunity also to enquire about the Nires, too. He learnt that there were eight of them. Kahei had been widowed the previous year, and besides him there were his son and heir, Naohei, and this son's wife, Michiko. Naohei was going on thirty-five, but he had married as soon as he returned from Manchuria at the war's end. Since then, he'd had three children. Apart from Naohei and his lot, Kahei also had another son, Shohei, aged twenty-five, and a daughter, Fumiko, who was the youngest of the siblings. She had two elder sisters as well, but of course they had been married off.

"But tell me," Kosuke Kindaichi interrupted the woman, "what I just read in the paper left a rather curious impression on me. If I understand correctly, Onda's daughter is the same age as the Yura and Nire daughters, as well as the proprietress of the Turtle Spring's daughter, and they were all in the same class at school together. Is that right?"

O-Ito paused. Kosuke Kindaichi couldn't see the expression on her face, as she carried on peeling peaches, her head down, but when she spoke, her voice seemed somewhat hoarse.

"That's correct, yes… Are you aware that the village chieftain is worried?"

"Worried? About what?"

"He says that the Besshos are well within their rights to build a house there, but is it right for Harue to bring her daughter back there? He's worried that something bad might happen…"

"And you share this concern of his?"

"No, but that's what he said… Then again, maybe he was just joking," she said. "Here, I've peeled all the peaches now. Are you sure you wouldn't like to try one?"

O-Ito looked slightly embarrassed and was trying to avoid Kindaichi's gaze.

"Ah, thank you."

As he brought the cool, refreshing slice of peach to his mouth, Kindaichi lapsed into thought. These people—that is, O-Ito and

Mr Tatara—knew something. Something important, connected to what happened back then, in 1932. But now was not the moment to press her further.

"By the way," said Kindaichi, his mouth full of peach, "I suppose you must know O-Rin? The village chieftain's fifth wife?"

"Why, yes, I used to know her quite well."

O-Ito had a look of wariness in her eyes.

"Have you heard that she's come back to him?" said Kindaichi with a chuckle.

There was that warm feeling in his heart again, but O-Ito reacted with only a look of contempt.

"Wh…whatever do you mean?" she asked, flustered.

"Well, they're both getting on in age, and so O-Rin has decided to take the initiative and reconcile with him. It was I who wrote the reply on Mr Tatara's behalf."

Kosuke Kindaichi proceeded to tell her how he had come to write the letter in question and how, only the previous evening, he had met, while crossing the mountain pass, an old woman who told him that her name was O-Rin. As the story went on, O-Ito's face turned pale, as though she had seen a ghost.

Surprised at this, Kosuke Kindaichi asked her:

"Are you all right? Is it O-Rin's return that's worrying you?"

"No, I'm fine, it's just…" she said, trying to catch her breath. "What exactly did the village chieftain say to you? About O-Rin's letter, I mean…"

"Only that he was delighted. He seemed to be overjoyed at the news… But won't you tell me what it is that's worrying you?"

O-Ito's face was so pale that she looked as though she were ready to faint. Kosuke Kindaichi was about to get up to help her when a group of young men and women came barging in, all jostling one another and shouting.

The First O-Bon Festival

No matter where you go in Japan, all inns have more or less the same configuration, with a long corridor running the length of the building from the front to the back and into a courtyard garden. This lively group of youths that had stumbled into the garden had in fact come from Onikobe. There were three boys, including Kanao, and three girls, and they were all in high spirits.

"What's all this?" said O-Ito. "What are you all doing here?!"

The sudden appearance of this group of youths seemed to be a good restorative for O-Ito, who had only moments ago been on the verge of fainting.

She hurriedly wiped away some tears with the cuff of her sleeve.

"Is it anything urgent?" she asked.

"Hello, Mother!" one of them cried out excitedly. It was Teru, O-Ito's young, rosy-cheeked daughter-in-law. "It's amazing! I've just heard from Shohei that Yukari Ozora's on her way here!"

"What? Here?!… No, surely she can't be!"

"Oh, but she is!" said one of the young men, helping himself to a peach and plumping himself down on the edge of the veranda. "The town hall just received a call from Kobe. She's going to stop here and rest a little before heading on to the village."

Kosuke Kindaichi recognized the young man. Whenever the young people of the village got together at the Turtle Spring, he was forever to be found at Kanao's side. They all called him Katsu, but he was undoubtedly the same Shohei that O-Ito had just mentioned—that is, Kahei's second-born son. When he spoke, his eyes rolled about mischievously, just like his father's. And though he wasn't as tall or as good-looking as his father, his hair was parted neatly on the left and he wore an open-necked shirt, which made him look trim and rather handsome.

"Good grief… Is this really true, Kanao?" asked O-Ito.

"Every word of it, Auntie," replied Kanao off-handedly and with a grin on his face.

"Her mother also called and asked us to tell you, since she didn't want you to be in a panic because of her daughter turning up unannounced."

"Harue did that, did she? It's kind of her to remember me."

O-Ito seemed flustered.

"That's why she's stopping here! Quick, there's no time to lose. We have to put our best foot forward."

"Come off it! Don't exaggerate!"

"What do you mean, Fumiko?"

"All I'm saying is that you exaggerate. Isn't that right, Yasuko?"

"I'll say…"

"Katsu, Goro, what do you think?"

"I'm saying nothing. After all, it's my aunt we're talking about."

"Enough with the 'aunt' business, Goro," said Kanao, still with his usual aloofness. "It isn't funny, you know."

Clearly, this Goro was Ryota Bessho's grandson. He must have been in his early twenties and, although Yukari was biologically his cousin, she was listed officially as his aunt on the family register because of her adoption.

"Hey, guys, you've got to try one of these peaches! They're so cold and fresh. Do you mind, Auntie?"

"Of course not, be my guest," replied O-Ito. "Don't worry, Teru, there are plenty more where those came from. Shohei, do you know what time Harue and Chieko will be arriving?"

"At around four o'clock, I think. It's almost two now, so there's still plenty of time."

"Well, well! And you all piled down here just to tell me this?"

"Not only that… We thought we'd take the opportunity to come and welcome her, seeing as she's such a distinguished guest."

"And that's why Fumiko and Miss Yura are here as well?"

For some reason, O-Ito's voice sounded a little choked.

"Oh, no, Auntie! They came along because if they didn't, people might think they were jealous of her success!"

"How could you say such a thing!" Shohei's sister, Fumiko, exclaimed. "If you're going to talk like that, we'll just go home, won't we, Yasuko?"

"I'll say…"

"All right, all right, I'm sorry! I take it back," Shohei apologized. "The fact is, it was Kanao who invited them, and of course, since it was him, they jumped at the invitation. If he told the girls in the village to jump off a cliff, they'd do it in a heartbeat."

"Well, he is the village Don Juan, after all!" added Goro, sinking his teeth into a peach.

"Oh, give it a rest, will you!" said Kanao, his suntanned face blushing a deep red. He then turned to O-Ito. "Is there anything you need to do to get ready for them? We'll lend you a hand."

"I hate to put you to the trouble, but my head's in such a spin. Teru, go and fetch the lady next door. She can help us clean the tatami room… You can all see Chieko here."

"I'll return to my room, then, shall I?" asked Kosuke Kindaichi.

"Ah, yes, of course… I completely forgot, Kanao, you must know this gentleman. He's staying with you in Onikobe, isn't he?"

"Yes, of course I know Kindaichi-san. How do you do?"

"Very well, I'll leave you all to it…"

After O-Ito left, Kanao turned to Kosuke Kindaichi, who had been watching Fumiko and Yasuko closely. He asked Kanao:

"I was wondering, Kanao, is it true that your sister, Satoko, was in the same class as the three of them?"

"Yes, but she didn't attend school regularly."

"I heard she has a weak heart, your sister?"

"Yes, that's right."

"But she did go to school?"

"She did, yes."

Kanao's replies seemed evasive. Goro, who was in the middle of peeling a peach, added:

"Back then, she was just a child. She wasn't aware of love." He then realized that all eyes were on him, and averted his gaze.

"What do you mean by that?" Kosuke Kindaichi was about to ask, but he stopped short, noticing how suddenly the atmosphere had changed.

There was a momentary awkward silence, which was broken only by Kanao:

"Oh, I forgot to tell you, Kindaichi-san. There's somebody waiting for you at the Turtle Spring."

"Waiting for me?"

"It's Inspector Isokawa. He said he'd managed to take some leave. He arrived a little before noon."

"Oh, really?" said Kosuke Kindaichi with a smile.

Doubtless the inspector really had taken some leave, but Kindaichi had been in Onikobe for more than a fortnight now, so he imagined that the inspector was really coming to find out whether there was any news. Kindaichi wanted to reiterate that he wasn't there to carry out an investigation on his behalf, but he couldn't help smiling: the old case had at last begun to pique his interest.

"What would you like to do, Kindaichi-san? My mother suggested that you could join us. We're planning to drive back as soon as Yukari gets here."

"Thank you, but I think I'll make my own way back on foot. I'll cross the pass once dusk has fallen. I suppose the inspector will be spending a few days in Onikobe?"

"Yes, he said that he'd come for the week."

"Oh, I see. Thank you."

The group of youths from Onikobe then set about their busy preparations for Yukari Ozora's arrival, leaving Kosuke Kindaichi to retire to his room and watch all the commotion from the sidelines. The long-awaited arrival of Yukari Ozora and her mother was upon them. At that moment, the two women were in a procession of motorcars that was slowly making its way through the fireworks and the crowds that lined the streets.

The eye of the storm is always calm, however. Though the whole of Soja seemed to have descended on the Izutsu Inn, Kosuke Kindaichi let all the clamouring outside simply wash over him, while he himself sank deep into thought. It wasn't Yukari Ozora's arrival that weighed on his mind so much as O-Ito's curious behaviour just moments ago. When she had learnt of O-Rin's return, her reaction had been closer to fear than surprise. Why was this?

On the opposite side of the garden, which had been watered for Yukari Ozora's arrival, stood a world of resplendent beauty, where these bright young things now greeted the pin-up girl of the day. By comparison, the news of O-Rin's return seemed a world apart.

And yet, her return did not belong to another world, for the two events were bound together by a strong, though unseen thread—one that was black and boded ill…

*

"Teru!" Kosuke Kindaichi called out, stopping the flustered-looking girl who happened to be passing. "Yukari Ozora has arrived, hasn't she?"

"Yes, she's having a little rest right now."

"Did she come just with her mother?"

"No, they came with her manager. He's the guy who claims to have discovered her…"

"Do you know what time they'll be setting off again?"

"Well, she just came out of the bath, so I'd imagine it won't be long now. Would you like to meet them?"

"No, it's just that it looks as though it would be a little tricky to leave here before they do. There are still lots of people waiting outside, aren't there?"

"Hordes of them!"

For Teru, the excitement was dizzying, as if there could be no greater honour than this visit.

A moment later, Kanao arrived.

"Are you sure you won't come with us, Kindaichi-san? We're about to set off."

"No, thank you, Kanao. I'll wait until all the excitement has died down."

"Yes, there's still quite a crowd out there!" said the young man, laughing.

A few moments later, after Kanao had gone, Kosuke Kindaichi could hear great cries of adoration coming from the front of the inn. The cars seemed to be having trouble moving off because of the surging crowds. Some shouting mingled with the cheers for a while, but eventually the sounds of the engines began to fade into the distance, and Kindaichi heaved a sigh of relief.

*

"I'm awfully sorry. I got so caught up in all the commotion that I forgot all about you."

It was some time later that O-Ito appeared, still excited by the recent events.

"Please, don't mention it. You've had quite a day. You must be exhausted," Kosuke Kindaichi replied.

"I really am, Kindaichi-san," she replied. "But it was so wonderful to see Harue again after all this time. I never thought she'd remember me. And all those gifts she brought me!"

Clearly, O-Ito was deeply touched by this, and she kept wiping tears from her eyes.

"Everything went well, that's the main thing," said Kindaichi. "And now that the sun's going down, I think I'll be off myself. Would you mind totting up my bill?"

"Oh! You're leaving us so soon?"

O-Ito looked as though she wanted to add something more, but, seeming to think better of it, she simply got to her feet instead.

An hour later, Kosuke Kindaichi found himself making his way over the mountain pass. Just as on the previous evening, everything around him was bathed in the reddish light of dusk. The fireworks in Onikobe had finally stopped, and the bustle of the day had now been replaced by a hush that stretched out as far as the eye could see.

Suddenly, though, Kindaichi heard footsteps coming up behind him. He stopped dead in his tracks. When he turned around, he was startled.

"O-Ito!" he cried. "What on earth are you doing here?"

"I'm on my way to see the village chieftain in Onikobe," she answered, drawing nearer. "I'm taking him this O-Bon present…"

Kosuke Kindaichi was once again startled by this revelation, which gave him an uneasy feeling. It was a strange hour of the day to be taking someone a present for the festival of the dead. They walked on together.

"I see, I see," said Kindaichi. "If you don't mind, I'd like to return to our earlier conversation. Is there some problem with O-Rin's coming back?"

"Kindaichi-san…" said O-Ito in a strangely subdued tone of voice. "You mentioned that you sent the reply on Mr Tatara's behalf. Only, where exactly did you send it?"

"Now, let me see… I don't remember the address, but it was somewhere in Kobe. West Yanagiwara, if my memory serves. It was to be delivered care of a Mr Maeda."

O-Ito's shoulders began to shake, and she moved in a little closer to him.

"Was it around here that you met O-Rin last night, Kindaichi-san?"

"Yes, just a little up ahead, in fact. It was she who greeted me, saying that she was on her way back to see the village chieftain…"

"Oh, Kindaichi-san!" exclaimed O-Ito, shuddering and clutching at his sleeve.

"Wh-what is it, dear lady? What's the matter? Is it something to do with this O-Rin?"

"Yes! You see, O-Rin died this past spring… The 15th will mark the first O-Bon since her death!"

O-Ito pressed her cuffs to her eyes and began to sob like a child.

Chieftain's Death

Kosuke Kindaichi stood dumbfounded in the fading twilight at the top of the mountain pass.

The spot where he had met the old woman calling herself O-Rin was just up ahead. It had been the same time of evening, and everything around had been bathed in the same half-light. She had been carrying something wrapped in a large *furoshiki* on her back, which had almost made her double over. Because of this, he hadn't been able to see her face, but he distinctly remembered the stray strands of white hair poking out from under the *tenugui* she had wrapped around her head. Even now, he could even hear her voice and the melancholy tapping of her straw sandals.

"But… how could you…" said Kosuke Kindaichi, faltering as he looked all around himself, before coming to his senses and saying in a more confident tone of voice, "Are you quite sure? How did you come by the knowledge that Mr Tatara's fifth wife had died?"

"But, Kindaichi-san, I'm sure of it. Why, I even attended the funeral in Kobe!"

"Let's keep going," he said, looking around again. "You can tell me about it while we walk."

She nodded, drying her tears on the cuff of her sleeve, and stuck close to the detective's side.

"Would I be correct in assuming you're somehow related to O-Rin, then?" asked Kindaichi.

"Yes, she was a distant relative of my late father's. She'd once been a geisha, you know. It was my father who introduced her to the village chieftain. The Mr Maeda in Kobe, whom you just mentioned, married my father's cousin and now runs a restaurant in West Yanagiwara. When O-Rin divorced the village chieftain, she went through some hard times, but after the war she took a job as a waitress in Mr Maeda's restaurant. She fell ill at the end of last year and then finally died this spring, in April..."

Once again, O-Ito took the cuff of her sleeve and dried her eyes. It was not her sadness at O-Rin's passing that made her weep like a child, so much as the shock that this woman had supposedly returned to the village of Onikobe.

"How old was O-Rin?" asked Kosuke Kindaichi.

"She was in her late fifties."

That certainly tallied with the figure of the old woman whom he had seen the previous evening.

"So, Mr Tatara was unaware of this? That O-Rin had passed away, I mean."

"That's what I find so strange about it, Kindaichi-san! When you wrote the letter for him, he really didn't know that O-Rin was dead?"

"He'd no idea. He seemed so happy."

"It's incredible! So, he really didn't know..."

"Didn't you ever inform him about O-Rin's death?"

"No, I didn't. He has always been very quick to anger, you see, so my husband and I kept our distance..."

"But then, why did you think he'd know about it?"

"Because the Maedas told us they were going to send out an announcement."

"An announcement of the death?"

"Exactly."

"But Mr Tatara didn't go to Kobe, did he?"

"No... And he's usually so observant when it comes to these things. Not only did he not show up at the funeral, but he didn't even send a letter of condolence. I thought that he must still be angry with her, and so I never mentioned O-Rin's name again in front of him."

Just then, Kosuke Kindaichi reached the spot where he had come across the old woman calling herself O-Rin the previous evening.

"This is where I met her," he said.

O-Ito let out a frightened cry and clung to Kosuke Kindaichi's sleeve. Her eyes darted about, and she grew deathly pale.

Overcome by fear, he felt the hair on his neck stand on end. He looked around himself, half-expecting to see the ghost of the old woman appear in the half-light. Nearby, at the foot of an enormous cedar, there was a little Shinto shrine, in front of which was a flower canister with a bunch of red dahlias wilting in it. From up there in the mountains, they looked down over the silent village of Onikobe, sunk in mist and twilight, with little trails of smoke rising up from the houses here and there. At first glance, it appeared to be a peaceful little village, but behind that façade lurked something sinister…

"I'll accompany you to Mr Tatara's," said Kosuke Kindaichi. "This whole business is rather concerning."

"Would you? That's awfully kind of you, Kindaichi-san. I have a bad feeling about this… a very bad feeling."

"Are you worried that O-Rin's ghost has gone to pay a visit to the village chieftain?" said Kindaichi. He chuckled, but as he hurried on, his throat grew dry and his laughter choked. An eerie sense of anxiety swelled within him, making him quicken his step.

"I don't know, but this is the first O-Bon since her death…" She sighed. "You don't suppose somebody could be playing some kind of practical joke on him, do you?"

"Do you know of anybody who would want to do something like that?"

O-Ito carried on a few steps, her head hung in silence, deep in thought. She then turned her glittering eyes towards Kindaichi.

"Nobody with anything to gain by it," she finally answered, smiling plaintively.

"Let's leave all that to one side for the moment," said Kindaichi. "Is there anybody in the village or the surrounding areas who could have known about O-Rin's death?"

"Hmm…" said O-Ito, cocking her head. "I doubt anybody would have known, unless the village chieftain himself had told them."

Mr Tatara must be a very proud man. It was the very fact that O-Rin had made the first move towards a reconciliation that had made him so happy. If she hadn't done that, then he would surely still have held a grudge against her. Or was it perhaps because of this grudge that he hadn't attended the funeral or sent a letter of condolence? Doubtless the mere mention of her name had been painful to him. Was such a man likely to tell all and sundry that O-Rin had died? Certainly not!

Kosuke Kindaichi stopped dead in his tracks. His reasoning was going around in circles.

O-Ito turned to him. "What's the matter, Kindaichi-san?" she enquired fearfully.

"Oh, it's nothing. Nothing at all…"

Kindaichi removed his hat and mopped the sweat off his brow.

"We should hurry," he said.

Frightened more and more, O-Ito followed him with quick little steps, giving him questioning looks from time to time.

Kosuke Kindaichi resumed his train of thought. What on earth was going on? Mr Tatara had been sent word of O-Rin's death from Kobe, so, naturally, he ought to have known that the letter had been forged. So why all this joy and unbridled happiness? Kosuke Kindaichi didn't know Mr Tatara all that well, but after everything that O-Ito had told him that day, he was beginning to wonder whether Mr Tatara wasn't playing some kind of game. Was Mr Tatara trying to pull the wool pulled over his eyes? And if so, why? To what end?

Then again, it was also conceivable that the man had known nothing of O-Rin's death in the first place. In that case, there were three possibilities. Perhaps he had never been sent the death notice to begin with. Alternatively, it could have got lost in the post. Or a third option was that it had arrived at its destination in the village, but that Mr Tatara hadn't seen it—which is to say that it had been either intercepted or misplaced.

One thing seemed certain, however: the letter from O-Rin was a fake. And what was more, the likeliest candidate to have written it was the old woman whom Kindaichi had seen crossing the mountain pass the night before.

Once again, a vague feeling of terror swept over Kosuke Kindaichi. According to O-Ito there was nobody who stood to profit by playing a practical joke on Mr Tatara, and this was what made it all the more terrifying.

"By the way…" said Kindaichi, turning to O-Ito, who was walking just behind him. "About what happened back then, in 1932, when the husband of the present owner of the Turtle Spring was killed…"

"Yes?" O-Ito narrowed her eyes, hearing this unexpected mention of the old murder case. "What about it?"

"I heard that on that evening, when Genjiro was killed, O-Rin had an argument with Mr Tatara and ran away…"

"That's right. She came and stayed with us."

"With you?"

"Yes, my father advised her to go back the following morning and even offered to accompany her there. The village chieftain had a similar idea to come and find her, but what with everything that happened, he couldn't. As for us, we thought it would be better for her to wait a couple of days, to let things settle down first, but that was when O-Rin took her chance to disappear. The police searched for her and discovered that she even had another man in her life. Afterwards, the village chieftain was furious with us because he assumed we'd helped her escape."

"Why had they argued in the first place?"

After a moment's silence, O-Ito answered:

"The village chieftain has always acted like the spoilt child he was when he was little. Sometimes you get the sense that he's an understanding, compassionate man, but at other times there's just no reasoning with him. They do say, don't they, that you never know what goes on behind closed doors, but when he started getting into money troubles, he just grew more and more irate. In the end, he treated O-Rin so badly that she just couldn't take his violence any more."

By the time they reached the foot of the pass, it was already dark. Fortunately, however, Kindaichi and O-Ito had both brought torches with them, so they had no trouble finding their way in the dark.

As they passed by the village hall, they could see the lights and hear the noise of the reception being given in Yukari Ozora's honour. When they paused to look, they saw several figures come rushing out, and a group of five or six spirited youths heading off in the opposite direction.

From the village hall it was a walk of about twenty-five minutes to Mr Tatara's little cabin. The road leading there skirted around

77

the foothills of the mountains, so even though the distance wasn't very far as the crow flies, it still took them quite a bit of time to get there.

The cottage itself was set on a hillside, a little off the road leading back to the village, and, as the reader is already aware, there was a marshland stretching out behind it. The locals called this "the man-eating marsh" because if you fell into it, the mud was reputedly so deep that you would never be able to get out again.

After they had passed the last few huts on the outskirts of Onikobe, the darkness seemed to grow thicker, but sure enough, up ahead in the velvety night, stood Mr Tatara's cabin. No lights were on, and this unnerved them both. Mr Tatara was not the type to go out for a night-time stroll, and it was still much too early for him to be asleep.

"Hello? Mr Tatara? Are you there?" called O-Ito, her voice already shaking. "Mr Tatara, it's me, O-Ito!"

"Mr Tatara, it's Kosuke Kindaichi! You're not in bed, are you?"

The two of them called out to him in turn two or three times, but all in vain. They looked at each other, their faces tense and pale.

"Maybe he's gone out," said O-Ito, trying to dispel her worries, but the tremor in her voice betrayed her true fear.

"Let's try inside," said the detective.

The door was unlocked.

Kosuke Kindaichi entered first, followed by a jittery O-Ito. Their torches were enough to illuminate the interior of the cabin. There was nobody in the larger room, where Kindaichi had sat only a few days previously. He crossed it. Just as he poked his head into the kitchen, he heard the flip of a switch behind him, and suddenly the room lit up. O-Ito had turned on the main light that hung from the ceiling, but as soon as she did, she let out a cry.

Startled by this, Kindaichi turned around to see her standing there, rooted to the spot.

He frowned. On the old mandarin crate that served as a table, there was a flask of sake, two cups, a plate of grilled fish, two lacquered bowls still bearing traces of soup, a dish of simmered vegetables and a plate laden with *inari sushi*. Beside all this stood a large candle covered in wax drippings, which had probably been used during the previous night's power cut.

None of this cosy scene, however, was what had made O-Ito cry out. Looking down from the makeshift table, Kindaichi saw that the light summer floor cushion and the tatami mat beside it were spattered with drops of blood, as if somebody had spat it out. But there was nobody in sight.

Kosuke Kindaichi took another look in the little kitchen, and suddenly his eyes fell on a water jug standing on the dirt floor, in the corner. Or rather, it wasn't it that caught his eye so much as the half-dozen flower stems in it. They looked like Chinese bellflowers.

He stepped into the kitchen and, intrigued by the sight, proceeded to pick up one of the flowers. That was when he heard O-Ito scream.

"Oh no, Kindaichi-san! You mustn't touch them! They're poisonous."

"Poisonous?…"

Kosuke Kindaichi hurriedly threw it on the floor.

"What are they called, these flowers?"

"Well, they're… aah!…" A look of terror flashed on O-Ito's face. She seemed to be struggling for breath. "I don't know the proper name for them, but in these parts they're known as 'chieftain's death'…"

The Salamander

Onikobe was now abuzz with rumours. First, of the much-fêted femme fatale who had returned to the village, and second, of the strange old woman who had been seen crossing the mountain path and calling herself by a dead woman's name… and the missing Hoan Tatara.

However, only the older people in the village were interested in the latter. The young people paid no attention to it whatsoever. For them, the village chieftain was just a relic of the past. Just as Mr Tatara himself had "renounced" the world, so too the world now renounced him—or had he been cast out by society even before that?

In any case, the youths of the village had better things to do that morning: they were all talking about last night's party and Yukari Ozora, who had captivated them with her charm, her beauty and that husky voice of hers, which had made her so famous.

And yet they were wrong to ignore the village chieftain. For, looking back on it, there was indeed a hidden link between the return of this "femme fatale" and what had just happened to Mr Tatara.

"Be that as it may, Kindaichi, it's all very strange…"

Dressed in an open-necked shirt and a pair of shorts, with an old, battered hat atop his head, Inspector Isokawa looked more like an inspector of public works, or even like the foreman of a construction site.

"How could he just sit down and start drinking with a woman he hadn't seen in twenty years? Was he really taken in by her?"

"Hmm…" said Kosuke Kindaichi, gazing at the old marsh in front of him and, as usual, vigorously scratching his bird's nest of dishevelled hair. "She could have fooled him for five, maybe ten minutes at most… If she came here directly after passing me, she would have arrived at around seven-thirty. In Soja, the power cut didn't happen until nine-thirty, so that means they would have spent two hours together, and then, even after the power cut, carried on chatting by candlelight."

"Which means that if it wasn't O-Rin, he would have known, surely?"

"Yes, I suppose he would…" mumbled Kosuke Kindaichi evasively. What he really wanted to know, however, was whether Mr Tatara had known about O-Rin's death.

Wandering aimlessly about the cramped little cabin now were three plain-clothes policemen who had just arrived from the neighbouring town, as well as the village constable, a certain Kimura. Perched at the edge of the old marsh, Kosuke Kindaichi and Inspector Isokawa sat waiting for them to carry out their investigation. On the opposite bank a crowd of curious onlookers had gathered.

Kosuke Kindaichi tried to go over the events of the previous evening in his mind once again.

Having sensed that something sinister had taken place inside Mr Tatara's cabin, he had suddenly grown more animated in his demeanour. He had instructed O-Ito not to touch anything and set about searching every nook and cranny. The first thing he had noticed was that there was no sign of the *furoshiki* that the old woman calling herself O-Rin had been carrying when he passed her. However, he was relatively certain that she had been there, for there were traces of muddy footprints left by her straw sandals on the floor at the entrance. Alas, any footprints that might have remained outside the cabin had been washed away by the thunderstorm.

So: an old woman going by the name O-Rin had arrived there yesterday evening, carrying a large bundle on her back. She had then stayed a good two hours or more, talking to Mr Tatara. Or at least, that's what it looked like. Finally, she had poisoned the man with these flowers, the so-called "chieftain's death", and he had begun to cough up blood and died...

This, more or less, was probably what had happened. But what had become of the body? The most obvious solution was that the strange old woman had got rid of it by throwing it into the marsh. According to legend, the marsh would have swallowed the body up and never spat it out again. But why would the old woman have needed to do such a thing? If she was going to hide the body, then why hadn't she got rid of the traces of blood in the room as well? Disposing of the body was a means of concealing a murder, so why had the old woman gone drawing attention by introducing herself to passers-by? Was Mr Tatara really dead? And where had the old woman gone, carrying that enormous *furoshiki*?...

Kosuke Kindaichi went into the kitchen again and peered down at the poisonous flowers. It was then that he suddenly heard what sounded like a splash of water. It seemed to come from inside the jug. The sound was very faint and quiet, but under the circumstances it assailed his ears like a clap of thunder. Startled by this, Kindaichi took another look at the water jug and once again he heard a splash coming from inside it. He reached for the jug and carefully shook the chieftain's death out onto the floor. Then he shone the light of his torch into the jug and peered inside. What he saw gave him an eerie sensation that raised gooseflesh all over his body.

Squirming around at the bottom of the jug was a monstrous, ugly creature that looked like a large newt or gecko. Its slippery blackish-brown body was covered all over in dark spots and hideous-looking warts, and its head was enormous and flat.

Intrigued to see what had alarmed Kindaichi so much, O-Ito had appeared at his side and now gasped as she peered into the jug with him.

"It's a salamander," she said.

Kosuke Kindaichi knew this perfectly well, but what was a salamander doing in the bottom of a water jug?

"Did Mr Tatara always keep a salamander?"

"No, it wasn't here the last time I visited him."

"And when was that, exactly?"

"It was on the 5th of this month."

"And what was the reason for your visit?…"

Kosuke Kindaichi's tone unwittingly had become interrogatory.

"I was bringing him an O-Bon present…"

Was that really so? When she had caught up with him on the mountain pass, she had said she was taking an O-Bon present to Mr Tatara. Had that been nothing more than a ruse?

"And how is it that you're so certain the salamander wasn't here then?"

"Why, because… I took some water from this very jug when I was making tea for the village chieftain."

That seemed plausible enough. And the 5th of the month was two days before Kosuke Kindaichi had written the letter on behalf of Mr Tatara.

"Are there a lot of salamanders in these parts?"

"I wouldn't say there are lots of them, but they're not exactly a rarity either… And besides, the village chieftain was—is—a keen fisherman."

In evidence of this, O-Ito pointed to the many kinds of dried, skewered fish, both large and small, adorning the walls of the main room.

Kosuke Kindaichi returned his gaze to the water jug...

Shortly after that, he left, urging O-Ito to accompany him back to the Turtle Spring. Outside, they found Inspector Isokawa waiting for them. They told him what they had found. Were it not for his presence, the local policemen would surely have laughed in their faces.

"But, Kindaichi," flatly intoned the inspector, gazing all the while at the white water-chestnut flowers that were in bloom all across the marsh, "do you suppose this is connected with the affair that took place here twenty-three years ago?"

However, Kosuke Kindaichi knew well that the inspector's tone merely camouflaged the sense of hope and excitement that was welling up inside him. For indeed it was a sense of hope—hope that these new developments might cast a light on this unsolved mystery from his past.

"I don't doubt it," Kindaichi replied, weighing his words. "Otherwise, it's hard to believe that somebody would go to all this trouble for a recluse like Mr Tatara... Inspector, can you tell me where Mr Tatara gets his money? The owner of the Izutsu Inn seems to be quite close to him, but even she says she's no idea..."

"I seem to recall the owner of the Turtle Spring telling me that he had some relatives in Kobe or somewhere. Could they be sending him some, I wonder?" said the inspector.

"He did have family in Kobe, yes. But Mrs Aoike told me that relative died three years ago. If he was receiving money, it would have stopped back then. I'm at a loss to explain it myself. Then again, his outgoings can't have been all that much, so he might have been able to put some money away while it was being sent

84

to him… At least, that's what O-Ito said. But then, is Mr Tatara really the sort to save for his future?"

"Good grief, Kindaichi!" the inspector finally exclaimed. "Surely you don't mean to suggest that somebody in this village was slipping him some money?"

Before Kosuke Kindaichi could respond, however, a plain-clothes policeman poked his head out of the cottage, looking around in agitation. The moment he saw the inspector, he came straight over, carrying a letter.

"Inspector, we've got it! We've found the letter from Kobe!"

Inspector Isokawa took the envelope, extracted its contents, looked them over and then handed them to Kosuke Kindaichi without a word. The detective practically tore the letter from his hands and immediately recognized it as the one Mr Tatara had shown him on the evening of the 7th.

Why hadn't the old woman taken it with her, though? Surely this was the most important evidence of all…

"Wh-where did you f-find this?" asked Kosuke Kindaichi. "In some out-of-the-way corner?"

"No, not really… It was in the letter box, together with some other letters and postcards."

Kosuke Kindaichi felt his heart clench. It was unfathomable. The case seemed so elaborately planned. And yet, to leave behind this important forged letter…

"Inspector, m-might I see that envelope?"

There was no doubt about it: it was the same envelope that Kosuke Kindaichi had seen only the other day. He stared at the familiar handwriting in silence before absent-mindedly turning it over. And what he saw there raised a small cry of surprise from him.

"What is it, Kindaichi?"

"Inspector!" exclaimed Kindaichi, trying to calm himself. "When I was addressing the letter for Mr Tatara the other day, I looked at the return address on the back. But just see the postmark on the front!"

The inspector looked at the envelope. He raised his eyebrows and bit his lip.

The postmark was difficult to make out, as if somebody had tried to rub it away with their finger. The date was almost illegible, but the very last digit, which should have been a "5", was clearly a "4". In other words, the letter had not been posted that year, but the year before.

Dead or Alive?

As I mentioned before, had it not been for Inspector Isokawa's presence in the village, this business involving Mr Tatara, no matter how hard Kosuke Kindaichi pressed, would have been treated as a simple missing-person case—blood or no blood on the tatami mat.

However, as Inspector Isokawa, who had an unusual interest in the 1932 case, happened to find himself in Onikobe, the strange disappearance of Mr Tatara, who had been an important witness all those years ago, as added to the bizarre circumstances surrounding his disappearance, attracted the attention of the investigating authorities.

On the afternoon of 12 August, the recreation room at the Turtle Spring was designated the incident room at the request of Inspector Isokawa. All throughout the day, until that evening, officers had kept arriving, one after another, from the prefectural police headquarters and the local police station.

For Inspector Isokawa, this was something of a gamble. It was possible, after all, that he was barking up the wrong tree. He could turn over every rock in the village and still find nothing. And then, to cap it off, after causing all that trouble, Mr Tatara could very well turn up somewhere out of the blue.

Among the officers who had arrived to take charge of the investigation was Deputy Inspector Tachibana, who had come all the way from the town of Emi, some twenty-five miles away. Most of the officers had driven there, but for the average person getting to Onikobe from Emi meant taking the Himezu branch line all the way to Himeji, the final stop, then taking a bus to Soja and then crossing the Sennin Pass. There was, of course, a police force in Soja itself, but unfortunately that village fell under the jurisdiction of Hyogo Prefecture—a fact that hampered the investigation.

At any rate, this team of investigators, led by Deputy Inspector Tachibana, was assembled in the makeshift incident room at the Turtle Spring at around five o'clock that afternoon.

Having heard a summary of the events from Inspector Isokawa and Kosuke Kindaichi, the deputy inspector frowned.

"So, what you're telling me, Kindaichi-san, is that the day before yesterday, on the evening of the 10th, a murder was committed at Mr Tatara's cabin while the storm was raging outside?"

"Not quite, sir," said Kosuke Kindaichi, slumping down in an armchair and tapping the arms one by one. "Right now, we can't say that with any certainty. That's why we'd like you to investigate…"

"Kindaichi…" It was Inspector Isokawa who interjected. "Under the circumstances, I think it would be better to tell the deputy inspector the whole story."

"By 'the whole story', you mean…?"

"That you got here before we did and you're a step ahead of us on this case. I think you should give your opinion on how we ought to set about the investigation. I'm sure the deputy inspector would appreciate hearing it."

"Yes, of course… By all means," said Tachibana emphatically. He proceeded to stare at Kosuke Kindaichi with an inquisitive gaze. A tall, robust forty-something-year-old, the deputy inspector looked like a man who meant business.

Kosuke Kindaichi by contrast looked sleepy. As was his wont, he scratched his scruffy mop of hair and smiled as he sat up in his chair. He extracted a notebook from the breast of his kimono and from it pulled out two or three sheets of paper that had been folded in four.

"I may be getting involved in matters that don't concern me, but I've noted down everything that's struck me so far. Would you care to take a look?" he asked, slightly intimidated.

"Yes, of course! Please!" replied the deputy inspector, leaning forward with an expression of determination on his face.

"Well, these are just a few miscellaneous notes that I took down as the ideas came to me. They're probably quite incoherent, but, who knows, you may just find them useful…"

"I'm sure they'll be most illuminating…"

After having practically snatched the sheets from Kosuke Kindaichi's hands, the deputy inspector unfolded them to discover an itemized list that was written in a hand so neat and meticulous that it looked almost like block print. It was so tidy, in fact, that it seemed quite at odds with the famous detective's dishevelled appearance. The list was as follows:

1. Is Mr Tatara dead or alive? If he is alive, where is he? And if he is dead, where did the culprit hide the body? Furthermore, why hide the body?
2. Is O-Rin dead or alive?
3. If O-Rin is dead, was Mr Tatara aware of the fact or not?

The following operate on the assumption that O-Rin really is dead:

4. Did the Maeda family in Kobe send Mr Tatara notice of her death?

5. When exactly was O-Rin's letter asking for a reconciliation sent?
6. Who was the first person to read the aforementioned letter?
7. Who was the woman calling herself O-Rin on the Sennin Pass on the evening of 10 August?
8. Did Mr Tatara really not notice, after spending more than two hours in the woman's company, that she was not O-Rin? And if not, why not?
9. On what has Mr Tatara subsisted since 1953?
10. When did Mr Tatara acquire the salamander, and why?

When the deputy inspector reached the final point, his eyes widened in surprise. He cast a worried glance at Kosuke Kindaichi, then, keeping his lips pressed firmly together, heaved a deep sigh.

"Well, we've certainly got our work cut out for us," he said with a chuckle. "Let's go through each of these points one by one, Kindaichi-san. Inspector Isokawa, we could use your expertise, too."

"Yes, of course. These are certainly some interesting points you raise," said the inspector, smiling at the very last one on the list.

"Well, then, let's start with point number one: 'Is Mr Tatara dead or alive?' Ascertaining this is going to be no easy task."

"First of all, we have to find the body."

"Precisely. The bloodstains alone aren't enough to prove that he was killed."

Inspector Isokawa nodded.

"But, Kindaichi-san…" Tachibana began.

"Yes?"

"The fact that you posed this question first… Does this mean that you think he wasn't in fact killed?"

"Not quite… I have doubts about my doubts, as it were."

Deputy Inspector Tachibana looked at Kosuke Kindaichi's carefree profile with a somewhat bemused look, but eventually returned his eyes to the notepapers.

"'If he is alive, where is he?'… Well, where indeed? 'And if he is dead, where did the culprit hide the body? Furthermore, why hide the body?' Now, what do you mean by that, Kindaichi-san?"

"You see, Tachibana," Inspector Isokawa quickly cut in, like a father appeasing a difficult child, "this is Kindaichi's method. He's always like this. He likes to consider every possibility… So, in this case, until Mr Tatara's body is found, giving us conclusive evidence that he was killed, Kindaichi thinks it's best to be open to the possibility that he's still alive."

"I see. Only…" Deputy Inspector Tachibana bit his lip. "If Hoan Tatara is still alive, then how do you explain the scene at the cabin?"

"It wouldn't take much to fake that kind of scene," said Kosuke Kindaichi.

"To fake it?…"

Visibly shocked by this idea, Deputy Inspector Tachibana raised his bushy eyebrows. He stared at them both in silence, as his mind finally began to grasp the complexity of this strange and mysterious affair. He then reread carefully the ten points on the piece of paper, his eyes wide with attention.

He cleared his throat after he finished.

"Let's turn to the second point. 'Is O-Rin dead or alive?' Meaning…"

"Well, I wrote that one down for the sake of it, really. That one, along with point number four, can easily be clarified by getting in touch with this Mr Maeda in Kobe."

"I see. Yes… Then with this third point, 'If O-Rin is dead, was Mr Tatara aware of the fact or not?' You mean that—"

"Deputy Inspector," said Kosuke Kindaichi, wearing a solemn look on his face, "this is the most crucial question of them all. There's scarcely any doubt that O-Rin is indeed dead. After all, the owner of the Izutsu Inn claims that she attended the funeral. Still, just to be certain, I think you should have this checked out in Kobe."

Kosuke Kindaichi proceeded to relate to the deputy inspector the story of how he came to write the letter on Mr Tatara's behalf and how Mr Tatara had seemed beside himself with joy.

"And so, we come to points five and six…"

"'When exactly was O-Rin's letter asking for a reconciliation sent?'… But isn't this the letter that Mr Tatara received only recently?"

Deputy Inspector Tachibana reached for the letter on the table and once again examined the postmark on the envelope. As we have already noted, however, the postmark was terribly faded, and only the last digit could be made out. To make matters worse, the sender had neglected to include a date on the letter.

"Still, Mr Maeda in Kobe should be able to shed some light on this."

"Yes, that's true enough. And, Tachibana, that's why the trickier question for Kindaichi here is really the next one, number six."

"'Who was the first person to read the aforementioned letter?' Meaning?"

"Take a closer look at the envelope, Tachibana."

Inspector Isokawa handed him the magnifying glass that was lying beside Kosuke Kindaichi. The deputy inspector took the envelope and turned it over. It had recently been opened with a pair of scissors, but, looking at it carefully with the magnifying glass, he could tell that it had been steamed open. Tachibana heaved a sigh so deep that it was almost like a spouting whale.

"Why, it looks as though this letter was steamed open by somebody before Mr Tatara got his hands on it. This person could have read it and kept it until just the other day. Then all they'd have to do was reseal the envelope and pop it discreetly into Mr Tatara's letter box. He'd have been none the wiser and would have thought it had just arrived…"

"No, that would be too simple," said Kosuke Kindaichi.

"Come again?"

The deputy inspector turned to Inspector Isokawa, looking rather perplexed.

"What I believe Kindaichi means," the inspector began, "is that it could have happened the other way around. For example, Mr Tatara could have received this letter more than a year ago and opened it with his scissors. But, since he had no intention of reconciling, he would have put it aside. It was only later, when he needed it, that he steamed it open and then glued it back together, trying to pull the wool over our eyes…"

"But… But…" The deputy inspector's own eyes looked dazzled. "But the scissor marks where the envelope has been cut open… They look as though they were made very recently!"

"But you can cut an envelope that's been cut already… It's child's play to cut it again and make it look fresh…" said Kosuke Kindaichi.

"My god!"

"But, my dear Tachibana, these are only possibilities that we're discussing," said the inspector.

"But you mean to say, Kindaichi-san, that we should not overlook these possibilities? At least, not until a body has been found… But then, how should we proceed?"

The deputy inspector was breathing rapidly and sweat was beading on his forehead. He wiped it away with the back of his hand and quickly turned the sheet of paper over.

"All right, point seven. 'Who was the woman calling herself O-Rin on the Sennin Pass on the evening of 10 August?'…"

Inspector Isokawa explained: "So, there are two ways of thinking about this… Supposing Mr Tatara really was taken in by the false letter: somebody unexpected must have disguised themselves as O-Rin and paid him a visit. But on the other hand, if it was all his doing in the first place, then it could have been a friend of his or even Mr Tatara himself. After all, nobody saw the old woman's face, and her voice was barely audible. What's more, Kindaichi here spoke to the owner of the Izutsu Inn, who says that Mr Tatara was very fond of the theatre. He was even an amateur actor in his youth."

Deputy Inspector Tachibana's eyes appeared to have glazed over. He looked totally bewildered. Kosuke Kindaichi took pity on him and tried to reassure him:

"Deputy Inspector, I don't like to complicate things unnecessarily, but I really do think there's something suspicious lurking at the bottom of this case… Shall we continue?"

"Yes, of course… Point eight: 'Did Mr Tatara really not notice, after spending more than two hours in the woman's company, that she was not O-Rin? And if not, why not?' Why not, indeed? Do you have any ideas, Kindaichi-san?"

"I'm not certain yet… But on this point, too, there are two ways of thinking about it. The first is that Mr Tatara really didn't notice anything was amiss. The second is that he did in fact notice, but overlooked it, or else pretended not to notice."

"You mean to say that while he was overlooking it and pouring out sake, this person poisoned him?"

"Well, logically speaking, that would appear to be the case," said Kosuke Kindaichi with a chuckle.

"But… but that's absurd!" said the deputy inspector almost with contempt. He was growing more and more frustrated with all these possibilities.

"Come, come, Tachibana. Let's move on to the next point, shall we?"

"Oh, very well… Point nine: 'On what has Mr Tatara subsisted since 1953?' Well, then?"

Inspector Isokawa explained, and, when he did, the deputy inspector's face once again took on a look of seriousness and surprise, and Tachibana lowered his voice:

"But, Inspector, are you saying that Mr Tatara could have been blackmailing somebody after the case back in 1932?"

"We don't know whether Mr Tatara was a blackmailer or not, but it is possible that he was being given money to keep quiet. In which case, point number nine offers us the link between this affair and the one that took place here two decades ago."

"I see. We'll investigate this thoroughly," said the deputy inspector, underlining this point three times. "Right, Kindaichi-san, that leaves just this last point: 'When did Mr Tatara acquire the salamander, and why?'"

"Ah, that one…" said Kosuke Kindaichi, scratching his dishevelled head again. "I only added that to make it a round number."

"You did what?" exclaimed Inspector Isokawa and Deputy Inspector Tachibana in unison. They both looked disappointed.

"Well, that, and the hideous salamander seemed somehow symbolic of this case."

Deputy Inspector Tachibana sniffed in annoyance and glared at Kosuke Kindaichi. Then, as though changing his mind, he bowed to Kindaichi and said:

"Well, thank you all the same. You've certainly been a great help, Kindaichi-san. It's clear that, first things first, we need to find the body of Mr Tatara."

"Yes, that's the most important thing. To establish whether Mr Tatara is dead or alive," mumbled the famous detective, a dark look in his eyes. He shrugged his shoulders apologetically, but the deputy inspector was no longer paying attention to him.

"Kato! Kato!" bellowed Tachibana, calling his subordinate in the next room.

And so, the curtain rose on the investigation led by the energetic Deputy Inspector Tachibana.

"She would measure by the barrel and drink through a funnel..."

The following evening, a number of festivities were due to take place: there was to be a concert given by Yukari Ozora, lantern dancing for the O-Bon festival, and even a singing contest for the young people in the village. However, Deputy Inspector Tachibana had asked everybody to cooperate with the police investigation until the festivities commenced. It was 13 August and Mr Tatara had not yet been found, so the possibility that his body was now at the bottom of the marsh seemed ever more likely.

The marsh itself was around half an acre in size and so deep that it had never dried up, not even in the most arid years—a fact for which the villagers were most grateful. But curiously enough, despite its size, nothing lived in it, except for salamanders, which could be seen there, slithering about with their slippery skin.

That day, the police, helped by the young people of the village, dredged the bottom of the notorious marsh. Rice-paddy boats edged their way through the water-chestnut flowers that were in bloom all across the surface of the water, while nets were cast and long bamboo poles were used to probe the depths of the marsh, but all to no avail.

Perhaps this was to be expected, however. The youths, who cared little for Mr Tatara, had no enthusiasm for the task, and it was not even certain that the man himself was dead, let alone that his body had been dumped in the marsh.

Yet if the search for the body was going nowhere, the investigation led by Deputy Inspector Tachibana was beginning to yield fruit.

First of all, an analysis of the bloodstains had been requested from the prefectural forensic laboratory, and the results, which had just arrived, confirmed the presence of a deadly alkaloid known as lobeline ($C_{22}H_{27}NO_2$), which was found in many varieties of marsh bellflower.

Marsh bellflower…

So, it really was the flower known as "chieftain's death", which could be found all around the marsh. Had Mr Tatara been poisoned with this flower, then?

Then there was the discovery made by Detective Kato during his trip to Kobe the previous day. His report confirmed that O-Rin Kuribayashi was indeed deceased. She had passed away earlier that year, on 27 April, at the home of one Kotaro Maeda, the owner of a restaurant called the Crimson Roof, which was situated in the West Yanagiwara district of Kobe. Detective Kato had even visited the doctor who had written out the death certificate and ascertained that she had died of kidney cancer.

Mr Maeda had, moreover, confirmed that he had sent word of O-Rin's death to Mr Tatara. He even insisted that Mr Tatara must have received it, since the postcard was sent together with the one that had been delivered to the owner of the Izutsu Inn.

Detective Kato had also learnt that O-Rin's letter of reconciliation had been written by Mr Maeda's daughter, Tatsuko. After inspecting the letter, the young woman had immediately confirmed having written it, but she did not recall the exact date. All she remembered was that it was during the warm weather the previous year—hence, probably in August or September 1954. At any rate, O-Rin had waited for an answer in vain. Then, once she had resigned herself to the unlikelihood of a reply, she had seemed to age very suddenly.

And yet, this unanswered letter that had cast O-Rin into the very depths of despair had now unexpectedly resurfaced, just as this bizarre sequence of events was beginning to take place.

Had O-Rin's letter and the postcard notifying Mr Tatara of her death fallen into somebody else's hands? Or had Mr Tatara received them and, for whatever reason, chosen to ignore them?

The next step in Deputy Inspector Tachibana's investigation would be to solve the mystery of where Mr Tatara's money came from.

"All I know," the owner of the Turtle Spring had said in a firm and decisive tone on the evening of 12 August, after having been summoned by the investigating team, "is that one of Mr Tatara's nephews lived in Kobe… His name was Junkichi Yoshida, and he was the son of Mr Tatara's younger sister. Ever since the war was over, he sent him money… but then he died in 1952 or '53, I believe. Mr Tatara even went all the way to Kobe to see whether he could find any other source of money, but nothing came of it. When he returned, he just kept saying that he was in trouble…"

"That he was in trouble?…"

"Yes, but shortly after that, the trouble seemed to go away. I asked him about it one day and he told me that Junkichi's younger brother had decided to carry on sending him some money. He was awfully happy about it."

"You wouldn't happen to know the name of this brother, would you?"

"I'm afraid not…"

"Do you have the address of this Junkichi Yoshida?"

"Hey, Chief, I've got a letter from him right here! Look, it's got his signature…"

It was Detective Inui who had just found several letters from Junkichi Yoshida among all the bundle that he had confiscated from Mr Tatara's cabin. They were all addressed from Kobe. This one even had a phone number.

"Good. Send somebody to carry out the usual checks. He ought to be able to give us an address for his brother."

"Yes, sir. If you've no objection, I'll go myself."

On the early evening of 13 August, Detective Inui had yet to return from Kobe, but they didn't have to wait for his report before doubt was cast on what Rika had told them.

Enquiries at the village post office revealed that Mr Tatara had not been in receipt of any remittances since December 1953. Moreover, not only did neither of the two banks in Soja have any record of deposits being made in Mr Tatara's name, he didn't even appear to have a bank account.

In short, it seemed increasingly likely that Mr Tatara's money was coming not from any outside source, but rather from within the village itself. What's more, it appeared that Mr Tatara had been deceiving Rika...

Deputy Inspector Tachibana was excited by these developments and wasted no time thanking Kosuke Kindaichi for his suggestions.

"Thanks to your help, Kindaichi-san, we've discovered this shady side of Mr Tatara's life far quicker than I anticipated."

"Now, all that remains is to establish who in the village has been paying him," said Inspector Isokawa, his excitement growing. He could sense the connection with the affair of 1932 gradually getting stronger.

"Why not call for the owner and question her again?" suggested Kosuke Kindaichi. "You could ask her who in the village was on good terms with Mr Tatara..."

"Ah! That's a fantastic idea! Hey, Kimura, go and ask the owner of this place to come and see us again, would you?"

"Right away, sir!"

Rika arrived soon after that and answered the questions put to her by Deputy Inspector Tachibana as follows:

"Who was on good terms with him? Hmm… He was so worldly and generous with his time that, as soon as anybody had a little free time in front of them, they'd head over to his house to hear him tell his stories. But truth be told, I'm not sure there was anybody who was especially close to him."

"So, what you're saying is that he wasn't a loner, but there was nobody he would really open up to?"

"That's about the size of it, Deputy Inspector, yes…"

"What about old Mr Nire?" Inspector Isokawa interrupted. "I bet he could tell a few stories…"

"Yes, now that you mention it, they did seem to enjoy talking together. Only, they didn't see each other very often. He had more to do with the cooper's wife…"

"By 'the cooper's wife', you mean…?" asked Kosuke Kindaichi.

"Of course, my apologies. I mean Mrs Yura. People in these parts tend to be called by their old guild names, you see."

"Ah, I see. So, you mean Ioko? The one who's in her eighties?"

"You're very well informed, Kindaichi!" said Inspector Isokawa, chuckling.

"It's just that the owner of the Izutsu Inn mentioned her to me only the other day…" Kosuke Kindaichi replied. "So, was Mr Tatara a regular at the Yura residence?"

"Yes, the old woman would invite him round… Despite everything, Mr Tatara as chieftain still enjoyed the highest social standing in the village. And besides, they were around the same age, so they had things to talk about. And whenever Mrs Yura made something really delicious, she would always have Atsuko take some to him. We'd also try to watch out for him as much as we could…"

It was none other than Atsuko's late husband, Utaro, who had been at the centre of the affair in 1932. The first thing that came to everybody's mind was the possibility that there could be some kind of hidden connection there.

"How exactly is this octogenarian's health? Is she old and frail? Bedridden?"

"Oh, no! She's as strong as an ox, that one. She even comes here to bathe from time to time. Of course, she's as bent over as a bow, but her eyes and ears are so sharp, you'd never know she was in her eighties…"

Rika looked at all three of them questioningly. She had a cold beauty—the kind one encounters so often in Kyoto—but she always maintained a certain modesty and sense of composure.

"You've been most helpful. Thank you," said Inspector Isokawa warmly. "I hope we won't have to disturb you again."

Rika smiled, bowed her head humbly and took her leave.

"Inspector, should we look into the connection between Mr Tatara and the Yura family again?" asked Tachibana.

"It couldn't hurt, certainly," said the inspector with a nod.

Thus, the investigation into the disappearance of Hoan Tatara was steadily progressing. Meanwhile, the young people of the village were making all the necessary preparations for the O-Bon festival. It was to be held at the village school, which had been built on top of the ruins of the residence where the shogun's intendant had once lived.

"What do you say, Inspector?" said Kosuke Kindaichi. "Shall we leave Deputy Inspector Tachibana to his investigation and go along to watch the dancing?"

By the time they had eaten dinner and polished off a bottle of beer each, it was nearly eight o'clock. The evening breeze carried strains of some traditional music issuing from a loudspeaker.

"So, Kindaichi, are you interested in the 'femme fatale' as well?" asked Inspector Isokawa, chuckling to himself.

"What do you mean, 'as well'?... Speak for yourself! Besides, who was it who tried to lure me here using the promise of this 'femme fatale' as bait?"

"Yes, you're right enough there. But let's go and take a look all the same, shall we?"

"Aren't we a bit old for that?"

"Nonsense!"

It was just after eight o'clock when they left the Turtle Spring, laughing and joking, dressed in their lightweight summer kimonos. It took almost an hour's walk to reach the centre of the village, so it was already nine by the time they neared the site where the shogun's intendant had once lived. The place would be crowded with people who had come from all over the surrounding areas.

"This is quite a turnout, Inspector!"

"Let's take a shortcut…"

Inspector Isokawa knew the way better than Kosuke Kindaichi, who had never set foot in this direction since arriving in Onikobe. After walking a short distance along a deserted road surrounded by hills and forests, they saw up ahead a stage that was lit, and around which there was a crowd of people moving about like ants.

"We've arrived just in time, Inspector! Isn't that Yukari singing now?"

Kosuke Kindaichi instinctively rushed towards the stage, but all of a sudden the inspector held him back, tugging at his sleeve.

"Just a moment, Kindaichi…" he whispered, motioning towards something a few yards ahead of them.

Kosuke Kindaichi looked, his heart pounding, and saw two women with their backs to him, loitering at the foot of one of those enormous red pine trees native to the region, as though trying to hide from public view. They were both dressed in summer kimonos, but one of them was wearing an *okoso-zukin* headscarf, the hem of which hung down to her shoulders.

"Who are they, Inspector?" asked Kindaichi, narrowing his eyes.

"It's Satoko… from the Turtle Spring. Haven't you met her yet?"

"No, never… Ah, and the other one is the maid, O-Miki, isn't it? But why is Satoko wearing a winter headscarf in the middle of summer?…"

"She has a birthmark that runs from her head all the way down her body… If it weren't for that, she'd be a pretty-looking girl. Let's slip past, pretending we haven't spotted them, Kindaichi. I feel so sorry for that girl…"

Before they could walk on, however, from the ruins of the old residence, three boisterous men and a woman suddenly came their way. As soon as she saw them, Satoko rushed to the woods to hide, but the others had already spotted her.

"Hey, is that you, Satoko? You don't have to hide away, you know!"

The voice belonged to Shohei. The other three were Kanao, Goro and Fumiko.

"Satoko, are you there?" her brother, Kanao, called out in a plaintive tone. "You haven't seen Yasuko, have you, O-Miki? She and Fumiko are supposed to be on next, and we can't find her anywhere."

O-Miki pointed to the woods and said something.

"What?!" cried Goro. "She went off with an old woman? Well, who was she?"

Hearing O-Miki's response, Shohei froze in horror.

"Hey, Kanao, you don't suppose it's the same oldie who turned up at the chieftain's house, do you?"

The very next moment, Inspector Isokawa and Kosuke Kindaichi found themselves standing before the group.

"What's all this, O-Miki?" said the inspector, adopting as neutral a tone as possible. "An old woman took Yasuko away somewhere?"

O-Miki said that she and Satoko had passed Yasuko along the way. At that time, Yasuko was accompanied by an old woman who was as bent over as a bow, with a *tenugui* tied around her head and wearing a pair of cotton work trousers and worn straw sandals.

"Did you speak to her at all, O-Miki?" asked Kosuke Kindaichi.

"No, Satoko didn't want anybody to see her, so we hid behind a tree."

Satoko stood there in silence, her face turned away. The *okoso-zukin* she was wearing had a gap only for her eyes.

"So, they didn't notice you then?"

"No, sir."

"And how did Yasuko look? Did she seem at all frightened?"

"No… Well, I can't really say for sure, actually. She seemed more surprised than anything."

"Kanao," said Inspector Isokawa, weighing his words as usual, "would you and your friends like to help us look for Yasuko? Go to the Yuras' house and see whether she's gone home… If she isn't there, send somebody up to the Turtle Spring to alert the police."

There was a tremor in the inspector's voice.

Little by little, the commotion grew, and as soon as the O-Bon dance was over, the village was combed through, but Yasuko was not discovered that night.

The corpse of Yasuko, the cooper's girl, was discovered only the following morning. And, just as in the *temari* song, she was found drinking through a funnel...

PART II

What the Second Little Sparrow Said

Round the Fire Stories

Up in the gently sloping hills above Mr Tatara's cabin by the marsh, there was a waterfall. The term "waterfall" may be something of an exaggeration, but there was a drop of around twelve feet at one point in the rock formation, and it was there that clear spring water cascaded down over the surface of the rock face. The locals called this feature "the bench waterfall" because halfway down the drop was an outcropping that looked remarkably like a bench, on top of which water pooled before overflowing and trickling down into the basin below, which was shaped like an irregular semicircle, about six feet wide and a foot and a half deep. From there, the water flowed down into the marshland, but this was where Mr Tatara always came to fetch his fresh water.

It was in this basin that the corpse of Yasuko Yura was found. Her body was lying in the shallow waters, her head resting on a rock and facing skywards. But these words do not do justice to the incredible scene. In her mouth there was a large glass funnel, almost eight inches in diameter at the top, while wedged into the rocky outcrop above stood a one-and-a-half-gallon barrel that was collecting the falling water. As the water filled the slightly tilted barrel, it allowed the overflow to trickle down into the funnel sticking out of Yasuko's mouth.

For those who didn't know the *temari* song of Onikobe—and no doubt also for those who did—this discovery caused an electrifying shock. At first, nobody could grasp the meaning of this bizarre tableau or what the murderer had been trying to show. The sheer incomprehensibility of it made it impossible not to feel a gut-wrenching sense that there was something strange and sinister lurking at the bottom of this incident. As in the *temari* song, the murderer had made the cooper's daughter drink through a funnel after measuring the water out in a barrel, but in reality the girl had been strangled first and then placed in this bizarre pose.

The body had been found by Kanao and Goro. They had searched for the girl high and low, but to no avail. Then, thinking that perhaps she too had been killed and thrown into the marsh, they decided to search the surrounding area, and that was when they found her.

At the time of the discovery, Kosuke Kindaichi and Inspector Isokawa were in the incident room at the Turtle Spring. They had been dozing off, but when the report came in, they bolted out of their chairs and rushed to the scene, where a large crowd had already gathered.

As Kosuke Kindaichi picked his way through the people to reach the small waterfall, he felt a shiver down his spine. He stood there beside Inspector Isokawa, as if glued to the spot, and a single, rueful groan escaped his throat.

It was not only Kosuke Kindaichi and Inspector Isokawa who were unable to move, however. From the officers of the investigating team, including Deputy Inspector Tachibana, who had already arrived, to the villagers surrounding the waterfall basin, everybody just stood there, gazing at this diabolical scene as though mesmerized.

And yet, although it was a terrifying sight, it also had a strange kind of beauty and allure. Yasuko's body was almost completely submerged, while the sleeves and hem of her yukata undulated in the ripples of the water. Doubtless, this bizarre image would imprint itself indelibly on the minds of all those who witnessed it, the vibrant patterns of her kimono, vermilion and indigo, dancing prettily at the bottom of the crystal-clear water.

Yasuko's face was almost entirely obscured by the large funnel. The overflowing water was trickling down from the glass funnel and onto her face. The enormous old barrel perched on the rock above the funnel added to the horror of the scene. As the water from the waterfall cascaded down into the barrel, tiny droplets would splash up, which, in the morning sun and against the dark background of the rock face, glittered with the seven colours of the rainbow…

This was the stuff of fairy tales… And yet they were all in the presence of a terrible murder.

Deputy Inspector Tachibana cleared his throat and spoke at last:

"Who on earth would do such a thing? And why the barrel and the funnel?"

His voice was full of indignation, and he sounded almost ready to lash out at Kosuke Kindaichi.

Unable to answer, Kindaichi merely shook his head in disbelief, while Inspector Isokawa, as though waking from a bad dream, answered in his stead:

"We'll investigate all that in good time, Tachibana. For now, though, we should photograph the crime scene. Is the photographer here?"

Fortunately, the police photographer had been summoned the previous day to take photos of Mr Tatara's cabin and had not yet left. His involvement led to a sudden flurry of activity around the waterfall.

Without waiting for Tachibana's response, Kosuke Kindaichi beckoned to Kanao, who was standing a little off to the side. Kanao approached, accompanied by Shohei and Goro. The three of them were inseparable.

"What is it, Kindaichi-san?" Kanao asked, his usual charm and composure now completely gone. The anger deep within him seemed ready to bubble over.

"Tell me, Kanao," said the detective, looking at him questioningly, "what is that strange mark on the barrel? It looks like a weight beneath two mountains."

Inspector Isokawa had also noticed the curious-looking mark that Kosuke Kindaichi had pointed out. The same symbol that had been branded on the side of the barrel was also emblazoned in enamel on the side of the glass funnel.

"Oh, that…" said Kanao, a little flustered. He turned to Goro, as though looking for help, but the latter turned away.

"Don't you recognize it, Kanao?" The weary-sounding question came from Shohei. After a whole night of searching, the young man looked drained and exhausted. "It's our logo."

"Your logo?…"

"Yes, our guild name has always been 'weigher', and that's our logo. It's a combination of two carpenter's squares and a weight. All of our things are branded with that logo."

"But, Inspector…" It was Kanao who now spoke, coming to Shohei's defence. "Anybody could get hold of those, though. Isn't that right, Goro?"

"What do you mean?"

"You'd better tell it, Shohei. The police will want to know this."

"All right," said Shohei with a firm nod. "You can't see it from here, Inspector, but during the war we built a winery just over that hill, where we'd press the grapes, ferment them, and then bottle them before delivering the bottles to the army—or something like that. We carried on selling the wine after the war, but not for long. Once alcohol became plentiful again, nobody wanted such a sour-tasting drink. We didn't shut the winery down

112

completely though, but it's in a terrible state of disrepair and lying half-abandoned. So, even though those things are technically our property, it wouldn't be hard for anybody to get their hands on them if they wanted to—as Kanao just said."

"Especially since it's my old man who's in charge of the winery," said Goro with a shrug.

"What do you mean by that?" asked Inspector Isokawa, exchanging a brief glance with Kosuke Kindaichi.

"Oh, just that my old man has a reputation in the village. He drinks all day long. There are a lot of funnels and empty barrels lying around the place; there's every chance he wouldn't notice if one or two were to go missing. Ah, here he is now…"

They turned and saw three men walking quickly in their direction. One of them, as Kindaichi well knew, was Shohei's father, Kahei. He had on a straw hat at a jaunty angle and wore his lightweight summer kimono hitched up and tucked into his obi. Behind him, running with short, hurried steps, was a stout little man of about forty-five, in overalls. With his red nose, he was undoubtedly Goro's father. They found out later that his name was Tatsuzo, and he was of course Harue's older brother. Finally, the third man, who was pushing a bicycle, was apparently called young Doctor Honda, and he must have been around the same age as Tatsuzo.

Seeing them arrive, the crowd of people parted to make way for them. When Kahei found himself in front of the waterfall, he stood there for a moment, his eyes wide and his breath short, before heading over to Kosuke Kindaichi as he mopped the sweat off his brow.

"Kindaichi-san," he said, "what's the meaning of all this? Why has poor Yasuko's killer staged this eccentric scene?"

"I was just about to ask you that myself."

"Come again?"

"What I mean to say is, did such a kind of torture ever exist in these parts?"

"… Of torture?!" said Inspector Isokawa, raising his eyebrows doubtfully.

"It reminds me of a foreign book…" said Kosuke Kindaichi with a nervous laugh.

I believe the "foreign book" in question was probably Arthur Conan Doyle's *Round the Fire Stories*. The collection's opening story, "The Leather Funnel", takes place in the France of Louis XIV and describes a form of torture whereby the criminal is trussed and laid on their back, while a funnel is inserted into their mouth and water poured into it until a confession is extracted.

"This whole area used to be under the control of a minor daimyo, so it's quite possible that this form of torture could have been employed…"

"Yes, quite," said Kahei, nodding. "I've never heard such a story myself, but if ever it did happen, you can be sure that Mr Tatara would have known about it. Although…" He stopped before he could finish that thought and instead merely sighed and asked: "What do you make of it, Kindaichi-san?"

Meanwhile, Tatsuzo rubbed his nose and assumed a knowing air.

"I have something that might interest you, sir," he said.

"Something interesting, eh?"

"It happened yesterday evening, you see. I was on my way back from the fields and took the path that passes by the old winery. Well, I had a thirst on, so I stopped here to get a drink of water. I'm pretty sure the barrel and funnel weren't there at the time, but…"

"But?"

"I went over to the winery to have a drink of the sour stuff, but then I came back along the same path, towards the waterfall—I had to go this way, because, as you'll know, the other road is blocked by a landslide after the rain the other night—when I got thirsty again. So, I came over to have another drink, and, as I got closer, I spotted something strange up on the bench. I tried to get a better look and saw that it was a barrel and a funnel. I even touched them just to be sure."

"Now, hang on a minute," Deputy Inspector Tachibana cut in. "At what time was all this?"

"Hmm… I got home around nine, so I must've passed here around half-past eight. It was already dark."

"And you left the items here, just as you found them?"

"No, I took them home with me," Tatsuzo said off-handedly.

Just then, however, the victim's mother and brother arrived on the scene, and an atmosphere of tension suddenly descended upon the crowd.

A Rivalry

Atsuko, the widow of Utaro Yura, was now approaching the waterfall in full view of everyone. She must be around sixty years old.

The owner of the Izutsu Inn had described Atsuko as imperious, and indeed, she cut an imposing figure for a woman of her years. She was tall and plump, and with her greying hair brushed neatly back without a single strand out of place, she looked a formidable woman. She had on a grey splash-patterned kimono, but, unlike Rika Aoike, there was a slight carelessness in the manner in which she wore it.

Atsuko didn't look much like her beautiful daughter, but such is the mystery of creation—and besides, Yasuko's brother Toshio, what with his pale, almost malnourished-looking complexion, didn't look much like Yasuko either. He was as broad as his mother, but not as tall, and everything about him suggested sluggishness.

Atsuko strode forward, seemingly unperturbed by the stares of the crowd, her eyes fixed strangely ahead. Arriving at the edge of the rock pool, she observed for a moment the body of her daughter immersed in the water without showing any emotion, before taking a deep breath and turning to Kahei. Since her arrival, she hadn't looked at him even once, although she had known that he was there. Pointing to her daughter's corpse, she cried out to him:

"Is this your doing, Kahei?!" she cried, her voice menacing and strangely guttural.

For a moment, Kahei didn't seem to understand the meaning of her words and just stared at her blankly. But then Atsuko spoke again in a lower voice:

"I asked whether this is your doing, Kahei!"

"Wh… What do you mean?"

Kahei appeared genuinely confused. He stared back at the woman in astonishment.

"Why would I do anything to Yasuko?! What you're saying is outrageous!"

"Oh, but it isn't, Kahei," said Atsuko, trying to corner him. "I know she was in your way. So, I'll ask you once again, Kahei, is this your doing?"

Kahei finally got a hold of himself. It wasn't anger so much as sympathy that filled his eyes now.

"No, Atsuko. I'm telling you: I didn't do this."

"No, of course not…"

Atsuko suddenly turned her face away, no doubt embarrassed by the look of pity she saw in his eyes.

These two had, at one time, been known throughout the village for their love affair and infidelities. But if Kosuke Kindaichi were to credit what Kahei had told him in the bath at the Turtle Spring, it had been Kahei who left Atsuko in the end.

"No, of course you didn't," she murmured again distractedly. "Forgive me for saying that. I shouldn't have accused you. Toshio, ask the villagers to get Yasuko out of there as quickly as possible and bring her home. I'll go back now and make the arrangements."

"Er, madam…" Deputy Inspector Tachibana called out, trying to catch her attention, but Atsuko didn't hear him.

Having said what she had come to say, she set off briskly down the path by which she had come. Her dignified silhouette made her even more pitiful in the eyes of Kosuke Kindaichi. Perhaps she was too proud to express her grief at the loss of her daughter, at least while Kahei was around.

After this brief quieter interlude, the area around the waterfall suddenly sprang to life. The villagers, who had been so astonished by what just happened that they were all nudging and winking at each other, began to get agitated as soon as Atsuko left. There were calls for Yasuko's body to be lifted out of the water. Fortunately, the police photographer had already finished his work.

Deputy Inspector Tachibana then asked the young people of the village to help with the body. No sooner had he spoken than Kanao jumped into the water. He removed the terrible funnel from her mouth and threw it angrily into the barrel. Then he took her soaking wet body in his arms, pushing away Shohei and Goro, who had come to help him.

"Should I lay her out on the ground?" he asked with an extraordinary look in his eyes.

Kosuke Kindaichi exchanged glances with Inspector Isokawa. A few of the youths ran off to fetch something. Meanwhile, oblivious to the water seeping into his clothes, Kanao just stood there, glaring at all the people around him. When his eyes reached Shohei, however, they came to an abrupt stop.

His gaze was so penetrating that Shohei instinctively recoiled, but still he glared back at him. There was such mounting intensity in their eyes that the people around them worried something explosive might happen at any moment. Just as they began to wring their hands, however, the group of youths arrived back, carrying a door panel, which they had taken from Mr Tatara's cabin.

At the request of Deputy Inspector Tachibana and Doctor Honda, the girl was laid out on this makeshift stretcher. A ripple of alarm suddenly passed through the crowd that was standing near the door. They had just spotted the strangulation marks freshly cut into Yasuko's neck.

"Yasuko! What have they done to you?" cried the victim's brother, Toshio, trying to cling to the body. But one of the policemen held him back, while Doctor Honda set about examining the body.

The merest glance, however, was enough to establish that she had been strangled.

Kosuke Kindaichi turned to Tatsuzo.

"You were saying, Tatsuzo?… I'm very keen to hear the rest of your story."

"Er… and which story would that be?" said Tatsuzo, turning to the detective in surprise. Suspicious, he frowned as he watched Kosuke Kindaichi scratching his untidy hair.

"You know, Tatsuzo," Inspector Isokawa cut in, "Kindaichi-san here is a renowned private detective. I'd like you to answer his questions frankly."

"Of course, of course," Tatsuzo replied, somewhat flustered, rubbing his red nose with the back of his left hand. "What is it that you'd like to know?"

"You mentioned earlier that you took a funnel and a barrel home with you. Do you still have them?"

"Hmm… I left them in the kitchen last night. They should still be there. Goro, you didn't see them, did you?"

"Can't say that I did, no," said Goro, wiping the perspiration from his forehead. Little by little, the summer sun was getting more intense.

"If they're still at your home, it means that the killer must have taken these from the winery later," said Kosuke Kindaichi. "You said earlier that you came across the barrel and funnel here at around half-past eight, but what time was it when you passed here the first time?"

"Hmm…" said Tatsuzo, cocking his head slightly. "I don't remember exactly, but I think it would have been between seven and a quarter past seven. It was starting to get dark already."

"So that was when you had a drink of water here, but the barrel and funnel weren't here at that point?"

"Yes, just as I said… Ah!" Tatsuzo's eyes suddenly widened as he turned instinctively to look towards the top of the road.

"What is it?"

"Of course, that's it," he said in astonishment, looking anxiously at the men around him. "At the far end of the marsh, there's a crossroads that leads off in four directions. When I got there, I saw someone disappearing into the vineyards. I didn't think much of it at the time and assumed it was just an employee who'd forgotten something, but now I remember they were carrying something that glinted in the fading light. It could well have been the funnel…"

"Was it a man or a woman?"

"It was already getting dark. All I could see was a silhouette."

Tatsuzo mopped the sweat from his brow.

"Well, Inspector, why don't we ask Tatsuzo to show us this place?"

"Would you mind, Tatsuzo?"

"Of course not."

The three of them headed off, leaving behind Deputy Inspector Tachibana, who watched them go with a somewhat puzzled look on his face.

After a short while, the path veered away from the edge of the marsh and came to a steeper section that led up a hill. To their right, at the foot of the hill, the marsh spread out, while to their left stood row upon row of grapevines, giving off their heady fragrance.

"By the way, Tatsuzo..." started Kosuke Kindaichi.

"Yes?"

"About what Mrs Yura said back there... She seemed to think that Kahei had something to do with all this."

"Yes, she did. But I can't believe that for a minute."

"She implied that Yasuko had somehow got in his way. Is there any truth to this?"

Unlike in the big cities, it was difficult to keep a secret in the countryside. It had not escaped Kosuke Kindaichi's attention that when Atsuko let those words slip from her mouth, most of the people standing there seemed to understand the meaning behind them.

"Well, er, she was probably talking about Kanao..."

"You mean Mrs Aoike's son?"

"Yes, that's the one. The lad who carried poor Yasuko out of the water just now..."

"But what does Kanao have to do with all this?"

"Well, it's like this, you see. He's a not a bad lad. He's handsome and hard-working, popular with all the girls in the village, if you catch my meaning. But of all the girls, Yasuko was by far and away the prettiest. And I don't think Kanao was exactly indifferent to her either. As you could probably see for yourself just now..."

"So, do you mean to say that Mrs Yura intended Yasuko to marry Kanao?" asked Inspector Isokawa, raising his eyebrows.

"Exactly, Inspector. I heard she'd even spoken to Mrs Aoike about it and had settled things."

"So, what happened?"

"Mr Nire went and threw a spanner in the works."

"How so?"

"Well, he too has a rather pretty daughter who's around the same age as Yasuko, and so he set about trying to persuade Kanao's mother to change her mind."

"And she did?"

"No, but she was certainly thinking about it."

So, it wasn't for his own gratification, but rather for his daughter's sake that Kahei had gone so often to listen to Mrs Aoike's shamisen playing. Kosuke Kindaichi was a little taken aback by this revelation.

"Ah, it was right here, sir," said Tatsuzo, suddenly stopping.

They found themselves at a small crossroads with a statue between the rows of vines, overlooking the far end of the marsh. Kosuke Kindaichi had walked this way once before, but he had taken the path to the right, which led to the rear entrance of the Turtle Spring.

"Where exactly did you see this figure?"

"It was over there, Kindaichi-san," said Tatsuzo, pointing to one of the fields on the left.

There were long, trailing bunches of amber-coloured grapes hanging from the vines, and a person could easily have hidden among them, not least at nightfall.

"Which direction did this figure come from?"

"I think they must have been coming from up in the hills…"

"But you aren't certain of that?"

"No, I wasn't really paying attention while I was walking. I only looked up when I heard footsteps. That's when I saw this person in the shadows carrying something gleaming, just before they disappeared among the vines."

"Where does this path leading off to the left take you?"

"To Sakura."

"Sakura?"

"It's a hamlet. There's a Buddhist temple there. And yes, of course… the path passes right behind the Mr Nire's house," said Tatsuzo, suddenly lowering his voice, seized by excitement. "Besides, all the vines you see here belong to the Nire family."

Tatsuzo glanced at Kosuke Kindaichi and Inspector Isokawa with a look of fear in his eyes.

Scratching his dishevelled hair, the famous detective gazed distractedly along the path leading off to the left.

"So, this winery is up ahead then?" he asked.

"Yes, that's right. You follow the bend in the path up there to the left, then carry on straight down the hill."

"What do you say, Inspector? Shall we take a look?"

Shiro Aoyagi, Silent-Film Narrator

The winery stood around fifty yards from the crossroads, at the foot of a large hill. The buildings, of course, were little more than barracks, but they appeared to have electricity. A number of utility poles stood at regular intervals, one of which was tilting over at an angle—evidence of the recent storm and the enormous landslide that it had caused.

The winery overlooked several hamlets that depended on the village of Onikobe. Tatsuzo ran down the steep slope ahead of Kosuke Kindaichi and Inspector Isokawa.

"Look," he shouted. "There's the temple at Sakura over on our right. And can you see that big mansion to the left of it? That's the Nire house. All the land you see here is owned by old Nire."

The temple at Sakura was set into the hillside on the near side of the hamlet; it was perched at the top of a stone staircase of about twenty steps and shaded by a number of mature chinquapins. Not far away, there was another enormous, elaborate roof, which was that of the Nire residence.

"Tell me, where is the Yuras' house?" Kosuke Kindaichi asked.

"You can't see it from here, but it's over in that direction," said Tatsuzo. "Do you see the big reservoir over there? Beyond it to the right lie the ruins of the residence where the shogun's intendant once lived and where the school now stands. The Yura house is just on the far side of it."

"And the village itself is just alongside that?"

It would have been about a mile from where they stood.

"Yes, exactly… You know, the Yuras' house is much older than the Nires'. When we were children, the Nires had a house just as small as mine, but the last two heads of the family made an awful lot of money."

"Now tell me, where is the house that Mr Tatara used to live in?"

"The chieftain's place? As the inspector knows, it stood on the site where the village hall now stands. See, over there, just to the left of the school."

"Ah, so the chieftain's house, as it stood when the tragedy in 1932 took place, no longer exists?"

"That's right, sir. He had to sell it in the end. Now, when was that?" Tatsuzo asked Inspector Isokawa.

"It was back in 1936, if I remember rightly."

"Ah, yes, that's right, Inspector. It was the year before all the trouble began in China."

"So, did Mr Tatara move from there straight into his cabin?" Kosuke Kindaichi asked.

"No, at first he lived in a little house he'd built by the reservoir. He stayed there for the duration of the war. At the time, he was still with O-Fuyu, his eighth wife. It was only last year, when she left him, that he moved to the cabin."

Tatsuzo seemed strangely moved by this. Inspector Isokawa, too, nodded silently in agreement.

"Just one last thing before we continue, Tatsuzo. Would you mind pointing out your own house for me?"

"Mine?! Mine is far too small to see from here."

"But I thought I'd heard that your niece had had a grand mansion built for you?" said Kosuke Kindaichi, shortly before realizing that he had put his foot in it. "Oh, forgive me. Of course, I mean to say your sister."

He tried to gloss over the mistake as quickly as he could, but Tatsuzo didn't seem to care much about it.

"She had it built for her grandparents, so it's got nothing to do with me," he said, practically spitting out the words. "Would you care to see the winery now, sir?"

There was a hint of irritation in his voice. Kosuke Kindaichi turned instinctively to Inspector Isokawa. Clearly, Tatsuzo seemed to have some kind of inferiority complex where his niece was concerned.

The winery appeared deserted, without a soul in sight. Right in the middle of it stood a large drum, with pipes leading off in all directions. At the far end of the room was an enormous vat that looked like the kind used for making sake, while at the near end, along one wall, was stack upon stack of barrels. On the opposite wall were stacks of thousands of empty bottles. Throughout the winery, the pungent smell of vinegar hung in the air, assailing their nostrils.

Tatsuzo stepped out briefly and came back, bearing a tray with three cups. He twisted the cork in one of the barrels, and there came a glugging sound as the poisonous-looking purple-red liquid came flowing out. Tatsuzo filled the three cups.

"Well, Inspector, Kindaichi-san? Would you care to try it?"

Kosuke Kindaichi and Inspector Isokawa took the cups being offered to them and each took a little sip, but immediately winced and set the cups down again.

Tatsuzo laughed. "I suppose we villagers are the only ones who drink this stuff these days," he said, taking another draught. "Still, it does the job quick enough."

Soon enough, the conversation returned to the subject of Tatsuzo's niece, Yukari Ozora.

"She's completely under the control of that damned manager, who takes advantage of her and her money," lamented Tatsuzo.

"Oh?"

"His name's Koreya Kusakabe. Surely you know the one I mean?"

"Ah yes, of course. Him. Isn't he the one who discovered the girl and practically raised her?"

"So he says… He's somehow managed to win over her mother entirely. There's a story going around that he's a returnee from Manchuria, but in truth nobody really knows who he is…"

"A returnee from Manchuria?" Inspector Isokawa exclaimed. "How old is he?"

"Hmm… I'd say he must be in his early fifties. I believe he's what they call a 'silver fox'. Harue's certainly head over heels in love with him."

"What was he doing in Manchuria?"

Inspector Isokawa tried to ask the question as nonchalantly as possible, but the words seemed to stick in his throat.

"I heard he was working for some film company out there. Though I don't know what he did for them exactly."

Inspector Isokawa shot a piercing look at Kosuke Kindaichi. He had growing suspicions.

The inspector wondered whether the man who was killed in the autumn of 1932 in Mr Tatara's cottage really had been Genjiro. The victim, impossible to identify, could have been Ikuzo Onda, the crook, and the real murderer none other than Genjiro. He could have killed the con artist and taken his money before vanishing. Meanwhile Genjiro's family, aware of what had happened, could have claimed that the body was his in order to protect him… For more than twenty years, this doubt had plagued Inspector Isokawa. If his suspicions were right, his only hope was that Genjiro might one day return to Onikobe under a false identity.

And now, a perfect stranger had arrived in the village. What's more, he was thought to be around fifty years old. In 1932, Genjiro Aoike was twenty-eight, which would make him fifty-one today. At the time, it was even rumoured that the murderer had fled to Manchuria, and here was this man who had supposedly returned from there…

"Tatsuzo," said Inspector Isokawa, trying to hold back his excitement, "do you happen to remember the murder of Genjiro Aoike, which took place back in 1932?"

"Why, of course I do! It's because of all that that Chieko was born," he said with a laugh.

Having poured himself several more cups of the sour-tasting alcohol from the barrel, Tatsuzo was growing more and more inebriated, and his nose redder and redder.

"Do you think it's true, what they're saying?" asked Inspector Isokawa. "That this is a continuation of the affair that took place back in 1932?"

"Who's been saying that?"

"I overheard Mr Nire discussing it with Doctor Honda as they were standing by the waterfall."

"I see…"

Inspector Isokawa cast a sidelong glance at Kosuke Kindaichi.

"But how old would you have been back then, Tatsuzo?"

"It was the year after I'd had to go for my army physical, so I'd have been twenty-two."

"So, you'll remember Genjiro Aoike well then?"

"Why should I?" Tatsuzo shot a suspicious look at Inspector Isokawa. "He was six years older than me, Inspector. He left school just as I was starting it. And when he left, he went straight to Kobe. I don't really remember him at all, I'm afraid."

"But what about after he came back?"

"Oh, no, Inspector. As you know all too well, the incident took place only a month after he came back. We lived at opposite ends of the village, so we hardly ever saw one another. All I heard was that he'd returned with his wife and child."

"Tell me," said Kosuke Kindaichi, "what exactly had this Genjiro Aoike been doing in Kobe?"

"Didn't I tell you?" retorted Inspector Isokawa, looking somewhat taken aback.

"I think you said only that he'd done various things in Kobe and Osaka."

"Did I now? Do you know what Genjiro did in the city, Tatsuzo?"

"Well, I had heard that he'd worked in Kobe as a narrator for silent films, and that he'd lost his job when the talkies came along…"

"A narrator for silent films?" Kosuke Kindaichi repeated, his eyes wide with amazement.

It would have been right around the time when, all across Japan, announcers and musicians employed by cinemas were losing their jobs in droves because of the boom in talkies.

"Yes, that's right. I forget his professional name, but, whatever it was, it was a romantic-sounding one. He was awfully popular with the young ladies in the audience," continued Tatsuzo.

"Shiro Aoyagi, wasn't it?" said the inspector. "They said he was one of the best-known film narrators in Kobe."

"Yes, that's it! Shiro Aoyagi. I remember now," said Tatsuzo, looking pleased with himself for no reason. By this point, he was totally inebriated.

Kosuke Kindaichi nodded. He finally seemed to have grasped why the inspector was so excited. In the inspector's mind, Genjiro Aoike and Koreya Kusakabe were one and the same person.

But wasn't there something a little off about this hypothesis? If what the inspector thought was true, Genjiro Aoike had fled after killing the con artist Ikuzo Onda. That this Genjiro, having decided to return to the village, would do so with his victim's former mistress and daughter, seemed a little too absurd. Even if Harue did not recognize Genjiro—or, what's more, even if her brother, Tatsuzo, did not recognize him—would it not have taken an extraordinary coincidence for Genjiro not only to meet Harue, but to turn the girl she had with Onda into a famous singer?

"Incidentally, Tatsuzo…"

"Yes?"

Tatsuzo had gone to remove the cork from the barrel again and refill two glasses to the brim with the thick purple-red liquid. Called by Kosuke Kindaichi, he teetered back towards him, carrying a glass in each hand.

"Did you ever happen to meet Ikuzo Onda?"

"Of course, many times. He was a smooth-talker, and my father was taken in by it—hook, line and sinker. When he found out that Harue had fallen pregnant by this con artist and murder suspect, he was furious, while my mother just cried and cried no end." He took another numbing gulp of the odious liquid. "But isn't the world a curious place, Inspector, Kindaichi-san? Now they're the ones who are in clover because of that child."

With that, Tatsuzo downed the contents of the glasses he was still holding, bowed respectfully and, as he did so, lost his balance and went crashing to the ground, whereupon he began to snore loudly.

Kosuke Kindaichi and Inspector Isokawa then quietly took a walk around, inspecting the winery. In a warehouse adjoining the building, they found a number of empty barrels and funnels stacked up on the shelves. A pane in the window had been smashed, and the latch on the inside was up. It was clear that anybody could have taken any number of barrels and funnels. The question now was why the assassin had insisted on using them.

Leaving Tatsuzo there, Kosuke Kindaichi and Inspector Isokawa left the winery and made their way back to the bench waterfall. A good dozen villagers were still loitering there, talking in small groups, but there was no longer any trace of either the corpse or of the deputy inspector. When they arrived back at the Turtle Spring half an hour later, they found Tachibana getting ready to question Satoko and O-Miki in the makeshift incident room.

The Girl with the Birthmark

"Ah, Inspector, you're just in time," said Deputy Inspector Tachibana. "I was just about to go over the events of last night with these two ladies once more. I'd appreciate it if you'd stay to listen in."

"Oh, I see. Well, yes, of course," replied the inspector. "Will you stay as well, Kindaichi?"

Inspector Isokawa's sojourn in the village had been supposed to be nothing more than a holiday. Under the circumstances, however, somebody would have to be dispatched from the prefectural police headquarters sooner or later, but until then the inspector had decided to undertake the role himself. In fact, later that day, he would receive a telephone call from the Okayama Prefectural Police Headquarters, putting him officially in charge of the case.

A playwright might have set the scene of this interview as follows:

Time:	10 a.m. on 14 August 1955.
Place:	The recreation room at the Turtle Spring, a large and dreary-looking room lit by a solitary ray of sunshine. On the wooden floor stands a table and several chairs.
Characters:	Satoko (22) and O-Miki (28). Deputy Inspector Tachibana, Inspector Isokawa and Kosuke Kindaichi. Two other policemen, one of whom is preparing to take notes.

Before the interrogation began, Kosuke Kindaichi looked at Satoko properly for the first time, but when he saw her face, he involuntarily lowered his eyes at such a pitiful sight.

In terms of her profile, Satoko would have been a real beauty. But what a cruel hand the gods had dealt her. Despite her fine features, half of her face was covered in a patch of red, so big that it almost resembled a map. This birthmark did not stop at her face, either: it reached down her neck and, judging by the back of both her hands, which peeked out of the cuffs of her summer kimono, all across her body. She was a girl with naturally smooth, pale skin, and so the contrast with the dark-red pigmentation of her birthmark was all the more conspicuous. In a girl of her age, too, it was all the more pitiful and tragic that nobody could help averting their eyes whenever they saw her.

One of the traditions in the region held that if, during her pregnancy, a mother were to see an especially powerful event—say, a conflagration of some kind—the child would be born with a birthmark. When Satoko's mother, Rika, had been pregnant with her, she had seen her own husband dead, face down in the *irori*, his features so horrifically burnt that he was unrecognizable. The legend told by the villagers was that Rika had transmitted the terrible shock of the discovery to her unborn child, resulting in Satoko's birthmark.

Satoko was so profoundly embarrassed by it that she usually hid herself away in her annex and, on the rare occasions when she went out in public, she would always wrap herself in a head-scarf devised to cover her face and wear gloves even in summer.

That day, however, Satoko had removed both to show herself in all her pitiful reality. The steely look in her eyes, as they met Deputy Inspector Tachibana's gaze, seemed to speak of this desperate attempt to resist the cruel fate that made her like that.

"You've nothing to worry about, Satoko," said Inspector Isokawa in a kindly tone. "Answer the questions truthfully and you'll be just fine."

"Thank you," she said, bowing to the inspector. "I understand."

She then turned towards Deputy Inspector Tachibana to show that she was ready for any question that he might put to her.

"Well, err… Shall we…"

"Yes?"

Now it was the deputy inspector's turn to feel embarrassed.

"Would you mind telling us what time you left the Turtle Spring on the evening in question?"

"I think it was just before eight when we left. Isn't that right, O-Miki?"

O-Miki nodded, clearly more frightened by the ordeal than Satoko was.

"I think it must have been ten or fifteen minutes to eight," the maid said, "because it was just after I'd cleared away the guests' plates after dinner…"

In that case, it would have been around five-past eight when Kosuke Kindaichi and Inspector Isokawa left, and it was only Rika who had seen them off at the door.

Deputy Inspector Tachibana turned once again to Satoko.

"Right," he said, "and where did you spot Yasuko with the strange-looking old woman?"

"It was a little past the temple at Sakura, very near to the bamboo grove on the Nire estate."

"Could you tell us a little more about what you saw?"

"Of course…" Satoko shuddered, but she continued nevertheless, all the while looking the deputy inspector directly in the eye. "As we approached the bamboo grove, we saw some people coming towards us, so O-Miki and I hid among the bamboo. Then we—"

"Just a moment, Satoko. Why exactly did you hide?"

"Because I don't like meeting people," she replied matter-of-factly, still staring the deputy inspector in the eye.

Deputy Inspector Tachibana looked embarrassed.

"Oh, I see. So, you were saying…?"

"After we hid in the bamboo grove, we saw Yasuko rush past with a strange-looking old woman."

"Can you tell me which direction they'd come from and where were they heading?"

"Yes, they were coming from the village and heading towards the temple at Sakura."

"And did you happen to see the old woman's face?"

"No, she was bent over at the waist. All I could see was the *tenugui* tied around her head."

"And you, O-Miki?" asked the deputy inspector. "Did you see her face at all?"

A woman of few words, O-Miki replied simply: "No, I'm afraid not, sir."

"But what about Yasuko?" the deputy inspector asked, turning back to Satoko. "Did she look scared?"

"No, nothing of the kind. I'd sooner say that she was the one who seemed to be hurrying the old woman on. I seem to recall having overheard them talking about the village chieftain."

"About the village chieftain?" retorted Tachibana.

Kosuke Kindaichi's and Inspector Isokawa's ears pricked up at this. Even the policeman taking notes beside them looked up at Satoko, surprised to hear it.

"What exactly did you hear them say?"

"Well, I couldn't hear them very well, you see… All I heard was his name being mentioned."

The men exchanged tense looks with one another, and Inspector Isokawa leant forward to speak:

"O-Miki, what about you? Did you hear Yasuko mention the village chieftain?"

"Yes, err…" As she looked around nervously at all the anxious faces, O-Miki was at a loss for words. "I believe so, sir. I think I heard Yasuko ask where the village chieftain was…"

"O-Miki!" The deputy inspector's tone was understandably rather harsh. "Didn't you know that the chieftain disappeared right after the arrival of a strange-looking old woman in the village?!"

"Yes, sir, I'm sorry," she said, her face burning. "I had heard that, but it didn't occur to me that this could be the same woman."

One more word from the deputy inspector and she would have burst into tears right on the spot. He looked angry, and fixed his eyes on O-Miki's profile, but he was loath to admonish her.

To break the awkward silence that had fallen, Inspector Isokawa turned to Satoko.

"What about you, Satoko, did you know about this?"

"No, Inspector. If I'd known about it, I'd never have let Yasuko go. When I think about my poor brother…"

Once again, Satoko began to tremble, and now tears wetted the tips of her long eyelashes.

"What does your brother have to do with this, Satoko?" asked Kosuke Kindaichi.

Satoko glanced momentarily in his direction before lowering her eyes once again.

"He was in love with her," she said. "And she was in love with him. She had even asked her mother for permission to marry him. And…"

"And?"

"And our mother had agreed to the match. She said that Yasuko would make a very good wife. She was so happy about it. And now this has happened…"

Unable to hold off any longer, Satoko began to cry out loud and wiped her face with the sleeve of her kimono.

Moved by this spectacle, O-Miki, too, suddenly burst into tears, cursing herself and saying that it was all her fault. Her sobbing was so violent that they were forced to suspend the interrogation.

Angered by this, the deputy inspector pulled a wry face, but he knew that he had little choice but to wait for the girls' crying to abate.

At last, after they had both stopped weeping, Kosuke Kindaichi broke the silence.

"Tell me, O-Miki, at approximately what time was it that you saw them? Yasuko and the old woman, I mean."

"What can I say, Kindaichi-san?" she said, still snivelling. "We went straight to the old ruins, and we hadn't been there five minutes when Kanao and his friends spotted us…"

It had been around a quarter past nine when Kanao saw them. If they had been there for five minutes, that would put the time of their arrival at ten past nine. Assuming they had left the Turtle Spring at ten to eight, that would mean they had taken an hour and twenty minutes to make their way there. That seemed like an awfully long time for anybody to walk that distance, but perhaps it was only to be expected if they had hidden from time to time so that Satoko could avoid meeting people along the way.

Kosuke Kindaichi and Inspector Isokawa had set off from the Turtle Spring fifteen or twenty minutes after them, but they had not encountered Yasuko or the mysterious old woman along the way. Therefore, they must have taken the road that skirted the temple at Sakura and then turned off towards the waterfall at the crossroads.

If only Kosuke Kindaichi and the inspector had quickened their pace and arrived at the temple road even five minutes earlier, they might have come across Yasuko and the old woman. They had missed each other by a hair's breadth. The very thought sent a shiver down the detective's spine.

"So, Satoko, we may assume that the old woman had been sent by the village chieftain to fetch Yasuko, may we not?" said Kosuke Kindaichi.

"Yes, that's what I thought at the time," she replied, wiping away her tears, and shuddering as though having just replayed the scene in her mind.

"And you, O-Miki, what do you think?"

"Yes, that's the way it seemed to me, too," she replied in a voice that was barely audible. She slumped over on the table, her shoulders convulsing from the violence of her sobs.

The men all looked at one another in silence.

Was Mr Tatara dead or alive? The question that Kosuke Kindaichi had posed two days previously had suddenly become of vital importance and now stared all those investigators present in the face. An eerie sensation, like a cold hand gripping your neck, suddenly took hold of them.

"Damn it!" Deputy Inspector Tachibana exclaimed, before hastening to assure the young ladies that the current situation wasn't their fault.

He persisted in asking them whether they had seen anything else of note, but he was unable to extract any further insights from them.

Finally, after the two women had left, Tachibana turned angrily to Kosuke Kindaichi.

"Kindaichi-san, what is all this? This whole case is beyond me."

"I'm in the dark just as much as you are, Deputy Inspector. I'm afraid there's nothing for it but to persevere with the investigation. We must keep trying."

"But where do we even start with this?!"

"We must do whatever it takes to find Mr Tatara," said Kosuke Kindaichi, his voice grave and sombre. "Dead or alive…"

The deputy inspector's despair reached a peak when Inspector Isokawa then told him about the barrels and the funnels they had discovered earlier that day at the winery.

"I'm afraid I don't follow you, Inspector. Do you mean to say that the murderer took a barrel and a funnel to the waterfall in advance, but that Tatsuzo, completely unaware of their purpose, made off with them, and so the murderer had to go back to the winery to fetch another pair? Have I understood this correctly, Kindaichi-san?"

"That's about the size of it, assuming of course that the barrel and funnel taken by Tatsuzo are still in his kitchen, as he claims they are."

"But, Kindaichi-san, why would the murderer do such a stupid thing?!"

Inspector Isokawa intervened: "Come now, Tachibana, this is no time to lose your temper… Kindaichi-san isn't a clairvoyant, now, is he? You'd better send somebody round to Tatsuzo's to check whether those items are still there."

The inspector's sound advice immediately prompted one of the policemen to rush out, but, as it turned out, the barrel and the funnel that Tatsuzo had taken home were indeed in his kitchen, just as he said they would be. In retrospect, it seems clear that the murderer made a fatal error in this.

Just as the policeman was leaving to check on this, O-Miki returned:

"Inspector... Kindaichi-san..."

"Yes? What is it, O-Miki?"

"The mistress is worried. You haven't had your breakfast yet. Would you like me to serve it here? Or would you prefer to take it in your rooms?"

It was true enough. They had not yet had breakfast, and it was already half-past ten. Kosuke Kindaichi suddenly felt hungry.

"Shall we have breakfast in our rooms, Inspector? In fact, O-Miki, I'd quite like to take a bath before I eat..."

"Very well, let's do as you suggest. O-Miki, could you make sure that the breakfast is substantial, as we'll probably have to go without lunch?" said the inspector.

"Of course, sir. I'll come and fetch you as soon as it's ready."

Just after O-Miki left, young Doctor Honda arrived by bicycle.

"I've brought you the post-mortem report, Mr Tachibana. You'll have the full details after the autopsy has been completed, but my father said you should see this now..."

"Thank you for seeing to this so quickly." The deputy inspector trained his eyes on the report. "'Cause of death: asphyxiation... probably strangled with a cord of some kind... this examination was made at nine o'clock on the morning of the 14th and the estimated time of death was around twelve hours previously...' So, the murder took place at around nine o'clock last night."

"Most likely, yes. I asked my father to be present, just to be on the safe side. You are going to have an autopsy carried out, though, aren't you?"

"Yes, I've requested that it be done here in the village. I contacted the prefectural police headquarters a short while ago, and Professor Ogata from the faculty of medicine is making his way here as quickly as possible… Ah, forgive me, Inspector, for having neglected to mention this to you earlier."

"No, that was quick thinking, Deputy Inspector. But tell me, Doctor Honda, how is your father getting on these days?"

"He's in fine fettle, Inspector. He was delighted to hear that I was coming to see you and asked me to tell you that you're always welcome at the house."

"That's very kind of him. Of course, if I'm not much mistaken, it was your father who wrote the report after the tragedy back in 1932."

"Yes, that's right, Inspector. And he hasn't had to do another one since then."

"Thank heavens for that."

Kosuke Kindaichi had been listening to their conversation with great interest when O-Miki returned to inform him that his bath was ready.

Morocco, the Accursed Film

It had already gone eleven o'clock by the time Kosuke Kindaichi and Inspector Isokawa stepped out of the bath and sat down to a hearty breakfast.

The meal was comprised of miso soup with *nameko* mushrooms, salt-grilled salmon, stewed vegetables, and an egg each—and although it was an altogether simple affair, the delicious miso soup filled their empty stomachs.

It was O-Miki who served the food, but as soon as she cleared the trays away, Rika came in, carrying a dish of peaches.

"You must be exhausted after all that work last night!" she said.

She had changed and put on some light make-up, but she still looked wan.

"Yes, it's quite an unexpected turn of events," said Inspector Isokawa. "Will you be going to offer your condolences today?"

"I went along earlier, but I couldn't stay long. I'll go again in a little while."

"And Kanao?" asked Kosuke Kindaichi.

"He's on his way there now," Rika replied, her nose sounding congested. "There was some talk of their marrying, you see. Kanao and Yasuko, I mean…"

"Ah, so nothing had been settled?" asked Inspector Isokawa.

"Weren't the Yuras enthusiastic about the idea?" Kosuke Kindaichi added.

"Oh, they were. It's just that ever since the war, you see, people generally leave it to the young people to decide for themselves. Mrs Yura said that's how it should be."

"But Kanao can't have been against it, surely?" said Inspector Isokawa.

"No, I don't think so… He seems so dejected today, and it pains me to see him like this." Rika dabbed her eyes with her handkerchief.

"I hate to bring it up," the inspector continued, "but back there, by the waterfall, Mrs Yura said something terrible to old Mr Nire. Did you hear about it?"

"Yes, it's already made its rounds in the village," the proprietress replied. "Mrs Yura does seem to have made her mind up about it. But I doubt the old man would ever have done such a horrible thing…"

"I quite agree," said the inspector. "But we couldn't let something like that just slip past without making a few enquiries. I asked a couple of people in the village, and I heard that old Mr Nire had offered his daughter Fumiko in marriage to Kanao."

"Yes, that is true…"

Rika seemed too embarrassed to say anything more.

"So, what exactly was going on?" Inspector Isokawa pressed on. "Forgive the intrusion into your private affairs, but if there's even so much as a shred of suspicion, we need to know about it."

"I feel so ashamed to tell you gentlemen."

"Ashamed? Why?" asked the inspector.

"Well, as a mother, I just didn't know which way to turn. Yasuko and Fumiko would both have made good daughters, and they were equally pretty. So, I began to consider which of them would be of greater help to me… I was only thinking of my child's future. Put yourself in my place!"

"But that's only natural. So, who did you settle on?"

"Well, things were almost settled with the Yuras, when old Mr Nire came to see me."

"And that's when you began to waver?"

"Yes, but there was something else as well."

"Something else?"

"Well, you know just as well as I do, Inspector, how it is for my poor Satoko. Despite all the love that a parent can give, I doubt she'll ever marry. It's a great source of worry for me. Old Mr Nire said that if I accepted Fumiko, that would make Satoko his son-in-law's little sister. In other words, she too would be provided for. And so, I began to have my doubts. I was sure that Mr Nire would keep his promise. And at the same time, I had a suspicion that the Yuras wouldn't care to trouble themselves with Satoko."

Kosuke Kindaichi felt deeply moved, listening to Rika's story. Inspector Isokawa simply shook his head at this sad tale.

"Besides," Rika continued, "Kanao loves his sister very much, and I knew that if I told him about Mr Nire's promise, he would understand. That's why I began to hesitate even more."

"You mean, you haven't told him about Mr Nire's proposal?" asked the inspector.

"No… I couldn't bring myself to do it. Satoko has her pride too, after all." Rika let out a sigh and sniffed. "At any rate, it's all my fault. It's all because I hesitated so much. But what on earth could have possessed the old man to do something like that?"

"He must have realized that you were unable to make up your mind," said the inspector.

"Though he would hardly have gone to such bizarre lengths to do something like that to the body, now, would he?" Kosuke Kindaichi added casually.

As though the remark had jogged her memory, Rika asked:

"Ah, yes… You must have dealt with a lot of strange cases in the past, Kindaichi-san. But just this morning Kanao told me

144

that you've never come across anything quite like this. What do you suppose it all means?"

"This is certainly a first for me, that's for sure. I don't suppose there are any old legends or the like around here that could have something to do with it?"

"I couldn't really say, Kindaichi-san. I'm not from these parts. If there were, though, Mr Tatara would be the one to know." Suddenly, a look of fear flashed in Rika's eyes. "Why, yes, of course! O-Miki just told me that the old woman who took Yasuko was doing it on the instructions of the village chieftain…"

"Well, we can't be sure about that just yet," said Inspector Isokawa. "But what do you think? Is Mr Tatara dead or alive?"

Rika looked at Inspector Isokawa and Kosuke Kindaichi in astonishment. A shiver ran down her spine.

"If you're none the wiser, Inspector, then surely you can't imagine that somebody like me would know any better."

"No, perhaps not," he replied.

"Although…" Rika paused, unsure whether to speak. "Even if he is alive, I doubt you'll hear about it. To be honest, I've always been a little afraid of Mr Tatara."

"Afraid? How so?"

"I'm not sure quite how to explain it… I'm not saying he was a bad man, but when you withdraw from the world like that, you end up closing in on yourself. Take, for example, the stories that everybody talks about, only then to forget them the very next day. Well, he held on to them, you see, deep inside himself. And then he'd start laughing to himself… He wasn't malicious exactly, but there was always something about him. And then, of course, in 1932…"

"Oh?" interjected Kosuke Kindaichi. "What happened in 1932?"

145

"You must be familiar with the case, Kindaichi-san?"

"I have heard bits and pieces about it…"

"Well, I hardly knew the man at the time, so I'm not too sure of the details, but… when the tragedy happened… or rather, afterwards, I had the feeling that he knew more than he was letting on about that Mr Onda."

"Oh? For example?"

"I can't really recall now. But I do remember that one day, while we were talking about him, he said that there was somebody else in the village who knew a secret about it, and that all it would take was one word from this person, and they would lose face and be sent packing. He laughed as he said it."

"Was he talking about a man or a woman?"

"I tried to get it out of him, but he just wouldn't tell me."

"When was this, Mrs Aoike?" asked Kosuke Kindaichi.

"It was just after he moved… He'd often come up here to use the baths, so we chatted a fair bit. Before, when he lived in the village, we were closer in terms of distance, but we hardly saw one another."

"When exactly did Mr Tatara move?"

"If I remember rightly, that would have been at the end of May last year. It was before the rainy season, in any case. He'd just split from his wife, O-Fuyu, and that's why he'd gone off to sulk in the wilderness. It must have been around then that he made the remark about sending somebody packing."

"Hmm, I wonder who it could have been…"

"He even added something that sounded quite frightening," said Rika.

"And what was that?"

"He said that one of these days, depending on how things turned out, he would reveal everything and plunge the whole

146

village into chaos. There was a terrible look in his face as he said it, too. I can see it even now."

"And he didn't say what this was all about?"

"No… He said only that it had nothing to do with my husband's murder."

O-Ito, the owner of the Izutsu Inn, had also said that Mr Tatara knew a great many things about the incident of 1932. Kosuke Kindaichi and Inspector Isokawa both wondered what secrets he might have been able to reveal.

A heavy silence descended upon them. But suddenly Kosuke Kindaichi broke into a broad grin.

"Tell me, Mrs Aoike," he said, "I hadn't been aware until recently, but I believe your late husband had a rather unusual profession."

"Well, err, yes…" replied Rika, taken unawares by the question and blushing.

Inspector Isokawa came to her rescue:

"The thing is, Mrs Aoike, Kindaichi here just learnt that your late husband worked as a narrator of silent films."

"That's right, he did."

Evidently, Rika was little inclined to discuss the subject, but Kosuke Kindaichi was unfazed by this and continued smiling, seeming to be enjoying himself.

"You know, Mrs Aoike, hearing the inspector speak just a moment ago reminded me that in 1932 I would have been twenty. I'd graduated from high school the year before and was enrolled at a private university in Tokyo, although I spent most of my time hanging around the Kanda district, where my lodgings were. It was just then that the talkies were becoming popular, and the silent-film narrators were being put out of a job…"

Kosuke Kindaichi spoke with such enthusiasm that Rika took the bait.

"Then, Kindaichi-san, you must recall the film *Morocco*?"

"Yes, yes, I remember it well. It was directed by Josef von Sternberg and, unless I'm mistaken, starred Gary Cooper and Marlene Dietrich."

"That's the one! It was shown in Kobe in 1931. My husband and I went to see it. I think it was then that he realized it was all over for him…"

"Among those early talkies, it really was a masterpiece."

"It may well have been a masterpiece, but it was also the first time that Paramount used subtitles. Until then, even for the talkies, they'd just turn down the volume and the narrator would do his job. Then everything changed, all because *Morocco* was such a hit. One by one, after Paramount, all the other companies started subtitling their films. And then it was curtains for the narrators…"

"So, *Morocco* doesn't exactly conjure up happy memories for you?"

"No, Kindaichi-san. When von Sternberg came to Japan after the war to film his picture about Anatahan Island, I was so pleased to read in the papers that his film had been panned by the critics."

"Oh, Mrs Aoike!" Kindaichi laughed.

"You may laugh, Kindaichi-san, but if only you knew how hard, how painful it was for me back then. The year when Kanao was born, my husband finally became lead narrator, and things were beginning to look up. If it hadn't been for the talkies, we'd have never come back here and he would never have died the way he did. When I think about it, I really can't stand the talkies."

Kosuke Kindaichi was moved to see tears welling in Rika's eyes.

"Forgive me, Mrs Aoike, but what was it that your husband planned to do here in Onikobe? Winemaking?"

"No… he wasn't cut out for it. He may have been born here, Kindaichi-san, but he hadn't worked the land a day in his life. In fact, he'd come back, intending to leave me here with his family."

This revelation came as news to Inspector Isokawa.

"And what did Genjiro intend to do while you were here?" he asked, looking at Rika in astonishment.

"Well, you see," she said through her tears, "he was planning to head off to Manchuria."

"To Manchuria?…"

Inspector Isokawa shot a glance at Kosuke Kindaichi.

"But you never mentioned any of this at the time, Mrs Aoike…"

"Didn't I? Well, if I didn't, it must have been because you never asked, Inspector. It certainly wasn't my intention to hide anything from you."

"No, of course not," said Kosuke Kindaichi, discreetly suggesting that Inspector Isokawa drop this line of questioning. He then nodded, encouraging Rika to continue.

"Well, the thing is, Kindaichi-san, I was pregnant at the time, and so my husband wanted go on to Manchuria ahead of me and send for me only after he'd set himself up there. That's why he'd brought me here, so that I'd be taken care of. It wasn't easy for me, you know. It was the first time that I'd met his family."

"Really? Only the first time?"

"Yes… You see, ours wasn't an arranged marriage, Kindaichi-san. His parents were real sticklers for tradition, and they were awfully angry that we'd married without their permission. At least, that's what I'd been told."

"Forgive me for asking, Mrs Aoike, but what was your profession when you married your late husband?"

Rika stared at Kosuke Kindaichi in silence for a few moments.

"I was on the stage," she replied at last.

"Come again?"

"I performed in a *yose* theatre, Kindaichi-san. It was a sort of vaudeville act. Half-a-dozen girls and I would go out on stage and take turns singing and playing the shamisen. I was only sixteen back when I started doing it."

As Rika looked at the famous detective, there were no longer tears in her eyes, but they were filled with an unparalleled sorrow. Once again, Kosuke Kindaichi couldn't help being moved by the sight of her.

"It was only natural that his parents were unhappy when they learnt how I earned my living," she continued. "Fortunately, Kanao was only two at the time. He was such an adorable child back then. Besides, my husband's older brother and his wife were childless, so the boy immediately became the apple of his grandparents' eye. That's why they agreed to let me stay until the end of my pregnancy. If only my husband had set off for Manchuria a little earlier, nothing would have happened to him, but alas…"

"But why didn't he?"

"He couldn't go abroad empty-handed. But after entrusting me to his parents, he couldn't very well go cap in hand, asking them for help, either. And so, it was while we were stuck there, losing time, that everything happened."

Slow and unhurried, Rika's story had unfolded. The memories that she was calling to mind were painful to her, but her dulcet tone was almost pleasant to listen to.

Just as Kosuke Kindaichi was about to ask about the events of that fateful night, O-Miki came in.

"I'm sorry to bother you, madam, but Kanao's been waiting for you for some time."

For a brief moment, Rika looked surprised. She then got to her feet.

"Oh, I completely forgot! And here I am, chatting away…"

She explained that Kanao had promised to take her to the Yuras' house on the back of his bicycle, and so he had come to pick her up. Looking at her watch, she saw that it was already twelve-thirty.

Rika made to leave, but then, as though remembering one last thing, turned and said, "By the way, did you gentlemen have the chance to see Yukari last night?"

"I'm afraid not," Inspector Isokawa replied. "We didn't have the time… Why? Do you think she has something to do with all this?"

"No, not exactly. Or, at least, not her but rather her manager… Now, what was his name?"

"You mean Koreya Kusakabe?" said Inspector Isokawa, looking pointedly at Rika.

"Yes, that's him! Mr Kusakabe. So, you haven't met him either?"

"No. Why do you ask?"

"It's just that I heard from Kanao that he'd been in Manchuria," she said, gazing pensively at the two men, before suddenly turning away. "I'm awfully sorry, gentlemen, but I really must be on my way."

And with that, Rika slipped out, as though trying to escape their inquisitive looks.

A Dark Secret

After Rika left, Kosuke Kindaichi had O-Miki lay out some bedding so that he could take a nap, but he was soon roused from his deep slumber by the shrill cry of the cicadas that were perched in a paulownia tree on the other side of the rattan blind.

When he looked beside him, he saw that Inspector Isokawa was no longer there. The watch lying by his pillow indicated that it was a little after five o'clock. In no hurry to get up, he quietly puffed on a cigarette and then, still lying on his stomach, clapped his hands to call the maid.

Before long, he heard footsteps coming along the veranda.

"Ah, you're awake already, Kindaichi-san? Did you sleep well?"

Resting her hand on the door frame, O-Miki wiped the sweat from her brow with the apron that she wore over her lightweight clothes.

"I slept very well, thank you. But where is the inspector?"

"A Mr Kimura from the police station came to collect him a while ago. I believe the doctor from Okayama has arrived."

"Ah, I see. When was this?"

"It was around two o'clock, sir."

In that case, Inspector Isokawa would not have had much time to sleep.

"I was going to wake you, too, Kindaichi-san, but you were sleeping so soundly that the inspector said not to disturb you. He told me to ask you to join him as soon as you were awake. We have bicycles here, if you would like to take one of them?"

"Perfect, thank you. Where is the autopsy being carried out?"

"I believe it's being done at Doctor Honda's surgery. But Kindaichi-san…" said O-Miki, kneeling down. "What exactly is an autopsy?"

"It's better you don't know, O-Miki. You'd lose your appetite if I were to tell you," said the detective, getting to his feet and changing into his old white-and-indigo kimono. "By the way, where are Mrs Aoike and Kanao?"

"They went together to see Mrs Yura earlier this afternoon, sir."

"Ah, I see. I take it they're preparing for the wake this evening?"

"Yes, sir, but what about the autopsy?"

"It'll be finished by then. We already know that strangulation was the cause of death, so this is just a formality… Incidentally, is Satoko around?"

"She's in the annex, sir, but I'm sure she'll go along this evening, too. Which means I'll be left alone here…"

O-Miki looked as though she could burst into tears at any moment.

"Come, come, O-Miki, there's nothing to be afraid of!" said Kosuke Kindaichi, trying to console her. He couldn't help feeling sorry for her, though. After such a terrible incident, it was only natural that a young woman wouldn't want to be left all alone out here in this sprawling inn. Worse still, the nearest building was Mr Tatara's cabin.

When Kosuke Kindaichi returned after washing his face in cold water, he found O-Miki tidying away the bedding, a forlorn look on her face.

"I think it would be quicker going via the back door, wouldn't it?" he asked as he put on his hakama. "I hate to ask, but would you mind opening it for me?"

"Of course not, Kindaichi-san. And anyway, that's where the bicycles are kept."

By the rear of the building, Kosuke Kindaichi found an array of farming implements, all clean and neatly arranged. There were two bicycles: a man's and a woman's, the latter probably belonging to Satoko. Besides these, there were also three wheelbarrows taking up a lot of space. As Kosuke Kindaichi, with a little help from O-Miki, extracted the bicycle from behind these, he spotted Satoko watching him from the window of the annex. She had not bothered to cover her face, and, when the detective smiled at her, she bowed without saying a word.

As he was about to leave via the rear gate, O-Miki asked:

"Kindaichi-san, will you be dining with us this evening?"

"I'm not sure," he replied. "If I do, don't worry. Something simple like *chazuke* will be just fine."

As he cycled off through the rear gate, it was half-past five exactly.

The path climbed towards the crossroads, but from there it was a pleasant downhill journey to the temple at Sakura, and so, though it took a little effort on the bicycle at first, it was much quicker than going via the path that skirted around the mountain.

As he cycled along, the sudden realization that the mysterious old woman had taken Yasuko along this same path in the opposite direction only the night before gave Kosuke Kindaichi gooseflesh. More than that, however, it made him wonder why Tatsuzo hadn't taken this shortcut.

A little before he arrived at the temple itself, he came across a massive earthen wall almost a hundred feet long with a gate right in the middle of it. Beside this gate stood a smart-looking mesh lantern on four legs, which illuminated a wooden plaque on which was written:

The heavy, elegant roof tiles atop the wall similarly testified to the wealth and power of the House of Nire.

As he came out onto the main road from under the shade of the chinquapin trees that stood behind the temple, Kosuke Kindaichi found himself in front of a bamboo grove. This must have been the spot where Satoko and O-Miki hid.

He arrived at a crossroads: in one direction, the road led up towards the winery, in another it went into the centre of the village, while behind him the road led back to the Turtle Spring. From his vantage point there, he could see that the road leading up to the winery had been blocked by a landslide. Below the road leading to the village stretched rice paddies where the harvest had just finished, as evidenced by the abundance of cut rice stalks.

Doctor Honda's surgery stood right opposite the village hall and the old ruins. A large crowd of onlookers had gathered outside, while a number of policemen and civilians came and went. Just like O-Miki, the villagers were doubtless curious to know what exactly an autopsy entailed.

Kosuke Kindaichi was shown by Detective Kato into the waiting room, where he found Inspector Isokawa discussing something with the victim's brother, Toshio, whose face betrayed a hint of tension.

"Excuse me for being late, Inspector…"

"Ah, Kindaichi, you're just in time!"

"Has the autopsy been completed?"

"They're still in there," said the inspector, pointing to the door leading into the examination room. "Would you like to be present for it?"

"No, thank you. Frankly, I'd rather leave them to it…"

"No stomach for it either, eh?" Inspector Isokawa laughed awkwardly but immediately carried on, lowering his voice, "We've just got our hands on a very important clue, Kindaichi."

"What is it, Inspector?" said the detective, instinctively lowering his voice as well.

"Well, I believe you know Toshio here? The victim's brother…"

"Yes, we met this morning, at the waterfall," said Kindaichi, bowing to the young man. "My condolences."

Toshio, who was still in his work clothes, sluggishly returned Kosuke Kindaichi's greeting and muttered something that the detective didn't quite catch.

"Toshio came to give me this," said the inspector, extracting a scrap of paper from his shirt pocket. "He found it a short while ago."

Having been folded in half three times over, the paper was quite crumpled, but when Kosuke Kindaichi opened it and spread it out on his lap, he let out an involuntary gasp.

If you want to know the dark secret of your father's death, meet me at nine o'clock this evening behind the temple at Sakura, where I shall reveal this to you.

Hoan Tatara

"Where did you find this, Toshio?" Kosuke Kindaichi asked.

"Inspector Isokawa asked me to search Yasuko's room for clues. When I did, I found this folded note hidden between the film magazines that were lying on her desk."

"And it was just the note? There was no envelope?"

"Err, yes, it was just this," mumbled Toshio in a low voice, still chewing his words.

Kosuke Kindaichi looked at the note once again. It had been written with a brush, but the handwriting was shaky, as though it had been done by an alcoholic. What was more, the writing was terribly uneven, which made it difficult to decipher.

The famous detective and Inspector Isokawa glanced at one another. In his mind, Kosuke Kindaichi could clearly see Mr Tatara's right hand with its persistent tremor.

"Toshio, if I remember rightly, your father died in 1935. What exactly did he die of?"

"It was his heart, Kindaichi-san… He died of heart failure caused by thiamine deficiency."

"Who was his doctor?"

"It was Doctor Honda… senior, that is to say."

"I believe that kind of heart failure can be terribly painful."

"Oh yes! I remember how he clawed at the tatami mats… The doctor gave him any number of injections, but nothing worked in the end."

Toshio swallowed the ends of his words. He had the bad habit of mumbling while looking away from the person he was talking to, all of which gave him an air of sluggishness and inattention.

"And, Toshio, do *you* believe that there is some mystery surrounding the death of your father?"

The man shook his head slowly.

"I've never really thought about it, Kindaichi-san," he replied. "He was in a whole lot of pain, though…"

As Toshio cast his mind back to that time, he seemed to have some doubts, but, as ever, he swallowed his words and returned his eyes to the piece of paper lying in Kosuke Kindaichi's lap.

"Exactly when in 1935 did your father die?"

"The anniversary of his death was on the 10th of this month."

"So, it happened during the hot season?"

"Yes… I've heard it said that the heat exacerbates that kind of ailment."

For a few moments, Toshio seemed restless.

"Inspector?" he asked hesitantly. "How much longer are they going to be with Yasuko's body? It's just, we'd like to hold the wake this evening…"

"Don't worry, the autopsy will be over shortly and the body will be returned to the family."

"I see, I see," mumbled Toshio, nodding. "In that case, Inspector, Kindaichi-san, would you like to come to the house this evening? My mother asked me to invite you. There'll be a meal for you, and I think she'd like to talk to you both."

Inspector Isokawa shot a look at Kosuke Kindaichi before he answered:

"That's very kind of you. Please thank your mother on our behalf. We'll come once we're finished here. I only hope she'll forgive us, as we aren't exactly dressed for the occasion…"

"It's fine. You are on holiday, after all," the young man said, looking up at the ceiling. "In that case, Inspector, I'll be off, and I'll let my mother know… Would you send a messenger to let us know when the autopsy's done? We'll send somebody right away."

Inspector Isokawa and Kosuke Kindaichi watched as Toshio lumbered out through the front door of the surgery with his slow, heavy gait.

Kosuke Kindaichi returned his attention to the note, looking at it again in more detail.

"Judging by the way it's been folded, I doubt it was sent in the post."

"Kato," said Inspector Isokawa, "would you mind going to Mr Tatara's cabin right away to see whether you can find identical writing paper?"

"Of course, sir. I seem to recall seeing a pad with paper that looked about the same size and type."

After he had left, Kosuke Kindaichi turned to the inspector.

"Where's Tachibana?"

"He's observing the autopsy. He's young, but he's made of strong stuff... Ah! Speak of the devil."

Just then, Tachibana appeared from the examination room at the back of the surgery, looking a little pale.

The time was half-past six exactly. Yasuko's final ordeal was over.

The autopsy revealed nothing of particular significance. The cause of death, as expected, was confirmed to have been strangulation. Professor Ogata and his assistant left immediately to return to Okayama, and, as soon as Yasuko's body had been taken away, Kosuke Kindaichi was introduced to Doctor Honda senior.

The doctor must have been over seventy and had long, white hair that he wore slicked back. He was overjoyed to see his old friend Inspector Isokawa again, but when the latter showed him the note, his eyes widened.

Deputy Inspector Tachibana was also surprised and looked in turn at Inspector Isokawa and Kosuke Kindaichi, his eyes full of suspicion. He pestered the inspector with all manner of questions to find out how they had got their hands on this note. The deputy inspector seemed to have misgivings about Kosuke Kindaichi.

"What do you make of this?" asked Inspector Isokawa, turning to Doctor Honda.

"Are you asking what I think about the cause of Utaro's death, Inspector?"

"Yes... His son told us earlier that he died of heart failure. Could there have been any mistake?"

"That's quite a question to ask an old friend, Inspector... But there's no mistake. He died of heart failure brought on by

159

thiamine deficiency. Their family has always had weak hearts. I'd wager that Toshio has one as well, judging by his pale complexion. But are you quite certain that this is Mr Tatara's writing?"

"What do you think, Doctor? Could Mr Tatara hold a brush in his right hand?"

"Hmm… It's not impossible, but he'd have to use his left hand to help. It would have been quicker and simpler just to write it with his left hand." He returned the paper to Deputy Inspector Tachibana and turned his gaze to the inspector. "At any rate, Utaro died of heart failure—of that much, I can be sure. As you're doubtless aware, the terrible events of 1932 had put even more strain on his already weak heart…"

"What do you make of Mr Tatara, Doctor?"

"What do I make of him?" Old Doctor Honda pulled a wry face. "Well, I don't like to speak ill of people, but to speak frankly, I don't like the man very much. He likes to play the misanthrope, but I get the impression that, really, he's always spying on everyone."

Doctor Honda's opinion was very similar to those given by O-Ito and Rika.

In other words, Mr Tatara was something of a crank.

A Woman in Her Eighties

It was around eight o'clock when Kosuke Kindaichi and Inspector Isokawa passed through the front gate of the Yura residence.

Stepping inside the house, they found the reception room crammed full of people who had come for the wake. Yasuko's body had been laid out in the back room, while the partition between the two front rooms in the house had been removed, so that as many as possible could attend. And since the mourners were almost all country folk, there was, for all the solemnity of the occasion, quite a bit of commotion. Although the Yura family's star was waning, there had been no shortage of food or housing in the provinces during the war, and so, unlike those families on the decline in urban areas, they hadn't had to worry about selling off their possessions. As a result, the family was able to receive its guests with all due ceremony. There was all manner of crockery, as one would expect for such a large house, and the mourners could help themselves to large platters of *inari sushi* and great bowls of chopped cucumber salad. The sake cups and flasks, as well as the dinner plates and even the ash trays, were all of good quality. And besides, in the countryside, where entertainment is scarce, the misfortunes of others can provide ready diversion. In a village where the people are partial to good food and drink, both celebrations and tragedies can be a great diversion...

By the time that Kosuke Kindaichi and Inspector Isokawa arrived, the reading of the sutra had ended, and sake was being served to the guests. As the two entered, the mourners all froze in an astonished silence and looked at one another.

Toshio's wife, Eiko, led Kosuke Kindaichi and Inspector Isokawa into the back room, where they bowed before the girl's mortal remains. They each in turn placed some incense on the altar and offered their condolences to Yasuko's mother, Atsuko, as well as to the rest of the family.

Beside the body, in addition to three Buddhist priests, were Atsuko, Toshio and his wife, Toshio's younger sister, Fusako, her husband and their two children, as well as a wizened old woman who held a rosary in her hand and who immediately drew Kosuke Kindaichi's attention. This had to be Ioko, Atsuko's mother-in-law, the eighty-three-year-old matriarch of the House of Yura. Her snow-white hair was gathered in a small bun at the nape of her neck, and her face was covered in wrinkles, but she was a beautiful old woman with dark skin. Naturally, the entire family was dressed in formal mourning costume.

"Kindaichi-san, Inspector, you'll be served in a separate room," said Atsuko in a stiff and formal tone. "They're just preparing the meal now, so if you wouldn't mind waiting a little while?"

"Thank you," replied Inspector Isokawa. Despite the wash he had just had at Doctor Honda's, he looked sweaty and uncomfortable and was waving his fan about frantically. "Only, please forgive our appearance…"

Kosuke Kindaichi meanwhile presented his condolences with simplicity, before looking around the enormous room with a detached air, discreetly exchanging greetings with those whom he already knew by sight.

After that morning's events, Kahei had not come, but sure enough, his son and heir, Naohei, who was reputed to be an upstanding young man, was there, drinking with young Doctor Honda and Tatsuzo. Naohei cut an imposing figure, much like his father, and, for a man in his mid-thirties, he had a rather casual manner about him. His hair was neatly parted on the left, and, with his black haori worn over a white kimono, he, too, was dressed in traditional mourning attire. Tatsuzo whispered something in his ear. Naohei's white fan paused while he smiled and bowed towards Kosuke Kindaichi, who promptly returned the greeting.

Naohei's younger brother, Shohei, was seated at the end of the room along with Kanao and Goro, but this little group was constantly coming and going, most likely because they had various jobs to attend to. The only one not stirring from his seat was Kanao, who had changed from his work clothes into a smart open-necked white shirt and neatly ironed gabardine trousers; instead, he just sat there, looking absent and forlorn.

"Thank you for coming, Inspector, Kindaichi-san." The voice belonged to Rika, Kanao's mother, who came smiling, a flask of sake in her hands. "I'm awfully sorry to have kept you waiting. I'm afraid your dinner isn't quite ready, so in the meantime would you care for a small glass of sake? Toshio, fetch two cups, would you?"

"Ah, thank you," said the inspector, accepting the cup that Toshio offered him. His wife Eiko, meanwhile, was busying herself, preparing a small dish of pickled cucumber.

Rika served them both and placed the flask on the banquet table.

The Inspector then suddenly turned and addressed the old woman beside him:

"It's been quite some time, madam, but I must say, you're looking remarkably well."

The octogenarian looked blankly at him.

"Forgive me, but who you might you be?" she enquired.

Inspector Isokawa laughed.

"It's only natural that you'll have forgotten me. Why, the last time you saw me was twenty-three years ago. The name is Isokawa. We met after the tragedy in 1932. I was just an assistant inspector back then."

Despite her advanced years, Ioko still had all her faculties and remembered the inspector very well.

"Why, yes, of course," she said. "I heard that you still visit the Turtle Spring from time to time. And you were there when... Well, I never! You haven't changed a bit!"

"Well, madam, a few grey hairs here and there. You know how it is."

Ioko laughed, her mouth like a drawstring purse.

"Come, come, don't talk nonsense. You're a spring chicken compared to me. How old are you now?"

"Ah, let's not talk of age, madam. We're both of us still a ways off a hundred!"

"That's very true," she said, laughing. "But tell me, Mr Isokawa, who is this young man standing next to you?"

Hearing himself referred to as a young man, Kosuke Kindaichi could not help breaking into a broad smile.

"This young man! Why, madam, this is the famous private detective, Kosuke Kindaichi. Surely you've seen his photograph in the newspapers? He's cracked all manner of impossible cases all over Okayama Prefecture. Kindaichi, old boy, this is Ioko Yura, the head of the household."

Instinctively, the inspector spoke to the old woman in a loud voice, as though she were hard of hearing, even though her ears seemed to work perfectly well. As a result of this, everybody in the room could hear him.

"A pleasure, madam..." said Kosuke Kindaichi.

Sensing the scrutiny of the entire room, he blushed with embarrassment as he bowed to Ioko.

"Well, I never!" said the old woman, gazing intently at the celebrated detective.

"He may not look like it," the inspector continued, his voice still raised, "but he's the greatest detective in all Japan."

As Inspector Isokawa spoke, he casually surveyed the room, attempting to judge the psychological impact of his words:

"Have no fear, madam. He'll catch and arrest the person responsible for the death of your granddaughter."

Embarrassed by all this attention, Kosuke Kindaichi ruffled his dishevelled hair as he still faced the assembly of mourners. It was not the effect of the inspector's words that bothered him, however. Instead, he was looking at the dishes that were passed around among the guests and at the amount of sushi that was being served.

Ever since the suspicious old woman had arrived on the evening of the 10th, pretending to be O-Rin, Mr Tatara's whereabouts had remained unknown. What was more, a full plate of *inari sushi* had been left behind. The source of this repast was still a mystery, but the investigators assumed that the old woman had brought it with her as a gift. Toshio, however, had said that the 10th was the anniversary of his father's death; in which case they would certainly have held a memorial service. Now, seeing all the food this evening, Kosuke Kindaichi wondered whether they hadn't served some at the memorial service on the 10th as well.

"Excuse me, Eiko," said the detective, stopping Toshio's wife. "It's improper of me to ask, but could you tell me whether these *inari sushi* are homemade?"

"Yes, they are," she replied, looking puzzled.

"I don't mean to be rude," he explained. "It's just that there was a plate of them found in Mr Tatara's cabin on the day he disappeared."

"That isn't surprising, Kindaichi-san. He took some home with him."

"What?" interjected Inspector Isokawa, looking anxiously at Eiko. "They came from your house?"

"Of course," she replied. "It was the anniversary of Mr Yura's death, so lots had been prepared to give to the guests as they left. Mr Tatara attended the memorial and, since he told us that he would be receiving a visitor from Kobe later that evening, we wrapped some up for him in bamboo leaves. He was delighted to take them home with him."

"Forgive me, Eiko," said the detective, "but how many exactly did you give him?"

"Old Mrs Yura told me to give six per person, so I wrapped up six and my mother-in-law, Atsuko, wrapped up another six. Isn't that right?" she said.

"Yes, yes, the girl's quite right," the old lady replied. "Was something wrong with them?"

"No, no, nothing at all," said Kosuke Kindaichi, scratching his head again and looking pleased with himself.

There was a hint of suspicion in Inspector Isokawa's eyes.

There were ten pieces of *inari sushi* left on the plate that had been found at Mr Tatara's cabin. Therefore, two must have been eaten by Mr Tatara or that strange old woman. The poison that had been discovered in Mr Tatara's blood, lobeline, was found in a plant that was common throughout the region: marsh bellflower, otherwise known as "chieftain's death". It was suspected, moreover, that somebody in the village had been paying Mr Tatara's living expenses in secret—or rather, to put it plainly, that he had been blackmailing somebody. Would it not be natural for the victim of extortion to harbour some murderous intent towards their blackmailer?

"So, you and your mother-in-law wrapped up the sushi in bamboo leaves?"

"That's right, Inspector. Old Mrs Yura put them in, one by one, with chopsticks, then handed them to me and my mother-in-law."

"Madam," said Inspector Isokawa, turning to the eighty-three-year-old woman with obvious curiosity in his eye, "are you on good terms with Mr Tatara?"

"You know, Inspector, as you get older, you get closer to those you've known for a long time. The village chieftain and I come from the same generation, and we enjoy talking together. He may have withdrawn from the world, but we get along just as well as ever, and he often comes to chat with me. Do you have any idea what's become of him, Inspector?"

"I'm afraid we're completely in the dark, madam."

As he stared at Ioko's wizened face, Inspector Isokawa knew that it was imperative, now more than ever, to know whether Hoan Tatara was dead or alive.

"If I might be permitted to ask a question, madam..." It was Kosuke Kindaichi who now intervened. "There is in these parts a plant known as 'chieftain's death', is there not?"

Turning to him, she replied that there was, and, as she did, there was a strange gleam in her eye.

"Only, it's a rather curious name. You wouldn't happen to know where it came from, would you?"

"Well, now that you mention it," she said, leaning in, "it was the Mr Tatara himself who told me about it. It was because of stories like that that we got on so well with each other, you see. Apparently, one of Mr Tatara's ancestors displeased the shogun's intendant here because he was too talkative, so the feudal lord had him removed. To kill him, he used the poison extracted from that very flower, and ever since then it's been called 'chieftain's death'. But, you know, Kindaichi-san…" She leant in even further. "When I was a little girl, there was a *temari* song that we used to sing in the village that began like this…"

Looking into Kosuke Kindaichi's eyes, she began to sing in her frail, shaky voice:

"In the trees in the garden behind our house,
Three little sparrows came to stay.
The first little birdie said to me:
In the faraway land where I come from,
Many are the pleasures of the shogun's…"

"Granny! Granny!"

Just then, one of Ioko's great-grandchildren came running in, throwing her arms around the old woman's shoulders.

"Granny, Granny! She's here! Yukari Ozora's here!…"

"What's that, dear? Miss Yukari's here?"

Eiko and Toshio's sister, who had been listening attentively to the old woman's song, both got up, and so nobody heard the rest. In hindsight, however, this was a great pity, for if Kosuke Kindaichi had heard the continuation, the tragedies to come could have been…

But let us leave that for the time being. For, just then, amid this scene of commotion, Fumiko and Satoko appeared on the veranda together with Yukari Ozora. The three young women, accompanied by Harue, the celebrity's mother, had come to pay their respects to their friend, Yasuko.

The Bastard Child

"Ah, Satoko!"

Even though Kosuke Kindaichi had seen Yukari Ozora any number of times in magazines, on the silver screen and on television, when she appeared in the flesh together with Fumiko and Satoko, right there on the veranda, he experienced an indescribable thrill in his heart. Rika, however, stood motionless beside him, holding a bottle of sake in her hands and looking dazed. She seemed to be overwhelmed by sadness.

Thinking back on it, each of these three young women had problems of her own. While Yukari's scarcely needs to be stated, it was only natural, now that Yasuko was dead, that Fumiko should suddenly become the focus of people's attention, perhaps even their suspicion. It wasn't clear to what extent she was in love with Kanao, but he was the Don Juan of the village, and it was widely known that he reciprocated her feelings for him to some extent. Yasuko, who now lay dead, had been her rival for his affections.

Satoko, meanwhile, was the daughter of the victim of the incident that had taken place twenty-three years ago. Moreover, the villagers also held her to be an indirect victim of the tragedy, convinced as they were that her birthmark had been caused by the shock that her pregnant mother had received upon seeing her husband lying there, dead and disfigured. Satoko, who, ashamed of the birthmark, had taken to never showing her face in public, now appeared that evening, impassive, in full view of everybody.

It was little wonder that Rika, her mother, had cried out in a pained, plaintive voice when she saw her.

Meanwhile, as the crowd of mourners watched, the women were ushered in. Of the four of them, Harue Bessho was the first to offer incense at the altar, after which she turned to Toshio and his wife and, in a low voice, offered her condolences.

Harue, who had been just sixteen back in 1932, must have been approaching forty now, although she could easily have passed for thirty-five, perhaps because she now lived in a world surrounded by youth. She was short and plump, and, with her round cheeks, she wasn't exactly pretty, but she had a certain charm about her.

Her daughter had inherited this charm. If beauty depends on the evenness of one's features, then Yasuko, now asleep for eternity, would have won, but where charm was concerned, neither Yasuko nor Fumiko could hold a candle to Yukari.

Unlike her mother, Yukari was rather tall. Of medium build, she was dressed in a black full-length evening gown that she would wear onstage. There was something daring and direct about the way she carried herself, and that something had earned her a reputation as a femme fatale, even though deep down, she was just like her mother, a village girl—and all this, of course, Kosuke Kindaichi could see at first glance.

"Thank you so much for coming, Chieko," said Rika, calling her by her childhood name.

When the famous singer, after burning some incense at the altar, arrived in front of Toshio to offer her condolences, the young man's wife was noticeably moved.

"This way, please," she said. "Harue, if you'd like to follow me."

They began to make such of a fuss of clearing a place for them, that Kosuke Kindaichi and Inspector Isokawa had no choice but to step back hastily.

"No, really, there's no need. I'd much rather help you in the kitchen," Harue began, seeming embarrassed not to be in traditional mourning clothes, even if she had donned for the occasion a black kimono tied at the waist by a dark-coloured belt.

"Oh, don't say that. I'm sure Yasuko would have wanted you right here," said Toshio's wife in her usual overblown way, making room for her to sit down. "Please, come and sit here beside Chieko."

Eiko was so busy fussing over them that it was only then that she spotted Fumiko and Satoko lingering awkwardly on the veranda, not daring to come in.

"Ah, Fumiko! Satoko! Come in and burn some incense, and then we'll sit you down here next to Chieko. You were all such good friends to Yasuko."

Fumiko and Satoko looked at each other to see which of them would go forward first. Finally, Fumiko went over and knelt before the altar, above which hung a small photograph of Yasuko. It didn't escape Kosuke Kindaichi's attention that her shoulders began to shake when her gaze fell on her friend's portrait. She burned some incense, then bowed to Toshio and the rest of the family.

"Fumiko, won't you come and sit over here?" Naohei, her brother, called out.

He was sitting with some other young people from the village at the other end of the room.

"Let her stay here for a little while, Naohei," said Eiko. "After all, it's the first time that the three of them have been reunited…"

"All right, then. Fumiko, you stay there. But what took you so long to get here?"

"Satoko asked me to accompany her…"

It was clear Fumiko wanted to get out of the way and join the young people at the far end of the room, but instead she sat down beside Yukari Ozora as unobtrusively as possible and muttered something feebly.

"Did Chieko and her big sister come to pick you up, Fumiko?" asked Shohei, getting to his feet.

"No, Shohei," said Harue, smiling. "We bumped into them at the front gate. But it's so lovely to see the three of them together again."

Having made her offering of incense, Satoko bowed silently to Toshio and the rest of the family and went to sit down next to Fumiko. Unlike her friend, who was trying to avoid the attention of the other guests, Satoko, much to everybody's amazement, held her head high, letting them all see her birthmark, a look of defiance in her eyes.

Thus there were two rows, more or less, of people scattered about near the altar: closest to the veranda were the three Buddhist priests, then Harue, Yukari Ozora, Fumiko and Satoko, and opposite them were Toshio, old Ioko, Toshio's wife, Eiko, Toshio's sister and her husband. A little further away, by the sliding doors, sat Kosuke Kindaichi and Inspector Isokawa. But Rika Aoike was nowhere to be seen. Doubtless, it was too painful seeing her daughter subjected to the stares of others.

"How about it, eh, Chieko? Why don't you sing us a song?"

Tatsuzo was starting to get drunk. From the sound of his voice, he seemed to want to quarrel with his niece (or, officially speaking, his sister), but Yukari Ozora dismissed his request with an embarrassed laugh.

"What's so funny?!" he pressed on. "After all, Yasuko went to the trouble of going all the way to Soja to welcome you, and now it's her wake. Why don't you sing something to pray for her soul?"

"No, I couldn't, even if I wanted to."

"And why not?"

"Because, with the shock of all this, I've lost my voice."

"The very cheek of it!" Tatsuzo's anger was deliberately exaggerated, but then he burst out laughing. "Did you hear that?" he said, turning to the other mourners. "Harue's done quite a job training her. She's quite adept at wriggling out of things, isn't she? Well, I for one can't stand it any longer!"

An audible murmur of disapproval passed through the room, but as soon as calm was restored, it was Kanao who spoke up from the far end:

"Yukari!"

At the strange sound of his voice, everybody turned around and saw the look of sadness in his face.

"About what Uncle Tatsuzo just said…"

"Yes?" Yukari replied solemnly.

"Are you sure you wouldn't like to sing something? Yasuko was such a fan of yours, after all."

Everybody looked at Yukari, curious to know what her response would be.

"Well…" she began, with a smile that revealed two charming dimples. "If you're really sure, I'll be pleased to sing later on. But right now, I need to rest awhile. We came here in such a rush, and I haven't caught my breath yet…"

"As you wish. But please do sing before you leave."

Kosuke Kindaichi could not help thinking that Yukari was a very intelligent woman. He had noticed how her voice had naturally regained the intonations of her native country, diffusing the atmosphere immediately.

"Ah, that's great news! I know that would have made Yasuko very happy," said Goro.

"I think you're the one who's going to be happier, Goro!" said Shohei, who, having worried about Kanao's dark mood, now ventured to make a joke.

"Tell me, Mrs Yura," said Yukari, addressing old Ioko and tilting her head slightly. With her bold fringe and long hair that fell over her shoulders, she looked every bit like the actress Machiko Kyo. "Would it really be all right for me to sing something?"

"Yes, of course, dear. Just because it's a wake, it doesn't mean that you have to cry the whole time. It would be lovely to hear you sing."

For all her years, Ioko was young at heart.

"Thank you, Mrs Yura."

"You know, dear…"

"Yes?"

"You really are as beautiful as they say."

"Oh, Mrs Yura, you really mustn't…"

"Now, now, dear, it's true. When I was girl, people used to say that beauty and talent never went hand in hand, but you have both. You really were born under a lucky star, dear."

"Really, you're making me blush, Mrs Yura."

The old woman's words had caught the ordinarily unfazed celebrity off guard, but they had also helped restore the lively atmosphere in the room.

It was at this point that Rika Aoike reappeared and whispered in Inspector Isokawa's ear.

"Oh, of course," he replied. "Kindaichi, it would appear they're ready for us next door."

Kosuke Kindaichi and Inspector Isokawa slipped away discreetly through the sliding door and were led into a small adjoining room where dinner was served to them.

As they began tucking into their repast, they were left alone in the company of Atsuko.

"I believe there was something you wanted to tell us?" the inspector said, wielding his chopsticks and tucking into the grilled sweetfish. "Well, we're all ears."

"Ah, yes, that," said Atsuko, pouring the inspector a drink. "It's a bit of a delicate matter, truth be told."

"I understand, dear lady, but in cases such as this, there are always a lot of things that are hard to say. But you must tell us, otherwise we won't be able to do our jobs properly, and we'll never catch Yasuko's murderer."

"Yes, I do appreciate that, Inspector," she said, glancing around and lowering her voice. "I'm sure that you both must have heard what I said to Kahei this morning by the waterfall."

"We did indeed."

"I'm sure you must both think it shameful of me, but I assure you, I had good reason for saying it."

"So, tell us, what was that reason?"

"Well, it's like this, you see," she said pouring both the inspector and the famous detective another cup of sake each. "The fact is that Yasuko was practically engaged to Kanao—you know, from the Turtle Spring? It had all been agreed."

"Ah, that… We were already made aware of this, Mrs Yura. We are also aware that old Mr Nire waded in and did everything in his power to convince Mrs Aoike to have the boy marry his own daughter, Fumiko. That's why Mrs Aoike had begun to get cold feet…"

"But, Inspector, do you know *why* she began to get cold feet?"

The two men looked at each other and then at her and saw that there was a wicked smile at the corner of her lips.

"What exactly do you mean by that, Mrs Yura?"

"Only that…" she began, but immediately stopped herself. "Oh, that's the last of the sake, I'm afraid… Please, wait a moment while I fetch some more."

Atsuko's reason for stopping mid-tale and getting up like this was probably to check that nobody was eavesdropping, but it could also have been to give herself time enough to gather her thoughts. She returned presently, carrying a large flask of sake.

"Please, won't you have some more?" she asked.

"Thank you," said the inspector. "You were saying…?"

"Ah, yes. Well, you see, Kindaichi-san…"

"Yes?" he replied.

"There's a world of difference these days between us and the Nires."

"'A world of difference'? Meaning what exactly?"

"It's all to do with money. After all, isn't everything? You see, our family is getting poorer and poorer, while the Nires… Well, they're like the rising sun. And with a girl as beautiful as theirs, why do you suppose Mrs Aoike was so hesitant to make her decision?"

"I had assumed it was because she felt honour-bound to you, Mrs Yura," said Inspector Isokawa.

"Oh, you're way off the mark, Inspector!" Atsuko's lips creased into a sneer. "After all, we only had a verbal agreement. We were yet to announce the engagement officially."

"So, what you're saying, Mrs Yura, is that there was another reason for Mrs Aoike's hesitation?"

"Why, yes, Inspector! Accepting Fumiko made sense in financial terms. She would have brought with her an enormous dowry. But then, Mrs Aoike would have been the laughing stock of the entire village."

"But why?"

"Why, because that girl, Fumiko, is a bastard child."

"A bastard child?"

Inspector Isokawa practically choked on his sake. Kosuke Kindaichi, who had been nibbling on a boiled shiitake mushroom, was similarly stunned and looked at Atsuko with half the mushroom still in his mouth.

"You need only ask the villagers. Everybody knows about it. Only nobody ever discusses it openly, because they're too afraid of the Nires' power. An open secret, you might call it…"

"Do you mean to say that Fumiko isn't Kahei's daughter?"

"Precisely. You see, Kindaichi-san, Fumiko—"

Atsuko suddenly stopped mid-sentence, because Yukari Ozora's dulcet voice had come wafting through the air.

"Crimson leaves scatter in the field,
The fragile remnants of summer days gone by…"

It sounded like the song "Fallen Leaves".

The First Night of Revelations

"But surely…"

Atsuko stopped instinctively to listen. The song flowed gently, while the voice was almost husky.

"That song…" she said, looking questioningly at Kosuke Kindaichi and Inspector Isokawa. "Can that really be Chieko singing?"

"It's her, all right… You can tell by the way she sings that it's no amateur."

"But if it's *the* Yukari Ozora, wouldn't you like to go and watch?"

"Oh, but we already saw her when she arrived with Fumiko and Satoko to offer her condolences. Her mother, Harue, is there as well."

"Well, I never…"

Atsuko looked in astonishment at the two men, before quietly listening to the song again. Kosuke Kindaichi, however, couldn't help but notice a fire burning in her eyes.

Yukari's low, husky voice was full of charm, and she had chosen a song that suited the circumstances perfectly. After singing it first in Japanese, she sang it again in French, and, when that rendition came to an end, the hitherto silent room erupted in a storm of applause. It was then that a violent shudder suddenly ran down Atsuko's back.

The song appeared to have moved her profoundly, for she extracted the cuff of her undershirt from beneath that of her mourning clothes and pressed it to the inner corners of her eyes.

"I'd no idea that Yukari, Fumiko and Satoko were even here," she said, sniffing.

"Didn't Mrs Aoike inform you that they would be coming?" the inspector asked.

"No, she didn't say anything to me…"

"It was Kanao who asked Yukari to sing, as a tribute to Yasuko."

Hearing this, Atsuko suddenly began to sob violently, still clutching her cuff. Kosuke Kindaichi and Inspector Isokawa looked at each other.

Why had this formidable woman, who only moments ago had shown no trace of emotion, suddenly begun to cry? Had Yukari's song touched her heart so deeply?…

"It pains me so much to see that my Yasuko died so cruelly, while her childhood friends are still alive and well."

Could Kosuke Kindaichi and Inspector Isokawa really believe the words that Atsuko spoke in between her sobbing? Whatever the case, they now watched on somewhat disappointedly as her shoulders convulsed. Although the change in manner was rather sudden, perhaps it was only to be expected of a grieving mother.

Having calmed down at last, Atsuko now wiped away her tears.

"Forgive me," she said. "It isn't very becoming for a woman of my age. What must you think of me…"

"Not at all. It's only natural after what's happened. Why, it would be odd if you didn't cry. But, Mrs Yura…" said the inspector.

"Yes?"

"Well, I'm not sure it's right to bring it up at a time when you're so upset, but what you were saying earlier about Mr Nire's daughter, Fumiko… I'd like to hear a little more about that, if you'd be so kind."

"Oh, that," said Atsuko hesitantly. "Well, you see, Inspector, it's a bit cruel of me to talk about it, given she's right next door."

"I think we'd like to hear it, all the same."

"Very well," she said. "I started it, so I suppose I really ought to finish it. But where to begin with it all?"

"How about this?" Kosuke Kindaichi intervened. "What if the inspector here were to ask you a series of questions. Would that be all right?"

"Yes, I think that would be a very good idea, Kindaichi-san."

"All right, then, let's do as you suggest," said the inspector. "But I'd like you to help with the questions, too, Kindaichi."

"Understood, Inspector."

"Well, now, Mrs Yura... The first thing to establish is that, if Fumiko is not Kahei's daughter, is she the result of some infidelity on the part of his wife? That is to say, would I be right in assuming that Kahei's wife had a lover?"

"No, Inspector, that isn't it at all," Atsuko hastened to explain. "What I meant was that Fumiko is not the daughter of Kahei and his wife."

"So, whose daughter is she then?"

"Truth be told, we don't really know who the father was. What I can tell you, though, is who her mother is. It's Kahei's sister, Sakie. She was the youngest of all the siblings. She's married now and lives in Tottori, but everybody in the village knows that she was the one who gave birth to Fumiko."

"I see," said Inspector Isokawa, casting a glance at Kosuke Kindaichi. "So, then, you have no idea who the father might be?"

"It's a bit of a strange story, Inspector..."

"Strange in what way?"

"Well, it's like this, you see. There were six siblings in all, the eldest of which is Kahei and the youngest, as I just mentioned, is Sakie. Though they are siblings, there is an age gap of almost twenty years between them. Anyway, Sakie attended the girls' school in Soja before she went off to live with the eldest of her sisters in Kobe, where she enrolled in one of the technical institutes. Only, while she was there, she fell pregnant by someone."

"I see, I see," said the inspector. "And then what happened?"

"Well…" Atsuko hesitated, blushing. "Since it happened in the big city and not in the village, and since nobody had any idea who the father might be, one day Mr Tatara ventured…"

"Hmm? What did Mr Tatara venture?"

"He suggested that it could have been Ikuzo Onda."

"Onda?!" exclaimed the inspector, his voice echoing in the room like a clap of thunder. Taken aback by his own reaction, he quickly glanced around, before lowering his voice to ask, "You mean that con artist? The very man who killed Rika Aoike's husband, Genjiro?"

"The very same, Inspector," said Atsuko squarely, her tears now having been replaced by a look of steely resolve.

No longer the meek and gentle creature who had been sobbing only a few moments ago, she was once again the woman who would casually utter all manner of cruelties in order to hurt Fumiko. The sharp, lacerating look in her eyes now appeared to confirm this.

After a moment of tense and awkward silence, Kosuke Kindaichi cleared his throat.

"I'm sorry," he said, "but what was it that made Mr Tatara say that? Was it pure speculation? Or did he have proof?"

"It was like this, Kindaichi-san. As I say, you know Mr Tatara had family in Kobe. Well, one day, he took the train from Himeji to visit them, and that's when he saw them together, in the same carriage—Onda and Sakie. Of course, they pretended not to know each other, but later on, in Kobe, he saw them again, walking side by side."

"Did you know this Onda chap well?" asked Inspector Isokawa. "I believe he once lodged with you, didn't he?"

"Yes, but he didn't stay with me for long… He really had a way with words, you know. He could charm the birds down from the trees."

"Mrs Yura, do you think that Mr Nire is aware that Fumiko's father is Ikuzo Onda?"

"I believe so, yes…"

Kosuke Kindaichi remembered it now. When he had first met Kahei in the baths at the Turtle Spring, the old man had seemed especially keen to talk about the incident that took place back in 1932. Doubtless, he, too, was keen to learn the true identity of Ikuzo Onda—not least since he could well be raising the man's child as his own daughter.

Who, then, had this Ikuzo Onda been in reality? In the autumn of 1931, he had shown up unannounced in the village, where he had been the subject of much speculation, only then to vanish again the following year, leaving behind in his wake a bloody murder and no clues as to his real identity. He had also left behind Chieko in Harue's womb and, if Atsuko's story was to be credited, Fumiko in Sakie's.

Kosuke Kindaichi remembered another thing. It was what the owner of the Izutsu Inn had told him during his trip to Soja:

"I still can't believe that Mr Onda would have done a thing like that," she had said. "I mean, he was no angel when it came to the ladies, but all the same…"

O-Ito must known what had happened. Perhaps Sakie, like Harue, meet Onda at the Izutsu Inn. And if she did, then perhaps even the village chieftain had gotten wind of their affair. Kosuke Kindaichi realized that he would have to question O-Ito further on this.

Inspector Isokawa looked baffled by this unexpected revelation.

"But," he said, "that would make Yukari Ozora and Fumiko Nire half-sisters."

"Exactly, Inspector," said Atsuko rather stiffly, the expression on her face every bit as hard as before.

"So, do they and the villagers know all this?"

"I don't believe so, no," Atsuko replied. "Everybody knows that Fumiko is really Mr Nire's niece, but I doubt they're aware that her father was Ikuzo Onda. And I doubt Mr Nire would have had the heart to tell her, either."

"So, how was it that they managed to keep up all this pretence?"

"Well, it was like this, you see. Hideko, Mr Nire's wife, who died last year, came from Shirozaki in Hyogo Prefecture. They said she was going to give birth back home and sent Sakie with her. Of course, Sakie had to withdraw from school to go. When the baby was born, Hideko brought it home and passed it off as her own, while Sakie went back to Kobe, where shortly afterwards she married a man originally from Tottori. He later took her there with him. It was all quite straightforward, really."

All the while, as she made this cruel revelation, Atsuko's face remained as cold and implacable as ever. Her frozen expression was reminiscent of a Noh mask.

Inspector Isokawa cleared his throat awkwardly.

"So, then, Mrs Yura, are you implying that all this has some connection to Yasuko's murder?"

"No, Inspector, it isn't so much that..." Atsuko blushed momentarily, but soon regained her composure. "That isn't what I'm saying at all. All I meant by it was that, when it came to the prospect of marriage, Mr Nire ought to have known better than anyone that Fumiko couldn't have competed with our Yasuko."

"I see," said Kosuke Kindaichi, nodding. "So, is that why you said what you did this morning by the waterfall?"

"Yes, but it just slipped out, Kindaichi-san. I know it was an awful thing to say, and in hindsight I'd take it back if I could, but I was in shock. I just couldn't think of anybody else who would have done such a terrible thing to her."

"It's perfectly understandable under the circumstances, Mrs Yura. There is one thing I'd like to ask you, though…"

He questioned Atsuko about the barrel and the funnel. She said that she, too, found the items bizarre, but that they didn't suggest anything to her in particular. When she was asked whether she knew of any local legend or tradition that mentioned anything like it, she explained that, hailing as she did from another region, she had only come to the village when she married and knew nothing of the old legends in this part of Japan. For those, she said, he would have to ask Mr Tatara or old Ioko.

The topic of conversation then naturally turned to Mr Tatara. Atsuko expressed much the same opinion as Rika: he was a treacherous sort and she had always thought it prudent to be wary of him. The news that the so-called "chieftain's death" might have been mixed in with the sushi that she and her mother-in-law had given him on the anniversary of Utaro's death, however, visibly surprised her.

"But that's impossible!" she exclaimed. "Though, I suppose somebody could have added the poison later. The area around Mr Tatara's cabin is full of it, after all." Atsuko lapsed into silent thought. "We had nothing to do with it, in any case. As Eiko already told you, Ioko passed them to us one by one with a pair of chopsticks so that we could wrap them up in bamboo leaves.

It's too far-fetched to suggest that Ioko or I or even Eiko could have done something as underhand as putting 'chieftain's death' in there at the same time," she added with a laugh.

And yet, the laughter with which she had punctuated her reply seemed so forced and unnatural that Inspector Isokawa and Kosuke Kindaichi could not help exchanging a meaningful glance.

When they moved on to the subject of Hoan Tatara, Atsuko clearly began to show a subtle reluctance to talk. Then, when the conversation had turned to the question of whether Mr Tatara was dead or alive, and, if he was dead, whether the *inari sushi* that he had taken home with him had been adulterated with "chieftain's death", Atsuko had suddenly seemed to grow agitated. But why?

Once she had settled down again, Inspector Isokawa said:

"By the way, thank you for your help earlier, Mrs Yura."

"Whatever do you mean, Inspector?"

"Your help in finding the note that lured Yasuko out, the one in which she was told that she would learn the secret of her father's death…"

Inspector Isokawa fixed Atsuko in his probing gaze.

"Oh, that…" said Atsuko, who, having been caught off guard earlier, had already regained her usual cold, rather formal demeanour. "What I can't quite understand, though, is why Yasuko was taken in by such a letter… There was no secret surrounding my late husband's death. Just ask Doctor Honda."

Inspector Isokawa looked as though he was about to say something, but Kosuke Kindaichi quickly cut in:

"We've already taken that liberty, Mrs Yura, and there doesn't seem to be any doubt about it. Yet, as you say so yourself, the question remains: why was Yasuko 'taken in' by this letter? Do you have any idea?"

With her usual steeliness, Atsuko returned the famous detective's gaze.

"Kindaichi-san, you know how girls of that age are... They're prone to imagining that the world around them is more complicated than it really is. If you were suddenly told that there was some mysterious secret lurking behind your father's death, wouldn't you be curious to know what it was? Of course, I don't suppose she suspected that anybody was out to kill her, not even in her wildest dreams."

As a shadow suddenly darkened Atsuko's eyes, her face was overcome by sadness, and she began to cry again.

"Why, yes, of course," said Kosuke Kindaichi, nodding sympathetically. "I see."

Koreya Kusakabe

It was not until later that it was discovered, but that evening something odd happened at the Yura residence.

It was around nine o'clock. Inspector Isokawa and Kosuke Kindaichi were with Atsuko in the small room adjoining the large hall where everybody was gathered. Masako, a young neighbour who had come to help with the wake, had gone with a wheelbarrow to fetch some firewood from the shed at the bottom of the garden, because they had run out of it in the house. To get to this shed, she had to pass by the annex.

It was rumoured that the Yuras' annex had once overflowed with treasures, but that, since the end of the war, it no longer contained anything of real value. The building, certainly, was not well maintained, and in the moonlight one could very clearly see the weeds that were growing on its dilapidated roof. Masako placed some firewood in the wheelbarrow and, just as she was about to retrace her steps back up the path to the kitchen, she casually glanced over at the wall of the annex. And what she saw there stopped her dead in her tracks.

There, on the wall, was an enormous shadow, covering it almost entirely, and so at first Masako couldn't quite make out what it was. But when at last she did recognize the shape, her heart froze in terror. It was the silhouette of an old woman bent double.

Trembling from head to toe, Masako looked around to try to establish where the shadow was coming from, but another outbuilding, where the male servants had once lived, blocked her view of the spot where it seemed the old lady must be standing.

The girl suddenly took fright. From the outline, it was clear that she was looking towards the main house. Abandoning the wheelbarrow, Masako mustered all her courage and stealthily made her way back to the kitchen.

"The old woman… The old woman…" she kept crying, as she collapsed onto the wooden step by the back door.

"What on earth's got into you, Masako? Didn't you bring the firewood?" said another one of the neighbours, who was tending the fire in the kitchen stove, staring at her in bewilderment. Her eyes were full of tears from the smoke.

"No, no, no! There was a strange old lady out there, lurking in the shadows. I'm not going back out there…"

"A strange old lady?!" asked Rika Aoike, who had just that moment come in from the main room to fetch another flask of sake. "Masako, what do you mean?"

"Oh, Mrs Aoike! There's a strange-looking old lady down there! She's hiding in one of the old outbuildings. I saw her shadow cast on the wall of the annex. She's come to take somebody else, I'm sure of it! I won't go out again! I won't!"

Rika silently went over to the back door and put on a pair of straw sandals that were lying there.

"And you're sure you saw the shadow on the wall of the annex, Masako?"

"Oh no, madam, you mustn't! You mustn't go alone!"

But, leaving Masako behind, Rika rushed outside, after which two more women came into the kitchen. When they heard what had happened, the three neighbours and Masako decided to go and take a look together. When the four of them arrived at the annex, they found Rika Aoike quietly putting the wood that Masako had dropped into the wheelbarrow.

"Where exactly did you see the shadow that scared you so much, Masako?"

"It was over there, on that wall! The silhouette was so big that it made her look like a giant!"

The four women looked at where Masako was pointing and exchanged glances. The wall was not lit by the moon. Even if somebody had been standing in the shadow of the outbuilding, there was no way that their shadow could have been cast there.

"You must have been dreaming, Masako. Or could there perhaps have been a light coming from somewhere?"

"It wasn't a dream! I swear, I really did see it! There was a giant silhouette taking up this entire wall…"

But no matter how Masako insisted, no matter how she stamped her foot on the ground, nobody believed her. Still, just to make sure, the group walked around the annex and took a good look at the outbuilding, both inside and out, but nobody saw anything out of the ordinary.

In the end, it was decided that Masako had been hallucinating, and, as she herself also came to believe this version of events, the little episode remained known only to these five women—that is, until the incident that happened later…

Meanwhile, it had been a very busy day for Kosuke Kindaichi and Inspector Isokawa. Half an hour after they learnt from Atsuko the surprising circumstances of Fumiko's birth, the two of them left the wake with Yukari and Harue, parting ways with Fumiko and Satoko at the front gate of the Yura residence. The four went to see Koreya Kusakabe, Yukari's manager who intrigued the two men so much, and were welcomed in the reception room of the new house that Yukari Ozora had had built for her adoptive parents.

It was just past ten o'clock.

Koreya Kusakabe was a muscular, handsome man of around fifty. His thick head of silver hair was swept back completely. A returnee from Manchuria, he had a wild, rugged look about him. Yet his violet-tinted glasses, which he wore even at night, lent him a rather suspicious air. He had on a pair of shorts and a garish Hawaiian shirt that showed off his strong arms, and on his left wrist he wore a gold watch.

"Well, well, Kindaichi-san," he said. "I've heard so much about you, but I never expected to find you here of all places."

"Err, thank you," he responded with a slight bow. As he did whenever he felt shy or embarrassed, he scratched his bird's nest of hair. "I'm sorry to barge in on you at such a late hour…"

"Not at all," replied Koreya Kusakabe, glancing discreetly at the tasteful clock that was placed on the mantelpiece. "It's only ten past ten. If this were Tokyo, the night would just be getting started! We have all the time in the world. Harue!"

"Yes?" came the reply.

"Would you mind getting some whisky for these two gentlemen?"

"I'm afraid we've already had quite enough to drink," said Inspector Isokawa, breathing heavily and unwittingly proving his point. "If it's all the same, I wouldn't mind something cold…"

"Just bring some juice, Mother!" called Yukari Ozora. Still dressed in her evening gown, she went over to sit on the arm of the armchair where Koreya Kusakabe was and put her arm around his neck with the air of a spoiled child.

"I sang at the wake this evening," Yukari told her manager.

"You did what?"

"It's true. Yasuko's fiancé asked me to…"

"Oh? She had a fiancé?"

"Yes, he's the one you were complimenting last night. The one you said had a good voice."

"Ah, yes, Kanao…"

"That's him, yes. He just looked so sad. Whenever I looked at his face while I was singing, I felt as though I could cry myself. He didn't even try to wipe away his tears."

"What did you sing?"

"'Fallen Leaves'."

"Ah…"

"I think it was a good choice. Don't you?"

Just then, Harue brought in a silver tray with several glasses of juice. Yukari stood up to serve them to Kosuke Kindaichi and Inspector Isokawa. She seemed to have a very considerate nature.

After giving a glass to Koreya Kusakabe, Harue was about to leave again, when he stopped her.

"Ah, please stay, Harue. I'm sure that Kosuke Kindaichi and the inspector will have some questions for you. I'll leave you all to talk, shall I?" he said, rising from his chair.

"Actually, Mr Kusakabe," Inspector Isokawa quickly put in, stopping him with a gesture of his hand, "we'd like you to be here as well. You must be aware of the incident that took place here in 1932?"

"Why, yes, of course," he said, sitting down again. "That's why we're here, after all."

"I'm sorry, come again?"

Inspector Isokawa stared intently at Koreya Kusakabe, whose gaze he could only guess at behind those tinted glasses. With a look of curiosity, Kosuke Kindaichi was also watching this hand-some, greying man.

If the inspector was not mistaken, this man was none other than Genjiro, and there were already hints that Rika was beginning to suspect as much…

However, Koreya Kusakabe adopted a very nonchalant tone:

"Well, now…" he laughed. "Shall I tell them, Harue?"

For some reason, Harue's cheeks were flushed, and she just sat there, awkwardly twisting a handkerchief in her lap. Suddenly, Yukari said quite frankly:

"It's all right, tell them. It's a pity that Mr Tatara's gone missing, but what luck that Inspector Isokawa happens to be here!"

"Yes, that's quite true, Yukari. Thank you. Shall I, Harue?"

"Fine, go ahead," she replied flatly, in a low and resigned voice. It did not escape Kosuke Kindaichi's attention that her cheeks, flushed only a moment ago, had in that instant turned pale and lifeless.

"You see, Inspector, Kindaichi-san… I intend to marry this woman. Yukari here is also in favour of it. From a legal standpoint, there's no obstacle to our getting married. According to the family register, Harue has never been married. Yet there is one thing that's still troubling her…"

"And that is…?" asked the inspector, staring all the more intently at Koreya Kusakabe and trying to conceal his growing curiosity.

"Well, you see…" Kusakabe hesitated. "It's to do with Yukari's father."

"Ah, I see," said the inspector. "You mean Ikuzo Onda. But surely he has no legal rights over Mrs Bessho?"

"No, that's quite right. As I said, there's no issue in legal terms. But what's troubling Harue is the possibility that he may still be alive, and what would happen then if he ever turned up out of the blue."

"But surely it's unthinkable that he'd come back. After committing such an appalling crime…"

"Yes, that's true enough, Inspector. Rationally speaking, at least. But there are such cases where people's actions cannot be explained by reason alone… In other words, what Harue would like to know is more fundamental: that is, whether Yukari's father is dead or alive. Put simply, if he's dead, she'll marry me, but if he's alive out there somewhere, she knows that she'll always be thinking about him and would rather live alone… As you can see, Harue has very old-fashioned sensibilities, and that's one of the reasons I love her. As I'm sure you can see, Kindaichi-san, we're in quite a bind…"

"Yes, I can see that," he replied, nodding. He cast a sidelong glance at Inspector Isokawa, who now seemed less cheerful than before.

The inspector seemed to have realized his mistake, and said:

"But why did you tell us that you had come here because of what happened in 1932?"

Koreya Kusakabe unhurriedly lit a pipe before answering.

"Well, Inspector," he said, "Harue can't quite bring herself to believe that Ikuzo Onda was wicked enough to do such a thing. The business with all the machinery may well have turned out to be a scam in the end, but she just isn't convinced that he originally set out with that in mind. Let alone intending to kill a man and then run off… No, even if he'd been forced somehow to take the man's life, he would surely have confided in Harue and taken her with him. And she may well have gone with him. She maintains that he knew just how much she loved him."

"I see. And so…?"

"She was still very young at the time, you know. And besides, she was so distraught and couldn't even explain to the investigators how she felt when they came to question her. Then, when she was evacuated here during the war, the village chieftain revealed something to her quite by chance. One of the men in charge of the investigation—in fact, it was none other than you, Inspector—suspected that it was not Genjiro who had been killed, but rather Yukari's father… It was a painful moment for Harue, to be sure, but it also provided a ray of hope for Yukari's future. Perhaps she wasn't the daughter of a murderer after all. Harue confided all this in me only recently. That's when we had the idea: to return to the village and ask the local chieftain for more details while there's still time."

Inspector Isokawa's hopes had been well and truly dashed. It was clear that the man who had just recounted all this was not Genjiro Aoike. The inspector was so dismayed that he did not even have the strength to ask any more questions, and so he let Kosuke Kindaichi take over.

"Mrs Bessho," he said, "was Yukari's father aware that you were with child?"

"Yes, of course he was."

"In that case, what, may I ask, was he planning to do about the situation?"

"My parents would never have accepted him into the family, so we planned to go to Manchuria as soon as the baby was born and arrangements could be made. We were going to ask for their forgiveness then and leave."

"This was why she was so convinced that he would have taken her away with him," said Koreya Kusakabe, "even if he had been forced to flee after committing a murder. Mr Tatara's explanations only gave credence to that belief."

"So, you didn't see the man who was killed in Mr Tatara's cottage?"

"No," she replied. "At the time, everybody thought it was Genjiro..."

It had already gone midnight, and Kosuke Kindaichi and the inspector were still listening to Harue recount the events of all those years ago, when suddenly Shohei and Goro came rushing in.

"Yukari! Fumiko isn't here with you, is she?"

"No," she replied. "We said goodbye to her about two hours ago outside the Yuras' house. She was with Satoko."

"Has Fumiko gone missing, Shohei?" asked Kosuke Kindaichi, who, like Inspector Isokawa, had bolted up from his chair with a start.

"Yes... Satoko said that they parted ways in front of our house. She saw Fumiko go inside, but now she's nowhere to be found! What if that mysterious old woman's been here again!?"

Shohei was trembling all over, a look of distress on his face.

That night, all the villagers set out with torches once again to find Fumiko. It was not until dawn the next day, however, that her body was discovered...

PART III

What the Third Little Sparrow Said

"Weighing up her coins, both great and small..."

Onikobe seemed to have fallen prey to some malign spirit. A spasm had passed through the entire village, which now lay completely paralysed with fear.

"Oh, what an O-Bon festival! What a festival of the dead!" lamented the old men of the village, while the young people panicked, wondering where on earth the old woman could be hiding.

In the event, it was the drunkard Tatsuzo who found Fumiko's body.

After two consecutive nights of scouring the countryside, Tatsuzo had begun to feel a little tired, and so, around dawn, he had separated from the search party in order to make his way over to the winery, where he wanted to have his fill of the sour-tasting drink.

As he uncorked a barrel and filled a thick-rimmed glass with the hateful purple liquid, his gaze was caught by something shiny not far away from him. The sky was starting to grow bright in the east, and the cool light of dawn was beginning to penetrate the interior of the winery. On the floor, three or four little golden discs glittered.

"Now, what could they be, I wonder?" he said to himself.

After taking only a sip from the glass, Tatsuzo set it down again and went over to look round. There, behind a mountain of wine barrels, he found Fumiko, still in her mourning clothes, lying strangled on the dusty floor.

News of the discovery spread throughout the village like wildfire, and, by the time that Kosuke Kindaichi and Inspector Isokawa, preceded by Deputy Inspector Tachibana, made their way up from the crossroads, they found a large crowd of unruly villagers already gathered and trampling all over the crime scene.

Tachibana was the very picture of rage. He rained curses down on the crowd, expelling every last one of them, apart from Tatsuzo, from the winery. He then cast an exasperated look behind the wine barrels and took a deep breath in an attempt to regain his composure.

For the first few moments, nobody dared to speak. Kosuke Kindaichi, Inspector Isokawa, the detectives and the officers—all of them stood there, frozen to the spot in stunned silence.

Sleep-deprived and still angry, Deputy Inspector Tachibana then suddenly turned his bloodshot eyes towards Tatsuzo and glared at him.

"Is this your idea of a joke, Tatsuzo?" Tachibana snapped.

"N-not likely, Deputy Inspector! She was already cold by the time I got here!"

"I'm not talking about the murder, you idiot!" (Tachibana already seemed to be at his wits' end.) "I'm asking whether it was you who slipped that strange thing in her obi."

"N-no! Not I, Deputy Inspector! Why, it was like that when I found the body!"

The deputy inspector, continuing to be beside himself, cast a furious glance at the body lying on the floor and then turned to Kosuke Kindaichi, ready to explode.

"Kindaichi-san, would you care to tell me what this means exactly? Why has the murderer done something as bizarre as this?"

He asked the questions in such a stern tone, as though wishing to pin the blame for what had happened on the private detective.

"Well, Deputy Inspector, it must have some meaning. I dare say it has some especial significance for the murderer."

"'Especial significance'?"

"Yes, Tachibana," muttered Inspector Isokawa, sighing. "Yesterday it was a barrel and a funnel, whereas today it's a balance scale and some coins."

The small group then fell silent once again as they looked down at the body on the floor.

Deputy Inspector Tachibana's anger and Inspector Isokawa's confusion were not without reason. Once again, the murderer had played a cruel game with the corpse.

Fumiko was lying flat out on her stomach. A balance scale had been slipped into her obi, and in its pans were several objects that resembled old-fashioned coins. What had caught Tatsuzo's eye not long before were these imitation coins of varying sizes, known as *mayudama*, which are made from little cocoons wrapped in gold paper and used to decorate willow branches during certain festivals. These were not made of the usual paper, however, but of thin metal, and they glittered in the light of that summer morning.

"Tatsuzo?" said Kosuke Kindaichi, his eyes bleary for lack of sleep. "Yasuko belonged to the family of coopers, and Fumiko belonged to the family of weighers, didn't she?"

"Why, yes! Yes, you're right!"

"Do you think this is some kind of lead, Kindaichi-san?" asked Tachibana.

"That seems to be how we're supposed to interpret it, yes. But what could the funnel and these *mayudama* mean?"

As he mumbled, Kosuke Kindaichi bent down to take a closer look at Fumiko's face. Everybody had been so distracted by the murderer's bizarre staging that they had forgotten to try to determine the cause of death.

Her face was pressed against the dusty floor, and her clothes were slightly dishevelled, but it was immediately apparent that she had been strangled. A ligature had left a thin mark around her neck, indicating that she had been killed in the same way as Yasuko.

Kosuke Kindaichi then looked at the *mayudama* on the balance scale, but suddenly he frowned, stood up and turned to Tatsuzo.

"Tatsuzo, did you move the body at all?"

"Well, err, yes, I did… I straightened it up a little."

"What about the *mayudama*?"

"No, I didn't touch them. I thought the murderer must be up to his old tricks again…"

Just then, young Doctor Honda arrived, together with the photographer and a group of forensic specialists, so Kosuke Kindaichi and Inspector Isokawa led Tatsuzo outside.

It was there, at the front of the winery, that they heard Shohei shouting.

"Hey, Kanao! Did you do this to Fumiko to avenge Yasuko's death? Hmm?"

Kosuke Kindaichi stopped in his tracks and turned to where this ruction was taking place. There, on the embankment in front of the winery, he saw the two young men staring each other down. Shohei had obviously intended his words to be heard by the famous detective and the inspector.

"What are you talking about?!"

"You were in love with Yasuko. After she was killed, her mother insulted my father. You could have done her in for revenge!"

"But that's absurd!"

"What's so absurd about it?! Ever since last night, you've been acting really strange, Kanao. You've been crying like a little girl. Go on, admit it! You killed her, didn't you?!"

"You bastard! How about you admit that it was your father who killed Yasuko!" shouted Shohei.

"What?! Why would he have done that?! Go on, tell me! Why would my father have killed Yasuko?"

"You really want to know, do you? Shall I tell you? It's because your father wanted to force a bastard child on me and Yasuko was getting in his way. That's why he killed her!"

"What are you talking about?" exclaimed Shohei. "What bastard child?! Tell me!"

"Oh, I'll tell you, all right! That little bastard was your sister, Fumiko! That's right! Fumiko, who's lying dead in that winery at this very moment! So there!"

"What did you say?! Let me go, let me go! I'll kill him! I'm going to kill you for that, Kanao!"

"That's enough, Shohei! Get a grip. You know that Kanao could never have done something as awful as that."

"Kanao! You didn't have to go and tell him that. How could you?! I thought he was supposed to be your friend!"

Goro and his friends had managed to separate the two frenzied young men, but Shohei, his entire face flushed, continued to struggle and shout.

"Let me go! Let me go!" he cried. "I'm going to kill him! I'm going to kill the son of a bitch!…"

"Shohei, enough!"

The voice burst like a clap of thunder from behind the circle of onlookers. An old man then pushed his way through the crowd of villagers and placed himself between the two adversaries. It was Kahei, who had come rushing upon hearing the news of his daughter, Fumiko's murder. His son, Naohei, followed behind him, pushing a bicycle.

"Please excuse him, Kanao," said Kahei. "He's on edge. But

equally, you've let your tongue run away with you, boy. As for you, Shohei, what do you think you're playing at?! How can you be so foolish to even think of fighting? Hasn't the village seen enough tragedy these past few days? Kindaichi-san, Inspector Isokawa…" His face darkened. "Pay no notice to what they just said, I implore you. They've hardly slept these past two days and they're upset, just like all the young folk here."

The inspector greeted the old man:

"I'm afraid it's your family this time, Mr Nire."

"So it's true, then… It's as though this village were cursed. May I be permitted to see Fumiko?"

At that point, the photographer emerged from the winery, having apparently completed his work.

"Of course. Please, step this way. Doctor Honda is here as well."

"Is that so? Very well, then… Naohei, come with me, please."

Unlike his father, Naohei, who was still young, had trouble hiding the emotions provoked by this latest tragedy. He glared at Kanao and, leaving his bicycle where it stood, followed his father inside the winery. No sooner had he entered, however, than Naohei reappeared.

"Inspector! Kindaichi-san!" he called out. "There's something I'd like to tell you later. Would you mind waiting for me in the winery office?"

As he spoke, there was a meaningful look in his eyes.

"Very well, we'll be waiting for you," Inspector Isokawa called back.

Fortunately, Kahei's outburst had been enough to put an end to Shohei and Kanao's quarrel, and so Kosuke Kindaichi followed the inspector into the office, which was every bit as dusty as the rest of the winery. Unable to find anywhere clean enough to sit, they stood by the window and silently took in the view stretching all the way from Sakura to the old ruins in the village.

The inspector approached Kosuke Kindaichi and said to him in a low voice:

"It would seem that the whole village knows about Fumiko, after all."

"There's no way of hiding such things in a village like this. It isn't the city."

"That may be so, but what does it have to do with her death?"

"What indeed?" said Kosuke Kindaichi vaguely. "This case is a mystery."

And with that he lapsed back into silence.

It was only after a long wait that the two men were finally joined by Kahei, Naohei and Deputy Inspector Tachibana.

"Where is Doctor Honda?" asked Inspector Isokawa.

"He's already left. He confirmed that the cause of death was strangulation, just like yesterday. But take a look at this," said a grim-faced Tachibana, throwing down the balance and *mayudama* on the dusty desk. "It's stamped with the Nires' logo."

As he gazed at the symbol combining two carpenter's squares above a weight, Kosuke Kindaichi felt as though he could hear the murderer's laughter ringing in his ear, and he couldn't help but shudder. Clearly, this was no ordinary killer.

"Is that balance scale from your house?" Inspector Isokawa asked in a whisper.

Kahei nodded silently. He had tears in his eyes.

"Yes, the stamped logo means that it must be ours, but who on earth would have taken it?"

Naohei's piercing eyes were fixated on the object.

"Could it have been used in the winery?" he asked.

"No, it's the wrong type. The ones they use here are much bigger."

"Then somebody must have taken it from our house?" continued Naohei.

"That's certainly what it looks like. But who could have got their hands on it, and how?"

"Look at these," said Naohei in a voice brimming with restrained anger as he threw down a handful of *mayudama* on the desk, similar to those that were found with Fumiko's body.

The three investigators looked agog.

"Where on earth did you find these?" Deputy Inspector Tachibana asked pointedly.

"I found them scattered in our garden."

"In your garden?!"

"Yes. When Shohei came to tell us the news, I rushed out the back door and found them just lying there. As he'd told us that some had been found near Fumiko's body, I went to check the shrine in the house. The *mayudama* were all gone."

"So, the *mayudama* are from your house as well, then?" the deputy inspector asked curtly.

"Yes, it certainly looks that way… But who would have taken them?"

Kosuke Kindaichi and Inspector Isokawa exchanged a bewildered look. The famous detective could still hear, right in his ear, the menacing laughter of the murderer.

"Put to sleep with chieftain's death..."

The post-mortem examination carried out by young Doctor Honda established that Fumiko had been killed probably at around midnight.

She had left the Yura residence at roughly ten o'clock, at the same time as Kosuke Kindaichi and Inspector Isokawa, along with Yukari Ozora and her mother, Harue, and Satoko as well. They had parted ways in front of the house, and Satoko had accompanied Fumiko home.

"We got to the house safe and sound," Satoko confirmed to Deputy Inspector Tachibana. "Then she said goodnight and went inside. There was nothing that seemed out of the ordinary."

Satoko seemed to have given up her headscarf for good and now appeared in front of everybody with her birthmark on full view.

Looking back on it, Satoko, on both occasions, had been the last person to see her friends alive. Was she herself aware of this fact? Her face was difficult to read, and she no longer seemed to care about the looks that it attracted.

At the Nire residence, nobody had noticed Fumiko return. Just after the two investigators and three women had left, Kahei had gone to play a game of *go* with old Doctor Honda, while Naohei and Shohei had stayed on at the wake. Naohei's wife, Michiko, had fallen asleep while putting her youngest baby to bed. Unlike the Yura household, the Nires had three servants, but they slept in another building in the grounds. Since Fumiko's corpse was found wearing sandals, it was assumed that she had probably sneaked out again, but why? Thinking that she might have received a letter like Yasuko, they combed her room but to no avail.

Back at the Yura residence, the wake had gone on until around half-past ten. Shohei had helped to tidy up, and it was a little after eleven by the time he got home. When he did, he found Naohei already there, but their father, Kahei, was nowhere to be seen.

Naohei's wife had noticed Fumiko's absence at around half-past eleven, just as Kahei came home, and the latter soon spotted that the sandals that Fumiko had worn to the wake were also missing. Shohei had then ridden his bicycle up to the Turtle Spring, where Satoko told him that she had seen Fumiko home. He was surprised also to note that Kanao had yet to return. After all, Kanao had left the Yuras' a little earlier than he and his friends had done. In fact, he had left the house right after Fumiko. Shohei insisted that, ordinarily, Kanao would have stayed longer than he and his friends did.

Kanao later explained that when he heard Yukari Ozora sing "Fallen Leaves", he had been overwhelmed with sadness and decided to leave shortly after Yukari did. As he was cycling home, however, he had stopped at the waterfall, and it was there that his mother, Rika, had found him, pensive, sitting with his head in his hands. Worried by his absence, she had suspected that she might find him there, but she'd had a hard time persuading him to go back with her.

Once back at the Turtle Spring, after much coaxing, they learnt from Rika that Shohei had just come by to enquire about Fumiko. Kanao then went to bed, but soon afterwards, his friends from the village woke him so that he could take part in the search.

If these accounts are all true, the following would appear to be what happened:

After leaving Fumiko at the front gate of the Nire residence, Satoko had hurried home to the Turtle Spring. The path would have taken her past the waterfall, where Kanao would stop a little later.

Fumiko, meanwhile, after saying goodnight to Satoko, had gone through the front gate of her house, but for some unknown reason went out the back door. The reason for assuming that she had gone out that way was that that the *mayudama* had been found there on the ground, along with a folding fan that belonged to her. This meant that she would have passed behind the temple at Sakura and taken the shortcut up towards the crossroads, so it was little wonder, given the distance, that Kanao would not have seen her.

But who could the murderer be?

Kanao said that he had been at the waterfall for nearly an hour by the time that Rika came looking for him, but that he hadn't seen a soul in the intervening time.

The balance scale and the *mayudama* that had been stolen from the Nires' house were no ordinary, everyday objects, and so nobody could say when they had disappeared for sure. On the other hand, the Nires and their servants were absolutely certain that the *mayudama* had not appeared in the back garden until that night, so perhaps it was Fumiko herself who had taken them. But if that were the case, why had she done so?

"What a dreadful business, Kindaichi-san. It makes me shudder just thinking about it."

It was around nine o'clock in the morning when Deputy Inspector Tachibana finished questioning everybody in the makeshift incident room at the Turtle Spring. Having established the above sequence of events, he and Inspector Isokawa were exhausted and in a state of shock.

Lost in thought, Kosuke Kindaichi just nodded silently. His little grey cells were racing to try to come up with a logical solution, but, weary as he was from a succession of sleepless nights, he felt as though his brain were filled with lead.

"Inspector," he said, "we should get some sleep. I'm afraid I'm not much use in this state."

"Yes, you're right. Tachibana, will you excuse us? I know you haven't had much sleep either, but..."

"No need to worry, Inspector, it's all right. I've got youth on my side," replied the deputy inspector, his face as grim as ever. He seemed especially annoyed with Kosuke Kindaichi.

Yasuko Yura's funeral was due to take place at four o'clock that afternoon. In the heat of the summer, it was impossible to delay it any longer. After asking O-Miki to wake them up in time for the ceremony, Kosuke Kindaichi and Inspector Isokawa went to bed at around half-past nine and, as soon as their heads hit the pillow, they both fell into a deep sleep.

They were woken by O-Miki at around half-past two and found that Rika, Kanao and Satoko had already left for the funeral.

"Sir," said O-Miki, frowning as she served them lunch, "is it true that they're also going to perform an autopsy on Fumiko today?"

She sighed.

"I'm afraid they've no choice, since it wasn't a natural death," said the inspector.

"Oh, it's just horrible," she said. "Two days in a row... And worse still, today, after the funeral at the Yuras' house, there'll be the wake at the Nires' house, so I'll be left all alone again. I'll be so afraid all on my own, so very afraid!"

She looked so forlorn.

"You'd better be careful then," said the inspector. "They say the old woman is on the hunt for more pretty young women to kill, don't you know!"

"Oh, Inspector! You ought to be ashamed of yourself!"

O-Miki feigned hitting him with her tray, but she didn't seem at all angry with him.

"Tell me, O-Miki, are there any bicycles? It would be much quicker than going on foot."

"There's only one left, so you'd have to share it."

"Oh, that's no trouble!"

Before leaving the Turtle Spring, the two went to check in the makeshift incident room and found Tachibana in conversation with Detective Inui, who had just arrived back from Kobe.

"Ah, sir," said the detective, standing up. Inspector Isokawa turned to him. "It looks like Mr Tatara was lying to Mrs Aoike."

"Oh? You mean about his nephew sending him money?"

"Yes, exactly, sir. After Mr Tatara's nephew, Junkichi Yoshida, died, he turned to Junkichi's younger brother, Ryokichi, who works in the shipping industry in Kobe. But whenever Mr Tatara asked for money, Ryokichi and his wife would always refuse. They hated each other so much that Mr Tatara didn't even go to the funeral."

"So, then, Mr Tatara was lying about his source of income…"

"There's no doubt about it, sir."

"What about you, Tachibana? Did you find anything at the scene of the crime?"

"Only a few footprints left in the winery by a pair of straw sandals. The villagers had trampled over everything!" The deputy inspector was still in a foul mood. The lines that creased his forehead seemed to be growing darker. "And outside the winery, it was nigh impossible."

"Yes, the fierce heat has dried the earth out. There wouldn't have been any footprints."

Not a single drop of water had fallen since the storm on the night of the 10th. The soil in the region was full of granite, and so in summer, as soon as the sun shone, it became as hard as a whetstone.

"As you were, then," said Inspector Isokawa. "We'll be at the Yura residence for the funeral."

"Very well, Inspector."

"Kindaichi, I'm afraid you'll have to ride on the back of the bicycle, since I'm the one wearing trousers."

"Forgive me, Inspector, but a man of your age—"

"What are you talking about?! A man of my age, indeed... I'm not for the knacker's yard just yet, you know. And don't you forget, I still practise judo."

Kosuke Kindaichi laughed.

"Forget I said anything! I'll be only too glad to hitch a lift."

They had slept so well that they were now both in fine fettle— a fact that made Deputy Inspector Tachibana, as he saw them exchange pleasantries like that as they left, all the more bitter.

They arrived at the Yuras' house just before the funeral procession was due to begin. The sound of sutras being chanted came from the main reception room. The entire house seemed to be packed with mourners.

The two men took seats at the very back of the main room and looked around. They spotted Kahei, who was sitting in his formal mourning attire, fanning himself. It was the 15th, the final day of the O-Bon festival, and the sun was so fierce and the heat so oppressive that the mourners were all dripping in perspiration as they listened quietly to the sutras. There was a sea of white folding fans in the room.

As Kosuke Kindaichi mopped the sweat from his brow, Rika Aoike made her way towards them through the crowd of people.

"Excuse me, Kindaichi-san, Inspector?" she whispered warily.

"Yes?"

"There's something I need to tell you… You seemed so tired this morning, so I didn't mention it."

Seeing the look on her face, the two men exchanged glances and stood up. She led them to the back of the house, where, by the annex, Masako was standing, surrounded by three women.

"Go on then, Masako," she said. "Tell Kindaichi-san and the inspector what happened last night."

Nervous and wearing a look of terror, Masako proceeded to tell them about the silhouette of the old woman that she had seen on the wall the previous evening.

"I didn't see her directly," the girl explained, "but from the way she was positioned, she must have been spying on us. The silhouette was so big that I didn't realize what it was right away. I was ever so scared!"

She seemed terrified by it even now.

"You see, Kindaichi-san," said Rika, "when Masako told us this, I rushed out to take a look, but I couldn't see the old woman anywhere. All I found was the wheelbarrow that Masako had left there. I was loading it up with wood when the others arrived with her. We told her that it was impossible to see a shadow on that wall when the moonlight was coming from this side, and we had a good laugh about it, sure that she must have been imagining things. But on second thought, I suppose the old woman could have been carrying a lamp. That could certainly have cast such a big shadow on the wall."

"Yes! Yes, you're right, Mrs Aoike!" said Masako. "It must have been just as you say. She must have been looking for Fumiko.

213

But nobody believed me. They all just laughed at me, and now look what's happened. I don't know what to say. It isn't my fault!"

Sensitive girl that she was, Masako burst into tears. The women around her looked at each other with a sense of regret.

"There, there, of course it wasn't your fault, Masako," said Kosuke Kindaichi. "Now, tell me, at what time did all this happen?"

"I'm not really sure, Kindaichi-san," said Rika. "Ah, yes, it was when you and the inspector were in the other room with Atsuko. If only we'd listened to her, rather than laughing at the poor girl…"

Rika sounded a little ashamed of herself.

Kosuke Kindaichi was contemplating all manner of things, such as measuring the distance between the outbuilding and the annex or standing by the outbuilding with a lantern to see what shadow it would cast, but, before he knew it, the chanting in the house stopped. The prayers had ended.

"Ah, Inspector, they'll be carrying out the coffin soon," said Kosuke Kindaichi. "We'll have to return to this matter later on, Mrs Aoike. In the meantime, don't go upsetting yourself, Masako. You aren't to blame for any of this."

When he and Inspector Isokawa then returned to the main house, the mourners were already on their feet, half of them loitering in the garden and the vestibule.

The two men took their places among the crowd, standing by the veranda, and just then Toshio's wife came over to them.

"Excuse me, Kindaichi-san, Inspector?"

"Yes, Eiko?"

"Old Mrs Yura is very keen to speak to you. If you'd like to follow me?"

"Of course…"

The two men exchanged a brief glance before entering the room. Ioko, the old woman, was sitting calmly in front of the coffin, an enigmatic smile playing on her pursed lips. Beside her stood Atsuko and Toshio and the rest of their family, and, a little behind them, the members of the Nire family, all watching curiously. Some other mourners stood there, eyes fixed on the old woman, wondering what was going to happen. Among them were Kanao and Shohei.

"Kindaichi-san, Inspector, thank you for coming to see me," said Ioko.

"Of course, Mrs Yura. I believe there's something you'd like to tell us?" said the celebrated detective.

"Well, you see, Kindaichi-san, I was going to tell you about this last night, when my great-grandchildren interrupted us... Isn't that right, Kahei?"

She glanced over at Kahei, who, dressed in mourning garb and carrying a white fan, was looking on with interest.

"The pastime had already died out in your and Atsuko's day, so you probably wouldn't know about it, but, when I was a girl, children used to sing songs while bouncing a *temari* ball," said Ioko, extracting from the sleeve of her kimono a brightly coloured embroidered ball for all to see.

Everybody's eyes widened.

"Now, listen very carefully, Kindaichi-san..."

The old woman stood up cautiously, took her right sleeve in her left hand and began to sing in a thin yet clear voice while bouncing the ball on the tatami:

"In the trees in the garden behind our house,
Three little sparrows came to stay.
The first little birdie said to me:

In the faraway land where I come from,
Many are the pleasures of the shogun's man—
Women, wine and hunting all day long,
But most of all he likes the women,
Oh yes, it's the women he likes.
So, he asked the local chieftain to find some girls.
And, sure enough, having hunted high and low, some girls he
   found,
But he talked and talked and talked too much,
And so to sleep he had to go,
Put to sleep with chieftain's death he was…"

Folk Traditions

Having finished her song while the mourners looked on in amazement, Ioko, still holding the *temari* ball in both hands, smiled and glanced at Kosuke Kindaichi, looking rather pleased with her performance.

Her face mixed the innocence of a child with the wicked cunning of an old woman of her years. The faint smile playing on her pursed lips seemed to mock the ignorance of everyone around her, including Kosuke Kindaichi.

The famous detective, however, had not yet grasped the importance of the *temari* song. Like everybody else surrounding Ioko, he just stared at her face with a look of astonishment.

"Why, yes," said Kahei, deep in thought. He had begun to wave his white fan nervously. "Wasn't there something about a barrel and a funnel in the song as well?"

Ioko smiled at him, as if to say: Bingo!

"You remember the song as well, don't you?" said Ioko. "Why don't I sing it for you all? Now, listen carefully …"

Once more, Ioko got to her feet, took her right sleeve in her left hand and began to bounce the *temari* ball on the tatami, while in a beautiful voice she sang:

"In the trees in the garden behind our house,
Three little sparrows came to stay.
The second little birdie said to me:
In the faraway land where I come from,
Many are the pleasures of the shogun's man—

Women, wine and hunting all day long,
But most of all he likes the women,
Oh yes, it's the women he likes.
A good little woman was the cooper's girl,
A pretty little thing, but she liked a drink,
All day long, she would guzzle it down,
She would measure by the barrel and drink through a funnel,
But before she'd had her fill, she was sent away,
They were all of them sent away..."

A cry rippled across the room. Kosuke Kindaichi was about to get to his feet, but, Ioko, unperturbed by the commotion, carried on bouncing the ball.

"In the trees in the garden behind our house,
Three little sparrows came to stay.
The third little birdie said to me:
In the faraway land where I come from,
Many are the pleasures of the shogun's man—
Women, wine and hunting all day long,
But most of all, he likes the women,
Oh yes, it's the women he likes.
A good little woman was the weigher's girl,
A very pretty thing, but rather mean,
She lived for money, weighing up her coins
Both great and small, all day and night,
But before she'd time to rest, she was sent away,
They were all of them sent away."

When the octogenarian had finished her song and, still holding the pretty embroidered ball in her hand, cast her gaze over the assembled mourners with a childlike smile on her face, everybody remained silent. Frozen there, they just looked at the old woman as though they had been hypnotized by some evil spirit. Even Kahei, who was ordinarily so calm, appeared dumbstruck by this latest revelation and, clutching at the white object in his hand, began fanning himself agitatedly.

Kosuke Kindaichi was agog. Twice he felt a curious shiver run down his spine, and his leg began to tremble. Suddenly, he asked in a voice that barely concealed his emotion:

"F-f-forgive me, Mrs Yura, but w-would you mind letting us hear that song again?"

"With pleasure, Kindaichi-san. I'll sing it as many times as you please."

And so, once again, Ioko straightened herself up, gripped her right sleeve and began bouncing the *temari* ball.

"In the trees in the garden behind our house…"

Her thin but crystal-clear voice carried, echoing throughout the room, which had frozen in perfect silence. When at last she reached the end of this awful song, there was a terrible commotion. Everybody wanted to give their opinion or ask her questions.

"Quiet, please!" Inspector Isokawa shouted, waving his arms about and trying to calm the audience. "Please, everybody, there's no use talking over each other like that. Why don't we let Kindaichi-san ask the questions? What do you say, Mr Nire?"

"I think that's a very good idea," said Mr Nire. "Kindaichi-san, please, ask away."

Kosuke Kindaichi felt the gaze of the entire room immediately shift to him, but he mastered his nerves and began:

"Mrs Yura, are you saying that the staging of these two crimes has something to do with the content of this *temari* song?"

"No, I'm not saying that at all. It's for you and Inspector Isokawa to determine whether the song has anything to do with these events. All I wanted to do was to bring it to your attention…"

"Thank you, Mrs Yura," he said, bowing his head slightly. "And you say the song is now almost completely forgotten? How old, roughly speaking, would a person have to be in order to remember it?"

"Well, you remember it, don't you, Mr Nire?" she said, turning to Kahei.

"Yes, vaguely… I remember hearing my late sister, Fukiko, singing it while she played with the *temari* ball. It suddenly came back to me when you sang the line, 'Put to sleep with chieftain's death he was'. But all that was such a long, long time ago!"

"And you, Mrs Yura," said Kindaichi, turning now to Atsuko. "Did you ever know a *temari* song like this?"

"I shouldn't think so, Kindaichi-san," old Ioko cut in. "Atsuko isn't from these parts. Remember, she only married into the village. Isn't that right, Atsuko?"

"It's true. This is the first time I've heard it. When I arrived here, the only *temari* song I knew was 'Thick hangs the mist on Mount Saijo, and fast flow the eddies in the Chikuma River…'— you know, the Kawanakajima song? Everybody knows that one. I'm sure you must have sung it in your day."

"Yes," said Kahei, waving his fan. "My younger sister used to sing that one… You had to lift your leg to pass the ball under it, and I remember that this made our mother angry because she thought it was improper for a young girl."

"So, there are probably not many people in the village who know the song you just sang then?" concluded Kosuke Kindaichi.

"I shouldn't think so. What do you say, Tatsuzo?..."

"Well, err..." he replied, stuttering. He had been sitting idly on the floor and now, having been called out by name for the first time, he rushed to his knees, startled. His nose was red, proving—as if any proof were needed—that he was still drunk.

"Your mother, who's three years younger than me, would certainly remember it."

"I'd be surprised if she did," said Tatsuzo.

"And why's that?"

"She's not like Mrs Yura here... she's completely senile."

Ioko pursed her lips and began to laugh in a refined sort of way.

"Come, now," she said, "I'm hardly any different. I'd completely forgotten it myself."

"But you just sang it to us!"

"Yes, but that's only because it all came back to me the year before last, when the village chieftain came pestering me with questions."

"The village chieftain?" Kosuke Kindaichi's ears pricked up, and he shot a look at Inspector Isokawa. "You mean that Mr Tatara came to ask you about this very *temari* song?"

"Yes... It would have been about two years ago now, if I'm not mistaken."

The inspector's eyes had a strange glint in them.

"But why," he said, "did the village chieftain want to ask you about this song, Mrs Yura?"

"Well, it was like this, you see," she said, grinning as she fingered the prayer beads that she was now clutching in her hand. "Are you listening, Kindaichi-san?"

"I'm hanging on your every word, Mrs Yura," he answered meekly.

For all his outward composure, however, Kosuke Kindaichi's heart was in turmoil and his chest was pounding.

"As I'm sure everybody here is well aware, the village chieftain always had his head in the clouds, and it was because of this that he lost his fortune. Well, two years ago, he apparently came across a little magazine. I forget what it is called, but it publishes articles on the strange ways and legends of people who live in the countryside. Perhaps it still exists. In any case, he had the idea of sending off an article on the *temari* songs of Onikobe, and that's why he came to find me. And do you know what, Tatsuzo? I must be going a little senile, because I had such trouble calling to mind the words. The village chieftain recalled them better than me… Anyway, we managed to remember the whole thing in the end, but it took both of us. If it weren't for him, I'd never have been able to sing it to you today."

"And the village chieftain sent the article to this magazine?" asked Inspector Isokawa.

"Oh yes. He even showed it to me. He was very proud of it," she said. "He read it to me because the print was far too small for an old woman like me to make out. Ah, he was such a kind man, the village chieftain!"

"But, Mrs Yura," the inspector hastened to point out, "we don't yet know for sure that Mr Tatara is dead."

"That's the problem," added Kosuke Kindaichi. "What do you think, Mrs Yura? Is Mr Tatara dead or alive?"

"Well," she said, "in the song, he's killed off with 'chieftain's death', but Mr Tatara wasn't the sort of man to fall into a trap. I doubt it would have been an easy task, getting rid of him. What do you think, Kahei?"

"Oh, I quite agree with you. Especially now that Yasuko and Fumiko have been killed just as it says in the song."

"Nobody in the village but the chieftain could have come up with such a bizarre idea," added Atsuko, immediately receiving a murmur of approval from many of the others present.

"Inspector," said Naohei enthusiastically, "what if we went to search for him in the mountains?"

"I think that's a good idea. Kanao, Shohei, I'm afraid you'll have to put your differences aside. Now isn't the time to fight. We need to get all the young people from the village together to go and comb the mountains."

"All right, let's get to work."

Thus did a reconciliation come about between Kanao and Shohei.

Meanwhile, Kosuke Kindaichi once again turned to old Ioko.

"You were saying that, in the song, the village chieftain is killed. Is that what the line 'And so to sleep he had to go' means? That he had to be killed?"

"That's it precisely, Kindaichi-san," she said, moving closer to him. "He explained all this to me, you see. As I was telling you just last night, there was, among Mr Tatara's ancestors, a village chieftain, and he was killed by the local feudal lord. And this was the one who liked women so much that he had the habit of taking any one of them who pleased him, regardless of whether they were young girls or married women. There was even a suggestion that when he tired of them, he'd throw them into the well on his estate. This is what the song means. Do you remember? At the end of every verse, there's the line: 'They were all of them sent away'. Well, apparently this means that they were killed. At least, that's what the village chieftain wrote in the magazine."

"And you don't recall the name of this publication?"

"I'm afraid not… But you could go and ask Junkichi Yoshida, the chieftain's nephew, who lives in Kobe. He ought to know."

"Why would he know?"

"The Yoshida family owns land in the Suma district of Kobe, so they're very wealthy. But Junkichi went to university—to Waseda in Tokyo—and among his friends there's one who took up studying folklore after the war and became a well-known professor."

"You don't mean Kunio Yanagida, do you?"

"The very one, Kindaichi-san," Atsuko put in.

"The chieftain was an avid reader of Yanagida's books," Ioko continued. "It was Professor Yanagida who came up with the idea for a sort of subscription magazine. Junkichi was the one who gave him the money to get it off the ground. And that was why Junkichi received the magazine every month from Tokyo. The village chieftain spotted it when he went to Kobe, and that's how he got the idea to write about the song in the first place. Ah! I remember now. The title of his article was 'On One of Onikobe's *Temari* Songs'. He sent it in and received a copy of the magazine himself when it was published. He was ever so proud of it! Didn't he show it to you, Kahei?"

"No, this is the first time I've heard of this."

"All the same, he was so proud to see his article in print. Every word of it just as he'd written it. Maybe he thought that the people in the village wouldn't understand. Did he ever show it to you, Eiko?"

"No, this is the first time I've heard about it, too."

"Ah, yes, of course. You'd gone back to have your first child."

"In that case, it must have been the August of the year before last. My first daughter was born on the 27th of August."

"Yes, I remember it was terribly hot at the time, wasn't it?"

"Thank you so much for everything, Mrs Yura," said Kosuke Kindaichi, addressing the old woman. "I shouldn't like to delay you any further."

Because of this interlude, the coffin was borne out almost an hour later than intended, but nobody complained. For the first time, in fact, we had a glimpse of a possible solution to this series of unexplained murders.

Fumiko's Mother

Just as O-Miki had said, the wake at the Nire residence would take place later that evening, after Yasuko's burial.

Kosuke Kindaichi and Inspector Isokawa had both been invited by old Mr Nire to attend the wake. As they had some time to spare, however, they decided to hop back on the bicycle and head over to Mr Tatara's home on the edge of the marsh.

The cabin had been turned over several times since his disappearance; however, nobody at the time had suspected that such a small magazine could conceal such an important secret. The two had consequently decided to go there and search for it, but, even after looking under the tatami mats, they were left empty-handed.

"Mrs Yura said that the article was his pride and joy," Inspector Isokawa remarked.

"Yes, but that was two years ago. He would still have been living in the village back then."

"That's true. Do you think he could have lost it in the move?"

"Frankly, I'd be surprised, Inspector, given that it was a prized possession."

"So why isn't it here?"

"Well, if it isn't here in the cabin, then I suspect somebody must have taken it. I doubt it would have been misplaced."

"Do you think it could have been Mr Tatara himself who got rid of it?"

"Let's leave that decision for later, Inspector. After all, we still don't know for sure whether he is dead or alive."

"But, you know, Kindaichi…"

"Yes?"

"I have to say, I really do admire your intuition, or your keen eye, or whatever you want to call it…"

"What do you mean, Inspector?" asked Kosuke Kindaichi, laughing.

"Just that ever since you laid eyes on Yasuko's body, you've been asking everybody you come across whether there wasn't a legend in the region that mentioned a barrel and a funnel."

"That's true… But never in my dreams would I have imagined that it came from a *temari* song!"

"That's only natural. After all, who could have thought that a song like that could exist? But why didn't old Mrs Yura sing it to us yesterday evening? If we'd known earlier, we might have realized that Fumiko could be the next victim."

"Didn't she say that her great-grandchildren interrupted her?"

"Well, yes, but just think of all the time we spent there with her… And if it was so important, then why didn't she tell us about it earlier? One could even surmise that she wanted to wait until Fumiko was dead before saying it."

"Yes, one could indeed…" murmured Kosuke Kindaichi distractedly.

Standing by the window of the cabin, he looked out at the white flowers of the water-chestnuts, which covered the entire surface of the marsh. What was he thinking just then? For he suddenly began to tremble…

"Inspector," he said, "I think we ought to ask all the elders in the village whether there aren't any other *temari* songs like this one."

"*Other* songs?!" exclaimed the inspector. "You think there might be others, Kindaichi?"

"Didn't the one that old Mrs Yura sang for us not strike you as a little odd?"

"Odd in what way?"

"Well, these songs would ordinarily have three, five or seven verses, all variations on a theme. And didn't you notice? In the song that Ioko sang, the first 'little birdie' sang about a chieftain, whereas the second and third ones sang about girls. In a traditional *temari* song, all three of them would have to be about girls—or about a chieftain."

"Yes, I see…"

"What I think is that, originally, there must have been two *temari* songs: one about the village chieftain and another about those girls with the guild names. Besides, most of the people in this village seem to have a guild name. I believe O-Miki told me that hers was basket-weaver, and I've heard it said that Yukari was born to the family of locksmiths. Yes, there must be a third verse, I'm sure of it…"

"But… Kindaichi!" Inspector Isokawa gasped, a shudder running through his body. "Are you saying that there's going to be another murder?"

"No," he replied emphatically. "All I'm saying is that we should bear this in mind. Don't you agree?"

"Yes, of course," said the inspector, regaining his composure. "Especially since the criminal appears to be so meticulous. After all, they've already succeeded with the daughters of the coopers and the weighers."

"That's right. That's why this criminal is doubly dangerous."

"That was a very good catch, you know, Kindaichi. You're spot on. The combination of the village chief with the three sparrows just isn't right. There has to be a third girl. Ah!…"

"Is something the matter, Inspector?"

"I have to take my hat off to you again, Kindaichi… I've only just clocked what you meant when you said that if the magazine

228

wasn't here, then it hadn't been misplaced but must have been removed. It's because Mr Tatara's article is sure to contain the third verse!"

"Yes, I believe so."

"But then, old Mrs Yura must know that too, mustn't she? It would be astonishing if she could remember the other verses so well but not the one that may yet save the life of another young woman."

"Hence her insistence that she, too, was going senile..."

"That devious old bitch!" exclaimed Inspector Isokawa, unable to control himself.

He looked around in panic, realizing what he had just said, before suddenly dropping his voice to a whisper:

"Do you suspect that she's involved in all this somehow?"

"I'm not so sure about that," Kosuke Kindaichi replied. "After all, it's a fact that she was the one who tried to tell us about the *temari* song last night. And we missed our chance because we were distracted by Yukari Ozora's arrival. But as you just said, Inspector, it was of such vital importance that she ought to have insisted on letting us know about it without delay. If she didn't do it, it was probably because, spurred on by morbid curiosity, she was waiting to see what would happen..."

"At any rate, if only we knew what this third verse was, we could set a trap for the murderer."

"Instead of asking around the village, Inspector, perhaps we'd have better luck having a discreet word with Tatsuzo's mother."

"What if, instead of going to the wake at the Nire residence, we were to go back to Yukari's house?"

"That's a good idea. Although I would like to attend the wake, too."

"But whatever for, Kindaichi-san?"

"I'm curious to see whether Sakie, Fumiko's real mother, has made the journey from Tottori."

"Yes, you have a point there," replied the inspector, clicking his tongue. "If they notified her by telegram this morning, she'd certainly be able to arrive in time for the wake this evening. Let's go, then!"

"Just a moment, Inspector."

"What is it?"

"I'd like to see whether the salamander is still here."

Kosuke Kindaichi walked to the kitchen to take a look in the jug. Sure enough, the horrible lizard was still there, motionless as if in hibernation, its skin glowing faintly.

"They can go a surprisingly long time without eating, can't they?"

"Yes, I believe so," said the inspector, peering with curiosity at the famous detective. He lowered his voice again. "You seem to have a special interest in that creature, Kindaichi. Do you think it's important to the case?"

Kosuke Kindaichi shook his head slowly.

"I don't know yet," he said. "But Mr Tatara captured it just before the events began. That's why I wonder whether it, too, has some role to play in all this."

The two men remained silent for a moment while they observed the dreadful creature, which still lay frozen at the bottom of the water jug.

"They do say that eating one can impart phenomenal vitality," murmured the inspector, as Kosuke Kindaichi replaced the lid.

"Shall we go, Inspector?"

The wake at the Nire residence was an even grander affair than the one at the Yuras' house. At around seven o'clock in the evening, when the two men arrived together on their bicycle, the entrance to the Nire house was so full of shoes that there was scarcely any space for them to put their feet.

Kanao was stationed at the entrance to welcome the guests.

"Ah, Kindaichi-san! Inspector! Wherever did you disappear to? Mr Nire has been looking for you."

"Oh, really? In that case, please inform him of our arrival, Kanao."

"Right away, Kindaichi-san."

All of the partition walls separating the three main reception rooms had been removed. The house was filled with people, and the heat was stifling.

The two men passed along the veranda to reach the back room, where the Buddhist altar was located, larger and more sumptuous than the one they had seen at the Yuras' house the day before.

They were burning incense when Naohei arrived in his mourning clothes.

"Kindaichi-san, Inspector Isokawa, thank you for coming this evening."

"Kanao told us that your father has been looking for us."

"Yes, he's expecting you. We've taken the liberty of having dinner prepared for you in a separate room. You can go through right away. Please…"

They were shown down a corridor to a smaller room, away from all the hustle and bustle of the wake. There, they were asked to sit in the place of honour, with their backs to the *tokonoma*, displaying Fumiko's photograph. Kahei arrived almost immediately afterwards, in the company of a beautiful woman in her forties. He greeted them affably.

"This is Sakie, my youngest sister," he said, indicating the woman in traditional mourning garb. "Sakie, these are

231

Kindaichi-san and Inspector Isokawa, whom I've just been telling you about."

The woman bowed.

"Allow me to introduce myself, gentlemen. I am the mother of
the girl who died today."

Without another word, she broke down in tears before
their eyes.

The Second Night of Revelations

After a few moments, Sakie wiped away her tears.

"Forgive me," she said. "I'm so embarrassed for you to see me like this. I won't cry any more, but, please, I beg you: bring my daughter's killer to justice!"

Tears welled in her eyes again, but now she tried desperately to stifle her sobbing.

"It's little wonder she's so upset," said Kahei, who was sitting beside her. "She's the one to be pitied most in all this. It happened before we had time to tell Fumiko who her real parents were... That's what I regret most in all this."

Kahei himself was also visibly moved.

"I'm awfully sorry to be troubling you with this, but it's all my fault, and I haven't even begun to explain it to you yet. Please, eat, and I'll tell you everything," he said, taking the flask of sake and serving them both.

Inspector Isokawa took a sip from his cup before setting it down and speaking:

"The rumour in the village was that Fumiko was not in fact your child, Mr Nire, but rather your sister's. Is that correct?"

"Yes, allow me to explain. You see, Inspector, there were seven siblings in total, six after the death of my elder sister. Sakie, the youngest, was the brightest of us all. When she finished the girls' school in Soja, her teacher encouraged her to carry on her studies, and so my father ended up sending her to Kobe, where she lived for a while with another of our sisters, who was married. There, she enrolled in a specialist institute, but in hindsight this

233

was a terrible mistake. No matter how intelligent a nineteen-year-old girl may be, she knows nothing of the world, and in the city there are all kinds of unscrupulous types just waiting to take advantage of her from the get-go. My parents knew this well enough, but they just didn't believe that it could happen to their own daughter. So, she left for Kobe in the spring of 1931."

Kahei broke off his monologue in order to offer the two men more sake and took the opportunity to pour some for himself, too.

"The following year, at the end of 1932, our sister brought Sakie back to the village and told my parents that she was with child. They could hardly believe it."

"Yes, I see," said Kosuke Kindaichi.

"As the youngest of all us siblings, she was the apple of our parents' eyes. She'd gone further in her studies than other girls her age, and she was exceptional in the village. My parents were so awfully proud of her. You can imagine, then, how they felt when she came back carrying a stranger's child!"

"I can just imagine!" said Inspector Isokawa, as Sakie refilled his cup for him.

"You see, Kindaichi-san, there are seventeen years between us. I was as protective of her as any father would be, because I'd taken care of her when she was little. To think, I even changed her nappies! She was the one of all my siblings whom I loved the most. So, when I found out what had happened to her, it made me so angry! You understand, Mr Isokawa, don't you?"

"Well, yes, of course!"

"Still, I couldn't bring myself to chastise her. She was pregnant, after all. We all questioned her to find out whose baby it was, but she always refused to tell us. Nothing could be done about the situation."

The inspector turned to Kosuke Kindaichi, who, engrossed in the dish before him, was silently eating a grilled sea bream.

"I see," said Inspector Isokawa. "So, what happened next?"

"Well, since we couldn't get anything out of Sakie, we turned to the sister with whom she'd been living in Kobe, but she was unable to tell us anything useful. So, we decided that I would raise the baby as if it were my own. Fortunately, my wife, who died last year, was from Shirozaki, where her parents ran an inn near a hot spring. They were both sent there, and Fumiko was born on the 4th of May the following year. We thought that we could keep up the pretence, but you know what people in the countryside are like. Soon enough, word spread throughout the village that Fumiko wasn't my daughter, but rather that of my sister and some unknown father. And the older Fumiko grew, the more bitter this became for her to bear, the poor child! It pains me to think back on it now."

While Kahei tried to control his emotion, Sakie bit her into handkerchief to stifle a sob.

"Sakie later married a man whom she had informed of her past and who took her away to Tottori, where she lived happily with her three children. But she could never forget Fumiko. How cruel it must be for a mother to see her illegitimate daughter die in such horrible circumstances, after a life of shame and without ever having had the chance to blossom as a woman!"

"Fortunately, my brother and sister-in-law," Sakie said, "loved her like their own daughter. Naohei and Shohei loved her, too, and I was reassured after my brother told me that he'd find her a good husband. You can't imagine how grateful I was for everything that he did for her. And now it's come to this…"

Sakie tried in vain to stifle another sob.

"Come on, calm down," said Kahei. "You know I can't stand to see you cry like that! And you'll end up spoiling our guests' appetite if you carry on. There, there, stop crying."

"I'm so sorry… I really don't mean to embarrass my brother like this. I'm just so terribly saddened by everything. Kindaichi-san, Inspector Isokawa, I hope you can find who did this and bring the killer to justice."

"Actually, we'd like to ask you some questions in order to do that," said the inspector, trying to move things along. Although he sympathized with Sakie's loss, her display of grief was making him feel uncomfortable. "Now that we know the circumstances of Fumiko's birth, would you mind telling us a little about her father?"

Kahei looked first at him and then at Kosuke Kindaichi, his eyes wide.

"I was under the impression that last night, during the wake at the Yuras' house, you spoke with Atsuko in private. Wasn't it in connection with all this, Kindaichi-san?"

"Well, yes, as a matter of fact it was."

"And didn't she also tell you about Fumiko's father?"

"She did."

"So, what did she tell you about him?"

"She believed that he might have been the con artist Ikuzo Onda…"

Kahei shot a glance at Sakie.

"Ah, so she knew it was him! But I wonder who could have told her that."

"Er, well, that's just it, Mr Nire…"

Kosuke Kindaichi seemed to struggle to answer, so Inspector Isokawa took charge:

"It was seemingly the village chieftain who told her."

"Was it now?" said Kahei, nodding, a bitter smile at the corner his lips. "Kindaichi-san, about that *temari* song, the one that Mrs Yura sang earlier today…"

"Yes?"

"Quite a little number, isn't it? 'And, sure enough, having hunted high and low, some girls he found, but he talked and talked and talked too much, and so to sleep he had to go…'?" Kahei gave a deep, mocking laugh. "Ah, Kindaichi-san, Inspector, what a business… Now listen very carefully. A long time ago, the village chieftain told me about Yasuko, that poor girl. He said that she, too, was Onda's daughter."

"What?! But, Kahei…" said Sakie, turning pale.

Startled by this revelation, Kosuke Kindaichi and Inspector Isokawa turned towards Kahei in unison, as though having been jolted out of their reverie.

Wearing that same bitter smile and with a roguish look in his eye, Kahei returned the two men's gaze, but finally looked back at his sister.

"Don't worry, Sakie, I didn't say that out of spite just to get revenge. I'm not so childish, you know. But it is better to inform them of the rumours going about the village. It could be useful to them. You've nothing to worry about in any case."

"You're right, Mr Nire," said Inspector Isokawa, still in shock. "So, if what you've told us is true, that would make Yasuko and Fumiko half-sisters."

"Inspector," said the famous detective, his leg shaking, "we mustn't forget Yukari Ozora, too."

The inspector let out a cry and looked at Kosuke Kindaichi, Kahei and Sakie each in turn, his eyes flashing. Sakie remained silent, dazed, her lips blanched; her cheeks were quivering and her shoulders convulsing. Clearly, all this was news to her.

"Do you have any proof of this claim, Mr Nire?" the inspector asked, his eyes glinting.

"The village chieftain undoubtedly had proof of this. But the only person who could say with any certainty is her mother. One thing is for sure, though: Mr Tatara had proof that there was an affair between Ikuzo Onda and Atsuko. Atsuko had four children. The eldest, Toshio, is thirty-four years old; then there was Jiro, who died during the war and who would have been thirty-three if he were still alive. Then there's Fusako, who's married and lives in Himeji—she's thirty-one. And finally, there's Yasuko, the youngest, who was born eight years after Fusako. Today, as I had to go to the village hall for Fumiko, I took the opportunity to check the Yura family register. And you see, Kindaichi-san…"

"Yes?"

"It's common enough to see a child born by accident eight or even ten years after his siblings, but they're very often a little backward. There is such a case even in my own family. But did you see how intelligent Yasuko was? And beautiful at that? She doesn't look at all like her siblings. That's why it seems perfectly reasonable to me that Mr Tatara should think that her father could have been Onda, given his relationship with Atsuko."

"And you're saying that the village chieftain had proof that Yasuko's mother was carrying on an affair with Onda?" the inspector asked pointedly.

"Yes, and I can even tell you when and how the village chieftain told me about it," said Kahei with an embarrassed smile, rubbing his large palms over his face. "This will be a difficult story for Sakie to hear, but I have to tell it in order to try to make amends. Kindaichi-san, this is what I mentioned to you the other day. For a time, Atsuko and I got along rather well. It was about a year after the death of her late husband, Utaro—in 1936. I was so in

238

love then that the whole village poked fun at me, and so I'd go to meet her in secret. My parents weren't happy about this, and they told me what they thought of it all time and time again. But they were the ones who wanted to keep Fumiko's true parentage a secret, and so, regrettable though it was, my parents found their hands tied. I don't want to say that I took advantage of that, but let's just say that I was very much in love. And when the village chieftain heard my mother crying, he told her to let me do as I pleased. And that's when he came to find me. He told me what I just told you, making me promise not to repeat it to anyone, not even to my parents. You can't imagine how surprised I was when I heard this. Needless to say, the scales suddenly fell from my eyes…"

Kahei blushed slightly and went on:

"Since two of Onda's daughters have been killed, I wonder whether this isn't where we should look for an explanation in this affair. That's why I wanted to tell you about it. Of course, if by chance this turns out to have nothing to do with the murders, then I would ask you all to keep this to yourself. That includes you, Sakie…"

Kosuke Kindaichi Departs for Kobe

"I understand exactly how you feel, Mr Nire," said Kosuke Kindaichi solemnly. "But I wonder: did Mr Tatara give you any concrete details of Onda's relationship with Atsuko at the time?"

"I'm afraid not. He began to tell me about it all, but since I didn't want to hear any of it, I turfed him out. It was only later that I thought it all over and decided that I was going to leave her. I didn't know what to do. She was in love, too, you see. In the end, everything went much more smoothly than I'd expected, though. I can still remember today how completely taken aback I was. Setting all that aside, however, if Atsuko knew who Fumiko's real father was at that point, then I believe that it must have been the village chieftain who told her. He could be very indiscreet, you know… Then again, he wasn't quite the blabbermouth people liked to make out. And even if he were as talkative as that *temari* song suggests, it would surprise me to learn that he'd said something like that with any malicious intent."

"You mean to say that he could have done this in order to abet your decision to break up with Atsuko, while doing the same to her so that she'd agree to break up with you?"

"Precisely, Kindaichi-san… The village chieftain could be a very stubborn man, but deep down he is kind and wants to help people. At any rate, I can see now our affair would have set a bad example for the young people in the village. And so, worrying about that, he must have taken drastic measures to end it."

"I see," said Inspector Isokawa, nodding automatically. "Then, if I understand correctly, while there can be no doubt regarding

Fumiko's parentage, we're still left with some reservations about whether Onda really was Yasuko's father. Is that correct?"

"According to her mother, at least. When we entered Fumiko's name in our family register, we begged her to divulge the name of the child's father, promising not to get angry, and that's when she finally decided to tell us. You can imagine our surprise, I'm sure. Afterwards, she explained to us that this Onda had spoken to her on the train to Kobe and that they'd hit it off. He was still living with the Yuras at the time, and it seems he claimed to have been a close relative of Atsuko's…"

"Sakie, as your brother has perhaps already told you, Inspector Isokawa here has already expressed some serious doubts concerning the affair that took place back in 1932. Specifically, he wonders whether it was in fact Ikuzo Onda who was killed, and not Genjiro Yura."

"Yes, Kindaichi-san. That's just what my brother was telling me before you arrived."

"What do you make of this hypothesis?"

"To be honest, I really don't know what to make of it… Looking back on it, though, it does seem strange that he just vanished without any trace."

There was a fearful look in her eye as she spoke.

"But don't you think the reverse would be just as odd, Inspector?" asked Kahei.

"How do you mean, exactly?"

"Well, if it had been Onda who was killed and Genjiro who was the one to run away… Wouldn't it be just as odd if he had disappeared off the face of the earth?"

"But that would be quite a different matter, Mr Nire," Kosuke Kindaichi countered gently.

"Different, how?"

"Don't forget that there was a nationwide search for Onda. If Genjiro was the murderer, then it would have been much easier for him to disappear."

"That's very true," admitted Kahei, nodding. "Inspector, when exactly did you begin to suspect that Genjiro could have been the murderer?"

"When I realized that Onda had quite simply vanished. That's when I began to wonder whether he in fact hadn't been the one who was killed. It was probably a good three or four months after the tragedy."

"And did you issue an arrest warrant for Genjiro at that time?"

"No, I was much too young and low-ranking back then… I did moot the possibility of it at an investigation meeting, but nobody took it up. If I'd only had a photo of Genjiro, then I might have been able to do something about it, but unfortunately there wasn't a single one…"

Kosuke Kindaichi let out a cry and turned to him in surprise.

"You didn't have a single photo of Genjiro?"

"No, we didn't."

"But don't you find that strange? He was well known in Kobe as a silent-film narrator. How can it be that there weren't any photographs of him?"

"It's precisely because of that that there weren't any. Genjiro's parents were very strict, and they were ashamed of their son's profession. So, when he returned to the village, apparently they burned all the photos of him."

Kosuke Kindaichi was silent for a few moments, lost in thought, but then he turned his attention to Sakie.

"Did you ever encounter Genjiro in Kobe?"

"No, never."

"I don't necessarily mean in person. Perhaps you went to the cinema one evening when he was narrating a film, interested to see someone from your home village?"

"No, Kindaichi-san, I couldn't have done."

"Oh? Why not?"

"Because it was only after Genjiro's death that we learnt that he'd worked as a silent-film narrator. And it was all the more surprising to learn that he'd been doing it in Kobe."

"I see… I believe he left the village shortly after finishing his studies at the primary school here. Do you remember much about him, Mr Nire?"

"No, I'm afraid not. Truth be told, it had almost slipped my mind that the owners of the Turtle Spring even had a son. Though I do remember that, when he was little, he was a sad-looking boy and a bit of a loner. That's why we were so bowled over when we found out that he'd made a name for himself in the film industry."

"But Mr Nire," said Kosuke Kindaichi, looking at Kahei and Inspector Isokawa in turn, "isn't it the case that your father paid Genjiro to investigate Ikuzo Onda?"

"What?" said Kahei, his eyes bulging. "Whoever told you that?"

"Why, it was Inspector Isokawa here…"

"Inspector, that is a false accusation! In other words, what you're saying is that because the tinsel business that Yura had foisted on the villagers had actually taken off, my father would have caused trouble for Yura and Onda out of jealousy?!"

"Well… that was certainly the rumour at the time."

"Somebody must have been pulling your leg, Inspector! My father was a hard worker, and he had far more drive than most. Yes, he could be stubborn and pig-headed, and yes, he had a sharp tongue. But he wasn't the kind of man who'd stoop so low as to throw a spanner in other people's work, no matter what they may say. My father was shocked to see how the tragedy unfolded."

The inspector made his apologies, looking a little sheepish, but Kahei carried on regardless:

"It's true that in those days our two families were rivals, and I can't speak for the Yuras, of course, but what I can tell you is that my father's only thought was for his work. At any rate, I certainly don't intend to make any more excuses for him... Were there any other questions, Kindaichi-san?"

"There is one other thing I'd like to ask Sakie..."

"Yes?"

"It's very indiscreet of me, but it's about Ikuzo Onda... Did he have on his body any identifying features? Something a stranger might not necessarily notice. A scar or a mole, for example?"

The famous detective's question, of course, made Sakie blush, but she showed no reluctance to answer him.

"To tell you the shameful truth, Kindaichi-san," she said, "I found myself with child after having relations with him only three times. We didn't exactly have the time to become well acquainted. So, as much as I'd like to, I really can't tell you anything. Perhaps Yukari's mother would be in a better position to answer your question than I..."

"Yes, of course. I understand. I'll try asking Mrs Bessho about it later."

No sooner had Yukari been mentioned than the first notes of "Fallen Leaves" suddenly issued from the big room where all the guests were assembled.

All four of them were listening in perfect silence, when Sakie asked in a quavering voice:

"Who is that?"

"Why, it's Yukari Ozora," Kahei answered. "I hear she sang last night at the Yuras' as well."

"It's the same song, too," said Kosuke Kindaichi.

As she listened to the singing with bated breath, Sakie soon found herself unable to hide her emotion and pressed her handkerchief to her eyes.

"Yukari doesn't know, does she? She's no idea that they were all half-sisters," she said, before breaking down in tears.

Kosuke Kindaichi and Inspector Isokawa looked at one another. They recalled Atsuko's reaction the previous evening at Yasuko's wake, when she had heard Yukari sing... Now they understood the reason for those sudden tears, when before she had shown no emotion.

The storm of applause that followed the song seemed to jolt Kosuke Kindaichi out of his drowsiness.

"We really must be going," he said, "but thank you for this excellent meal. You must have a lot to be getting on with."

"Oh, but won't you stay for another cup of sake? Sakie, would you do the honours?"

She hastily wiped away her tears and stood up.

Forty minutes later, Kosuke Kindaichi and Inspector Isokawa found themselves, just like the night before, in the reception room of the house that Yukari had built for her adoptive parents, along with Harue and Koreya Kusakabe. Yukari had yet to return from the wake.

They did not get what they had come for, however. Tatsuzo's mother had completely lost her memory and was in more or less a vegetative state. Her husband, Ryota, was in better shape, but he was a man, so it was not surprising that he did not remember the old *temari* song. And besides, having been adopted, he was not originally from the region.

"Does this *temari* song have something to do with the case, Kindaichi-san?" asked Koreya Kusakabe in a flash of curiosity.

"It's just terrible," added Harue with a penetrating look in her eyes.

"Indeed it is," said the inspector, "although I'd urge you to keep a good eye on your daughter."

"What?!… Chieko?"

"Are you saying that the killer could have Yukari in his sights, too?" asked the manager, sitting up in his chair in astonishment.

"Oh, no," the inspector replied, "but it's an altogether mysterious case. And I do think it would be a wise precaution to keep a close eye on her. And yet…"

"And yet what?"

"I'd ask that you do it in such a way that the killer wouldn't be aware that you're doing it."

"Oh, I see," said Harue, blanching and getting to her feet in a panic. "I think I'll run and fetch her now."

"Of course," said Kosuke Kindaichi. "Only, before you do, we have a few questions that we'd like to ask you."

"In that case," said Koreya Kusakabe, standing up, "I'll go and fetch her myself. I'll come up with some excuse. Don't worry, dear, it isn't even nine o'clock yet."

"Would you? Thank you."

Harue looked terribly frightened, her eyes wide and her trembling hand clutching a handkerchief. Once the manager had left, she turned to Kosuke Kindaichi and said:

"Now, what was it you wanted to ask me?"

"I'm afraid the question is of a rather delicate nature…"

When he asked whether Onda had any distinguishing physical characteristics, Harue fell silent for a few moments as she began to think. Suddenly, she looked up.

246

"Yes, of course… Now that you mention it, I seem to recall that his toes were a little peculiar."

"Peculiar in what way?" asked Inspector Isokawa eagerly. He looked as though he knew what was about to follow, and leaned in.

"His middle toe was longer than most people's. I even remember him telling me once that he would always get holes in his socks as soon as he bought them because of this."

As though electrified, the inspector stood up from his chair. Harue and Kosuke Kindaichi immediately turned to look at him.

"Does this mean anything to you, Inspector?" asked Kosuke Kindaichi.

"I can't say for certain," he replied, shaking his head, "but I do seem to recall that the feet of the corpse found at Mr Tatara's residence were just as you describe them. We'll have to ask old Doctor Honda, Kindaichi. Since he was the one who wrote the autopsy report, maybe he'll remember." He looked flushed, and there was sweat beading on his brow.

"But, Inspector, what became of the corpse?" said Kosuke Kindaichi, before turning to Harue. "Aren't people buried in these parts?"

"Well, yes, that is the custom, but…" Harue was so panicked that she seemed on the point of tearing her handkerchief into shreds.

"That's just it, Kindaichi," said the inspector. "This is why I, too, had my suspicions. Genjiro's body was cremated right after it was released following the autopsy. The family said that the body was unrecognizable."

"Do you suppose," asked Harue, "that it was really Onda who was killed, Inspector?"

"No, Mrs Bessho," said Kosuke Kindaichi, getting to his feet. "It's still too early to make claims like that. But you can be sure

247

that there will be some very surprising revelations soon. You must prepare yourself for this… Shall we, Inspector?"

And so they left, leaving behind a frightened Harue.

"Inspector, would you mind if I borrowed the bicycle?" asked Kindaichi when they were outside.

"Of course not. Where are you going?"

"I'd like to take the Sennin Pass over to Soja. I should still be in time to catch the last bus to Kobe."

"Are you intending to visit Junkichi Yoshida's family?"

"Yes, but there's something else… This entire case began in Kobe. I'm sure that the key to it is hiding there."

Inspector Isokawa stared at his friend.

"In that case, Kindaichi, I'll go with you."

"No, no, Inspector… It would be best if you stayed here and kept an eye on Yukari Ozora."

"Are you saying you think she's in danger?"

"It's pure conjecture, Inspector, but it's my belief that the third little sparrow had a tale to tell about the locksmith's daughter…"

The inspector just stood there silently for a moment in the dark, before replying in a hoarse voice:

"Understood. Take care of yourself, and I'll take care of the rest."

"I'd like to come with you to see old Doctor Honda, but I'm afraid I'd miss the last bus to Kobe… In the meantime, please, tell nobody that I've gone there."

"Of course."

"Till soon, old friend. I'll leave the bicycle at the Izutsu Inn."

With that, Kosuke Kindaichi hitched up the hem of his hakama, mounted the bicycle and set out over the starlit Sennin Pass towards Soja, determined to get his hands on some decisive evidence…

The Telltale Album

After watching Kosuke Kindaichi ride off on his bicycle, Inspector Isokawa headed straight to see Doctor Honda. The younger doctor had yet to return from the wake at the Nires' house, which suited the inspector perfectly.

Delighted to learn of his arrival, old Doctor Honda appeared immediately and invited him into a small, quiet tatami room at the back of the house, overlooking the garden. He asked his daughter-in-law, Kazuko, to serve them sake.

"But tell me, Inspector, where is Kindaichi-san?"

"He's gone to check on something," Inspector Isokawa replied. "We've been so rushed off our feet that we haven't had a moment's rest."

"I don't doubt it… So, do you have any idea yet who did it?"

"You can imagine how it is," said the inspector evasively. "Kindaichi-san is checking every clue systematically, whereas I'm still groping my way through the fog."

"The two of you work together, though, don't you?"

"That's correct, but he never says anything until he's about to lay his hands on the culprit. That's just his way. He appears to have some leads, although I've no idea what they are."

"It's a very curious case. I heard that it has something to do with a *temari* song?"

"Yes… In fact, that's what I've come to ask you about. You don't happen to know the song, do you?"

"I've been trying to recall the words to it, but I'm afraid I've drawn a blank. I remember that the song was popular when I was young, but, just like all the other boys, I didn't want to play with the girls, and so it's completely slipped my mind. If my wife were still alive, she'd remember it, I'm sure."

"Forgive me for asking, Doctor, but how old are you exactly?"

"I turned seventy last year."

"So, you're more than a decade younger than old Mrs Yura? What a pity there are no other women her age…"

"It's true that in recent years many of them have passed away. Have you asked old Mrs Bessho?"

"Haven't you seen what's become of her? She's practically a living corpse these days."

"You're right enough there," said the doctor, looking searchingly at the inspector. "So, there was another verse to the *temari* song, and you need to find out what it was?"

"Yes, that's what Kindaichi-san thinks."

Doctor Honda's daughter-in-law came in with the sake and some dishes with snacks.

"Here, help yourself. It isn't much, but I hope you like it."

"You shouldn't have," said the inspector, as the doctor poured him sake.

"Well, Inspector, I assume you didn't come to make a social call?"

"No, you're right there. There's something that I'd like to ask you. You're going to laugh at me again, but I still can't let go of what happened back in 1932…"

"For a man in your position, it's only natural."

Doctor Honda carefully refilled the inspector's glass, then his own, all the while keeping his eyes fixed on the man sitting opposite him.

"Well, here's the thing… It may seem trivial, but I still regret that we let the body be cremated so quickly after the autopsy."

"Yes, I remember your saying at the time that you suspected that the body perhaps wasn't Genjiro's but Onda's."

"Precisely, Doctor!" said the inspector, setting down his cup and looking him in the eye. "I'm sorry to drag all this up again, but you were the one who wrote the autopsy report at the time. I was wondering whether you might remember anything about the body?"

Honda looked at the inspector's face for a moment, then smiled bitterly.

"No, it is I who should be apologizing to you, Inspector."

"But what on earth for?"

"I was very young at the time, and it was the one and only time I ever had to write an autopsy report. When you started saying that the corpse might have been Onda's rather than Genjiro's, I took that as an insult. But thinking back on it, that corpse could well have belonged to either man. I just don't know. I only wrote down the cause and time of death, as well as the instrument that had undoubtedly been used. When you said what you did to me later on, I had the impression that you were accusing me of not having done my job properly. So, of course, I took umbrage, and that's why I was so resistant to your questions. I stated that the corpse was indeed that of Genjiro, but I realized later that the only proof I had was the repeated assertions of his family. I hadn't taken fingerprints, and you know as well as I do that the face was beyond recognition. Still, how I mocked you back then... Your idea seemed so far-fetched, and my sense of pride was hurt. I really am very sorry for the trouble I've caused you, Inspector."

"But in that case, Doctor," said Inspector Isokawa, leaning in, "what do you think now? About the body, I mean."

Old Doctor Honda's eyes were fixed on the man sitting opposite him.

"I still believe that it was Genjiro's, Inspector. Your hypothesis still seems too far-fetched to me, almost like something from a detective novel. However, that is my common sense speaking, and lately I've realized that if we put that to one side and operate solely on the basis of logic, there's a chance it wasn't Genjiro's body…"

"So, you're saying that it might have been Onda's body instead?"

"Not so much that. Rather, what I mean is that we had no conclusive proof telling us that it was Genjiro's body. But when I remember the grief of the family at the Turtle Spring, I'm still led to believe that it was indeed him."

"I see," said the inspector, nodding vigorously while the doctor replenished his sake cup. "Let's leave the identity of the deceased aside for a moment, Doctor. Do you recall there being any distinguishing characteristics on the body?"

"Distinguishing characteristics?"

"Yes, something that might not be noticed at first, like one arm longer than the other, or a peculiarly shaped finger?"

Doctor Honda stared at the inspector blankly.

"You wouldn't still happen to have the autopsy report, would you?"

"I'm afraid it was destroyed during the fire-bombings."

The doctor wanted to refresh the inspector's cup once more, but, realizing that the bottle was now empty, he clapped his hands to summon his daughter-in-law, who returned shortly afterwards with a full decanter.

"Kazuko, would you mind keeping the inspector company for a few moments?" said Doctor Honda, a look of agitation written across his face. "I'll be right back."

It was quite some time before he returned, however.

At the same time as this was going on, Kosuke Kindaichi found himself sitting in front of O-Ito, the owner of the Izutsu Inn in Soja, worrying about what time the last bus departed.

"You have to understand, Kindaichi-san, in my line of work it would be indiscreet of me to divulge the names of the people who've met here at the inn. Of course, if the police were to ask me, that would be another matter. I said as much the last time you paid me a visit."

"Yes, the village chieftain told you to keep quiet when you were worried about Harue's father."

"That didn't stop Harue and Onda's affair from soon becoming public knowledge, though. But in this business, it's better to keep quiet. As for the other one…"

"What do you mean by 'the other one'? Do you mean Onda's meetings with young Mrs Yura?"

"Yes… When I told the village chieftain about it, he got angry. He warned me not to breathe a word of it to anyone."

Kosuke Kindaichi's pulse quickened. He could feel his heart pounding. He would never have suspected that Atsuko would have met Onda only a stone's throw from the village. He had come to see O-Ito before leaving for Kobe only because he thought she might have heard something about their relationship from Mr Tatara.

"And did they meet here often?"

"Five or six times, perhaps."

"And which came first? The affair with Harue or the one with Atsuko?"

"That would have been Harue. He developed a taste for it with her, you see, and afterwards he started to bring young Mrs Yura."

"And did Mrs Yura show herself when she came here?"

"Not likely, Kindaichi-san! She always came wearing a head-scarf that covered her face. Even I didn't recognize who she was the first time. She never uttered so much as a word in my presence. But one day I caught a glimpse of her face in profile as she was rushing to the bathroom… You can't imagine what a shock it was. But luckily she didn't realize that I'd seen her."

"When did you tell Mr Tatara about it? Before or after the tragedy?"

"Before. That's when he got angry and told me not to tell anyone about it. He even advised me, in case it got out, to pretend that I didn't know anything. After that, it wasn't long before she stopped coming and I could finally breathe again."

"Very well. I ask only that you divulge nothing about our conversation to anyone for the time being."

"Of course, Kindaichi-san. It isn't every day that I talk about such things, you know."

Shortly after this, he took the last bus to Kobe…

Meanwhile, back in the village of Onikobe, the old doctor had finally returned, after an absence of around thirty minutes, bringing with him a dusty old album under his arm.

"I'm sorry to have kept you waiting, Inspector. Kazuko, thank you for keeping the inspector company. You may go now."

"Of course," she said. "Then I'll leave the decanter of sake here. If you need me again, just call for me."

Once Kazuko had gone, Inspector Isokawa approached the doctor:

"What is this, Doctor Honda?"

"You see, Inspector, I thought I had a duplicate of this autopsy report, so I was hunting high and low for it, but I just can't find it anywhere. I think I must have lost it. But then I remembered that I had this…"

"A photograph album?" said the inspector, leaning across the table with curiosity.

"Exactly. You see, Inspector, it was my first time working on a case like this, so I had some photos taken. This would have been just before you arrived from Okayama."

"And do you have photographs of the body?"

"I do, yes. Only, they aren't 'crime scene' photos. The local police took them while they were waiting for you."

The doctor dusted off the album before handing it across the table to Inspector Isokawa. Having practically snatched it out of the old man's hands, he opened it, his fingers trembling with excitement.

Pasted onto the first page was a familiar panorama of Mr Tatara's old estate. Without even pausing to look at it, however, Inspector Isokawa turned to the second page, where what he saw made him gasp.

It had been taken after the body had been removed from the *irori* and laid out on its back on a futon. A white cloth covered the face, but the sleeves of the kimono were burnt, and the two hands sticking out of the sleeves were horribly disfigured. Despite the twenty-three years that had passed since the tragedy, the inspector still felt as though it were only yesterday.

Two bare feet protruded from the bottom of the kimono and stood out clearly in the lower part of the photograph: the middle toes were a good half larger than normal.

The inspector let out a cry.

"What is it, Inspector?"

"Doctor, don't those toes seem abnormally long to you?"

"Ah, yes, that… I remember noticing it."

"You noticed it?"

"Yes, and not only that: I asked various members of the family about it after you raised your doubts. They all assured me that Genjiro had this particular trait."

"Yes, but they'd already seen the body, Doctor. Their testimony can't be relied on as evidence. Did anybody else tell you this about Genjiro? Or do you have any other proof of this?"

"I didn't push things that far. I wasn't as suspicious as you were, or perhaps I just lacked the imagination. I took the family at its word. That's how I came to the realization recently that I in fact had no real proof when I confirmed that the body was indeed Genjiro's."

Evidently, the family at the Turtle Spring had been lying. Having such long middle toes was not a common physical characteristic. Finding it in both the victim and the attacker would be too much of a coincidence. The corpse therefore had to be that of Onda. In which case, the murderer in the 1932 case had indeed been Genjiro, just as the inspector had assumed all along. That was why the family had wasted no time in having the body cremated. He could not help being proud of himself for having deduced all this correctly.

Just then, young Doctor Honda returned home. Inspector Isokawa looked at his watch: it was already ten o'clock.

The three of them raised their glasses.

"Inspector, you're very welcome to spend the night here with us if you like," the old doctor suggested. "Since Kindaichi-san has taken the bicycle, you can't very well go back to the Turtle Spring. Why don't we have a little more sake…"

At midnight, Inspector Isokawa collapsed into the guest-room bed at the Honda residence, by now completely drunk. Not half an hour had passed, however, when he was suddenly roused from his sleep by the young doctor.

"Inspector! Inspector, wake up! Somebody's gone missing again!"

"What?! Who? Yukari Ozora?"

"No, not Yukari... The young girl, Satoko, from the Turtle Spring."

"And when a lock breaks, the key won't fit..."

Not only had Inspector Isokawa drunk too much, but he had barely slept, and the effects of the alcohol, which would have worn off during sleep, were still permeating every cell in his body, including those in his brain.

He shook his head sadly and thought that it was at least a consolation that the victim was not Yukari but the girl from the Turtle Spring. Suddenly it struck him how truly awful this case was: the mere fact that the victim was not the one he had expected was the sole relief. Yet he could not hold back the anger and shame that he felt growing within him as he realized the extent of his negligence. Indulging excessively in alcohol, and during an investigation! One of the youths from the village came to pick him up on his bicycle and, teetering all the way, took the inspector to the village police station. By the time that Inspector Isokawa found himself in the presence of Deputy Inspector Tachibana, he could scarcely bring himself to look the man in the eye.

Even had the inspector not been drinking and been in full possession of his faculties, however, he would not have been able to prevent this latest disappearance. It had not occurred to Kosuke Kindaichi, either, that Satoko could be in danger. But nothing could justify the inspector's drunkenness the previous night, and now, uneasily, he listened to Tachibana's questions as though he were dreaming.

They were sitting in a small room at the back of the police station, the deputy inspector behind an old lacquered desk that had begun to peel, and Kanao in front of him. Sitting at another desk beside them was Detective Inui, who was taking notes.

The date was 16 August 1955, and the time was ten o'clock in the morning.

Satoko's body had been found in the small hours, at around six o'clock, between the temple at Sakura and the crossroads. It was Shohei and Goro who found her. The Nire residence was close to the temple, and the back door opened onto the path that climbed towards the crossroads. On either side of the road were terraced fields covered with vines. The boys' attention had been attracted by a dog barking as it dug the earth between two rows of vines. When they went over to take a closer look, they discovered the naked body of a young woman. It was Satoko's corpse.

She had not died in the same manner as her two friends. Unlike Yasuko and Fumiko, who had been strangled, she had been struck at the base of the skull with a blunt instrument. A single blow had probably been enough to kill her, because it seemed to have caused a skull fracture.

Another thing that distinguished this murder from the other two was that in both previous cases the bodies had been dumped at the scene of the crime, whereas in this instance the body appeared to have been moved.

The vineyard was situated just below the crossroads, where there stood a stone statue of the divinity Jizo. The murderer had probably hidden behind it, lying in wait for their victim, and struck the girl while she had her back turned to the statue. The red bib that adorned the statue's upper body was stained with blood, and the murderer appeared to have used it to avoid being splashed with the victim's blood.

But why would Satoko have gone there in the middle of the night?

The weapon that had killed her was also discovered nearby. It was a bottle from the nearby winery that had been filled with sand. The murderer had covered the neck of the bottle with a piece of cloth so that it wouldn't slip from their hands. After striking Satoko, they had got rid of the bottle by throwing it into the grass behind the statue. The glass had cracked slightly from the impact of the landing, not shattered, and was still filled with sand. Needless to say, it too was stained with blood.

But why had the murderer tried to hide the body this time? And, more importantly, why had the murderer stripped it?

When Inspector Isokawa rushed to the scene, he was so struck by the cruelty of the spectacle that he could not help but look away.

The cruelty did not consist solely in the wound that had been inflicted, which looked like a split pomegranate, but rather in the fact that the murderer had left Satoko only in her panties, revealing for all to see the irregular red mark that covered a third of her body, which had until then been so well hidden by her kimono.

Why had Satoko been subjected to such a cruel insult? To show her red birthmark not just in life, but also in death.

"You say you were taking your sister home on the back of your bicycle?"

Deputy Inspector Tachibana's voice rang loudly in Inspector Isokawa's ear, as he tried to concentrate on what he was hearing. He was sitting with his back to the wall in a corner of the room where the questioning was taking place. Although he still had a headache, his mind was now unaccountably lucid.

"Then why didn't you take her all the way home? Since you weren't far away, you could easily have taken her to the door, couldn't you?"

"You're right. I regret not having done that," said Kanao, sniffing, and wiping his tears on his sleeve.

It had been a terrible ordeal for him. Two days previously, he had lost his fiancée, and today it was his younger sister who had been killed—that unfortunate creature, to whom he was devoted, precisely because she was so pitiful.

This morning, in a kind of stupor caused by the terrible shock that he had just received, he had remained impassive, but now that the deputy inspector had pointed this out to him, he realized the extent of his carelessness and his negligence, and he could no longer hold back the tears.

"But she kept telling me that she'd be all right and there was no need to worry. And I was in such a rush…"

"A rush?"

"Yes, as you know, we'd decided to search the mountains for Mr Tatara and had agreed to meet at the village hall last night at nine o'clock to discuss and prepare for it."

"I see… So, what time was it when you and your sister left the Nires' house?"

"I think it was at around a quarter past nine. Mr Kusakabe—that is, Yukari Ozora's manager—he came to collect her and take her home. After that, Satoko felt lonely and went to ask Mother if she could go home, too. So, Mother asked me if I'd take her home on my bicycle. Satoko told me not to worry, but I insisted…"

"What was your sister wearing at the time?"

"She was in her mourning clothes, of course."

"And you left her near your house before returning to the village hall?"

"Yes, I dropped her off and then went to the village hall via the Nires', because Shohei and Goro were still there. The three of us went along together."

"And at what time did you get home?"

"It would have been a little after midnight. My mother, who'd arrived home before me, asked why Satoko wasn't there. I said I'd brought her back, so we asked O-Miki, who told us she hadn't seen her. Then I cycled down to the village police station, and that's when all hell broke loose…"

Kanao wiped his eyes once again with his sleeve, sniffed loudly and took out his handkerchief to wipe away the tears that continued to fall. But no matter how often he wiped them away, they kept coming.

"So, did your sister pretend to go home and then turn back towards the crossroads?"

"I guess so, yes."

"And why do you suppose she went back there?"

"I don't know… I… I…" said Kanao, choked with tears. "I feel like such an idiot!"

He buried his head in his handkerchief, sobbing violently. Nodding sympathetically, Inspector Isokawa, too, was gripped by an indefinable feeling of sorrow as he reflected on what a fool he had been.

As Kanao left the room after his questioning, Detective Yamamoto entered.

"Chief, I picked this up near the crime scene. I was wondering whether it could have anything to do with the case."

"Show it to me," said Tachibana, reaching out his hand.

"It's a key and a padlock," said the detective. "Only, the key doesn't fit the lock."

He was holding a small padlock and a key in his hands, but,

no matter how hard he tried, he couldn't get it to work. The key seemed to be significantly larger than the hole in the lock.

"That's strange. Here, let me try," said Detective Inui, grabbing the key from him and vainly trying to make it work. "It's obviously too big! The key doesn't match the lock."

"Lock…?"

Inspector Isokawa, who had been tormented by a throbbing in his head and a remorse for his negligence, suddenly looked up and saw the key and the padlock in Detective Inui's hand.

"Where did you find this?"

Although the inspector had spoken quietly, the strange fever in his voice made all three men turn immediately to look at him.

"Yamamoto just picked it up, Inspector."

Inspector Isokawa stood up, went over to Detective Inui and practically snatched the key and padlock from his hands.

"Yamamoto, where *exactly* did you find this?"

"It was lying in the grass behind the stone statue of Jizo, at the crossroads. Do you think it has something to do with the case, Inspector?"

He did not reply, but instead just stared at the lock and key in his hand, his eyes bloodshot.

"Do these items mean anything to you, Inspector?" asked Deputy Inspector Tachibana, almost shouting, his eyebrows furrowed and a look of consternation on his face.

But again the inspector did not respond. He just stared intently at the two objects, his jaw firmly clenched.

He could still hear the words that Kosuke Kindaichi had said to him the previous night, just before he left: "It's my belief that the third little sparrow had a tale to tell about the locksmith's daughter…"

But the locksmith's daughter was Yukari, not Satoko. Since she had been born to the Turtle Spring family, she had no guild name. Could it be that this lock and key were nothing more than a coincidence, and the fact that Satoko had been undressed an allusion to something else?

That evening, at around six o'clock, Inspector Isokawa received a telegram from Kobe:

"READ EVENING PAPER STOP KEEP EYE ON GIRL STOP RETURNING IMMEDIATELY STOP KK"

The Last Night of the O-Bon Festival

The entire village of Onikobe seemed to be in the grip of demonic forces.

It was the night of 16 August and the last night of the O-Bon festival. Fires were burning brightly at the entrances to the houses that were decorated for the occasion, but there was no joy in the celebrations this year, for, as soon as they had lit the fires, the villagers had all scurried back indoors, plunging the whole village into total silence.

The quiet tolling of a bell could be heard from a back room at the Turtle Spring. Satoko's wake was taking place. There were significantly fewer mourners in attendance than on the previous two evenings, partly because it was located far from the centre of the village, but Kahei Nire and Toshio Yura were there to represent their respective families.

Naturally, the topic of conversation focused on this series of murders, but, nobody having a satisfactory explanation to offer, it was concluded that nothing could be said until the hunt in the mountains had produced results, and until the fate of Mr Tatara, regarding which there were grave suspicions, had become clear. Yes, the figure to whom the villagers always returned whenever they thought of this mysterious case was Mr Tatara…

"Yasuko and Fumiko each had a verse in the *temari* song, but what about Satoko? Do you suppose there could have been another verse?" asked young Doctor Honda.

"But of course, Doctor," said Tatsuzo, the tip of his nose still as red as ever. "I'm sure of it. A verse about 'a pretty little thing from the Turtle Spring' who was put to sleep naked…"

In moments of crisis, he and Rika Aoike were always the first to rush out the door, but whereas she rushed to be first on the scene, he rushed for the bottle.

"Have you ever heard any *temari* songs of the like, Mrs Aoike?" asked Kahei.

"As you know, Mr Nire, I'm not from around here."

Rika had hastily applied some make-up to cover her reddened eyelids, but as she sat there, dressed in a mourning kimono with her thin shoulders slumped, she cut a pathetic figure, with none of the cool emotionlessness that Atsuko had shown two nights ago.

"I'd be surprised to learn that the daughter of the Turtle Spring figured in the *temari* song," said Toshio.

"What makes you say that?"

Kahei looked with interest at the young man who was unaccustomed to expressing himself so forthrightly in a conversation.

"Because it's a well-known fact that the hot-spring inns were always looked down on and that the local lords wouldn't so much as spare a glance for their daughters."

"Come now, Toshio! That isn't a very nice thing to say in front of Mrs Aoike! And don't forget, Satoko very nearly became your sister-in-law," Kahei gently chided him.

"I was only talking about how things used to be! They're different nowadays, of course," he hurriedly put in, suddenly flushed with embarrassment.

Doctor Honda came to his rescue.

"How long do you suppose all this will carry on?" he said, sighing. "Wakes three nights in a row, funerals three days in a row: even though I'm used to the misfortune of others, this is just too much to bear."

"I'm afraid we've put you to an awful lot of trouble, Doctor," said Rika, her shoulders still slumped. "The funeral will take place tomorrow, so I'd like to finish the wake by around ten o'clock this evening at the latest."

"Yes, that's a good idea," Kahei agreed immediately. "Our funerals may be over, but there are a great many things still to be done. I suppose it must be the same for you, Toshio?"

"Yes, a great many things..."

"But where's Kanao? I haven't seen him anywhere," said the doctor.

"They all went with the police to scour the mountains," explained Tatsuzo. "He said he would rather catch the criminal than stay for the wake..."

"Ah, I see..."

The doctor seemed almost disappointed, but Tatsuzo, who was starting to get a little tipsy, continued:

"One has to wonder what the police are playing at. What an idea to go traipsing around in the mountains now... Don't they understand that it's far too late, those fools?"

"I understand your frustration, Tatsuzo, but the police aren't just going to stand idly by. Whoever did this must be a cut above them, though..."

"You say that, but then what about this private detective? This Kosuke Kindaichi? What about him, eh?"

"What do you mean?"

"From where I'm standing, he's only held the investigation back. Dragging his heels like this... He's certainly put Tachibana's nose out of joint!"

"But Inspector Isokawa places great faith in him, you know. And besides, that's often the way these people operate. After all, a cat that meows catches no mice."

"Well, he seems awfully slow to me."

"On that note," said Rika, "where is Kindaichi-san? I haven't seen him all day."

"I heard he left for Okayama last night," said Doctor Honda.

"What? Why has he gone to Okayama?" asked Kahei, turning to him with a frown.

"Apparently, they think that this case has its roots in the tragedy that happened back in 1932. Inspector Isokawa told me that he'd gone to examine the original case notes in the prefectural police headquarters."

"They think it has to do with all that?!"

Now, every eye in the room was fixed on Rika, who had turned as white as a sheet.

Just then, O-Miki came in and announced the arrival of Inspector Isokawa. He was not alone, however: he was accompanied by Harue and her daughter, whom he had met on the way there.

Having offered their condolences to Rika, the three of them then went to burn incense.

"Inspector, is it true that Kindaichi-san went to Okayama last night?" asked Kahei, watching carefully for his reaction.

"Yes, it was a very sudden decision on his part."

"Do you know when he'll return?"

"Well, he only left last night, so I'd imagine he'll be gone for several days. After all, it's no easy task getting to Okayama from here."

"So, Kindaichi-san won't have heard what happened to Satoko yet?" Rika asked softly, her eyes full of tears.

"I'm sure he'll have read about it in the evening papers, but I haven't received any word from him," the inspector replied, frowning and running a hand through his thinning grey hair. "I should like to take this opportunity to ask that you all be especially vigilant this evening. As you're undoubtedly aware, the police have organized a search in the mountains with the help of the young people from the village. This means that security in the village will be reduced, so please take care and be responsible for your own safety."

"Do you mean that even more tragedy might unfold, Inspector?" asked Toshio.

"We cannot say anything until we find the culprit. For now, even you, O-Miki, must take care and remain alert. You know that the murderer only attacks beautiful girls like you!"

"Inspector, you're scaring me again!" cried O-Miki, frozen stiff in terror, two decanters of sake in her hands.

He laughed.

"Come, come, O-Miki," he said. "This is no joke. You too, Mrs Bessho, keep a close eye on your daughter."

"Of course, Inspector," Harue replied, looking even more terrified than O-Miki. "There are too many terrible things happening around here. In any case, we intend to return to Tokyo tomorrow, after Satoko's funeral."

"What's this, Harue? Running away already?" yelled Tatsuzo in a threatening tone from the other side of the room.

Tatsuzo's attempts to get his sister to loosen her purse strings seemed to have failed entirely, and his bloodshot eyes were now glaring at Harue.

"It isn't that we wish to flee, but we've visited the graves now, and we have work waiting for us in Tokyo."

"It has nothing to do with 'work waiting for you in Tokyo'! Just try to leave and you'll see: they'll take you for the murderer straight away. Is that what you really want?!"

"Don't be absurd, Tatsuzo!"

"What's so absurd about it? I, for one, find this Koreya Kusakabe very suspicious. Every time a stranger shows up in this village, it ends in murder. It was the same back in 1932. And now here he is…"

"Enough!" intervened Kahei, trying to restrain Tatsuzo with both hands. "You two are forever quarrelling when you see each other. I never saw a pair of siblings like it! If there really is reason to suspect Koreya Kusakabe, the police will take care of it. It isn't for you, Tatsuzo, to go around casting aspersions. As for you, Yukari…" Now, Kahei turned to the girl with a tender smile. "Here you are again in the middle of a drama. It's almost as though you came back just to sing at the wakes. Will you sing again for us tonight?"

Of all the assembled mourners, Kahei was the only one to know that the two young girls for whom Yukari had sung the day before were in reality her half-sisters. But that was not the case for this evening's victim, who was the daughter of her father's rival. Yet Inspector Isokawa's thoughts were elsewhere—or at least so it seemed. Kahei's curiosity now turned to whether Rika would allow Yukari to sing.

Feeling the gaze of all the mourners on her, Yukari stiffened.

"That's for Satoko's mother to decide. If she'd like me to sing, of course, I'll be very pleased to do so. But if not, then…" she replied tactfully, trailing off.

Once again, however, Tatsuzo began to bellow in his characteristically drunken, slurring voice:

"What a ridiculous idea! There aren't any young people here. Who's going to enjoy listening to a silly song like that?!"

"Tatsuzo, I won't allow you to disrespect my guests like this," said Rika, wiping away a tear. She then spoke directly to the girl: "But yes, Yukari, of course you may sing. Why should Satoko be the only one not given the honour?"

"As you wish, Mrs Aoike," she replied. "In that case, I'll go and rest for a few moments before singing for her."

Thus did Yukari come to sing "Fallen Leaves" for the third evening in a row.

Inspector Isokawa looked at his watch.

"Good grief," he said, appearing to have just remembered something. "Look at the time! I really must be going."

"Oh, but what's the rush, Inspector? Won't you stay a little longer, for Satoko's sake?"

"I wish I could, but it's this search in the mountains. I have to be there."

"You're taking part in it yourself, Inspector?" asked Kahei, his eyes wide with surprise.

"I'm too old to go running up mountains like a young man, but then nor can I very well just sit here, drinking sake. Not least since I ended up drinking too much at Doctor Honda's last night... Well then, if you'll forgive me?"

The inspector left the Turtle Spring at half-past eight that evening.

Ever since the heavy thunderstorm on the night of 10 August, the weather had been fine in Onikobe. That night, however, it looked as though it was about to break, and the gathering clouds blocked out the stars. As Inspector Isokawa rode his bicycle, the warm breeze caressing his cheeks, he raised a cloud of dust on the parched road.

After passing the path that led up to Mr Tatara's cabin, he skirted around the foot of the mountain and began to see little lights flickering amid the darkness of the hills surrounding the village. Evidently, the search had already begun. As the lights slowly advanced below the enormous dark clouds, they looked like ceremonial fires that had been lit to accompany the souls of the three girls who had met their untimely ends.

The inspector headed for the village police station with a feeling of excitement in his chest. There he was surprised to find, gathered together in a dimly lit room, Deputy Inspector Tachibana, Detective Inui and Kosuke Kindaichi, all of them engaged in an intense conversation carried on in hushed tones.

"Ah, Kindaichi!" cried the inspector.

"Inspector!" he responded, standing up together with the other men. "Where is Yukari Ozora?"

"I've just left her at the Turtle Spring."

"Is she safe?" asked Detective Inui, his teeth chattering.

"She is, yes. A plain-clothes officer is keeping watch on her, and Koreya Kusakabe is lying in wait outside the Turtle Spring. Did you find anything in Kobe, Kindaichi?"

"Take a look at this…" said Deputy Inspector Tachibana grimly.

He handed him a little magazine titled *Folk Traditions*. Fortunately, Mr Tatara's late nephew, Junkichi Yoshida, had kept a copy of it at home. Inspector Isokawa clenched his fists as he read the passage indicated to him:

The third little birdie said to me:
In the faraway land where I come from,
Many are the pleasures of the shogun's man—
Women, wine and hunting all day long,
But most of all, he likes the women,
Oh yes, it's the women he likes.
A good little woman was the locksmith's girl,
As pretty as they come, but rather stiff,
Then one fine day her lock did break,
And when a lock breaks, the key won't fit,
And since his key didn't fit, she was sent away,
They were all of them sent away…

Fire and Water

It was ten o'clock on the morning of 17 August. Kosuke Kindaichi and Inspector Isokawa stood, stunned, in the middle of the scorched earth.

Yukari Ozora's residence, which had been the envy of so many in the area, had now been reduced to a pile of ashes from which blue smoke was still rising here and there. The smoke stung the inspector's eyes, which were puffy from a lack of sleep. The heavy thunderstorm that had broken out at dawn seemed to have thrown the weather out of kilter, and the fine rain that had been falling ever since, now seemed to weep over the charred debris of the mansion.

Kosuke Kindaichi stood motionless amid the ruins, breathing heavily. He'd had to endure a terrible psychological shock, accompanied by great physical fatigue. Now he was faced with the feeling of nothingness that comes with the end of everything.

"Kindaichi," the inspector murmured distractedly, sounding almost apologetic as he watched the young men from the village silently clear away the rubble under the falling rain. "Do you think I opted for the wrong ploy last night?"

"No, Inspector," said the famous detective, looking at his friend in surprise. "You did everything right. It's because of your dogged perseverance that a twenty-three-year-old case has been solved at last. As for this," he said, turning to what remained of Yukari Ozora's large house, "nobody could have prevented it. It isn't your fault."

"It's a relief to hear you say that," said the inspector, still despondent. He turned again to his friend, seeming to search for something in his face. "You said that the old case was solved, though. Do you think that the same person was responsible?"

Seeing Kosuke Kindaichi nod silently, Inspector Isokawa's eyes lit up with surprise.

"But how?"

"I'll explain later... Ah! There's young Doctor Honda's wife." Kosuke Kindaichi gently took the inspector by the arm. "She's probably coming to get us because the bath's ready. I think the best thing for us both right now is to have a good soak and get some sleep. Shall we go and take up old Doctor Honda's kind offer?"

Under the drizzle, they left the rubble of the mansion and made their way over to meet Kazuko, who was coming towards them with an umbrella in her hand.

Here is what was running through Inspector Isokawa's mind:

Kosuke Kindaichi had suggested that the next victim could be the locksmith's daughter. And so, on the night of 15 August, Inspector Isokawa had been baffled when, contrary to what they had anticipated, the real victim turned out to be Satoko from the Turtle Spring. But when, on the morning of the 16th, a little later, Detective Yamamoto brought back a key and a padlock, which had been discovered not far from the scene of the crime, it occurred to the inspector that the murderer had indeed perhaps intended to kill the locksmith's daughter but ended up killing Satoko by mistake.

If what he thought was true, wouldn't the murderer then try to make a second attempt on the life of Yukari? So, full of hope, Inspector Isokawa came up with a ruse. He would send all the young people and all the policemen in the village to hunt in the mountains. This would give the murderer the impression that the village was temporarily defenceless. Harue would be asked to act as if she were going to leave the village with her daughter, Yukari, on the afternoon of 17 August to return to Tokyo.

The inspector had deduced that since Fumiko and Satoko had been killed just after the wakes, the murderer had certainly been in attendance there. It was reasonable to suspect therefore that they would also be present at Satoko's own wake. And even if they didn't attend in person, somebody close to them would surely be there.

Fortunately, Harue pulled off her part of the plan very well. In fact, she and her daughter had been so frightened that nobody questioned their desire to leave as quickly as possible. And so, the sole opportunity left for the assassin was the night of the 16th, especially as the village was completely unprotected that night. The only two people who knew about Inspector Isokawa's plan were Deputy Inspector Tachibana and Detective Inui. They, however, had pretended to take part in the search with the rest of the police, only to slip away discreetly and go back to the village police station. Having returned from Kobe earlier, Kosuke Kindaichi was also there, waiting with the others for the inspector.

The private detective had approved of the plan, and Tachibana, who had until then been rather reticent, agreed to it as soon as he read the article in the magazine. Inspector Isokawa was unlikely ever to forget what happened next.

At around ten o'clock, the policeman who had been keeping a close eye on Yukari returned to the station to report that she and her mother, accompanied by Koreya Kusakabe, had made it safely home to the mansion. When they left the Turtle Spring, the wake was not yet over, and Inspector Isokawa requested Yukari's residence be placed under immediate surveillance.

This house, recently built for her adoptive parents, was perched on a hill on the outskirts of Onikobe and, apart from Tatsuzo's house, which was nearby, was isolated in the middle of the vineyards and the forests.

Kosuke Kindaichi and Inspector Isokawa had arrived at the vineyards, where the police were already lying in wait just behind the mansion, at around a quarter past ten, and from there they could see the shimmering surface of the reservoir, which they had already noted from the winery, about 300 yards away.

At about half-past ten, they began to see the lights of bicycle headlights or electric lamps dotted around here and there. These must have been the mourners from Satoko's wake returning home. One by one, these lights disappeared into the houses. The last to return was Tatsuzo. They knew it was him straight away, because the light on his bicycle flickered from one side of the road to the other, and every now and then he would begin to croon in his hoarse voice. He arrived home, woke up his wife and then, amid curses, put his bike away before staggering up the hill. He passed around the vineyard to get to the garden of Yukari's house.

"Harue, wake up! I've got something to tell you!"

He circled the house two or three times without getting any answer from within. In fact, the lights had still been on a little before his return, but when they heard Tatsuzo coming from a distance, they had hurried to turn them all out. They did not want anything to do with him, so they pretended to be asleep.

"I saw the lights on earlier! If you don't get up, I'm going to set fire to this place and smoke you out!"

"Tatsuzo! Tatsuzo," pleaded his wife, who had come running. "Stop this! Aren't you ashamed of yourself? If you want to talk to them, you can do it tomorrow. Can't you hear our baby crying?"

Indeed, a baby had started mewling in the house below. Tatsuzo must have felt some embarrassment, for he gave up immediately.

"Well, in that case I'll stop for tonight, but I won't let her go back to Tokyo tomorrow. Just let her try! She'll see. They'll assume she's the murderer right away."

Grumbling and swearing, he stumbled back down the hill to his home, where again he shouted at his wife for a time. Before long, however, their lights went out one by one. Tatsuzo must have fallen into a deep slumber.

When Kosuke Kindaichi glanced at the luminous watch on his wrist, he saw that it was exactly half-past eleven.

It was thought that the murderer would take action within the next half hour or hour. The hunt in the mountains would soon be over, so the killer would have to put their plan into action quickly.

The five police officers who were on guard duty, however, had let the murderer slip through the net. In retrospect, it seemed likely that the culprit had taken advantage of Tatsuzo's outburst to sneak into the grounds unnoticed.

By this point, Kosuke Kindaichi and Inspector Isokawa were hiding in a vineyard overlooking the mansion, while Deputy Inspector Tachibana and Detective Yamamoto were concealed in the bushes on either side of the entrance to the house. As for Detective Inui, he was somewhere in the vineyard that Tatsuzo had climbed up. But there were inevitable blind spots, including one just below where Kosuke Kindaichi and Inspector Isokawa were standing. There was a fairly large shed there, the roof of which almost touched the eaves of the main building, preventing the two men from seeing what was going on below. The killer must have profited from the fact that everybody's attention was focused on Tatsuzo and crossed the vineyard from behind, hiding in the shadow of the shed and then waiting for the right moment.

At midnight, exactly half an hour after the lights had gone out in Tatsuzo's house, and when everybody in the mansion had just fallen asleep, the sound of firecrackers was suddenly heard, and a fire broke out in the shed. Had the murderer intended to set the fire in the first place, or had Tatsuzo given them the idea? The truth remains unclear, but in any case, nobody had envisaged anything like this.

The killer, however, had apparently not realized that the house was so heavily guarded. Kosuke Kindaichi saw the figure flee into the vineyards and was seized with fear when he heard screams coming from within. He hesitated, thinking that he recognized the old woman whom he had met on the Sennin Pass on the evening of 10 August. What should he do? Help put out the fire or go after the murderer? The famous detective took a snap decision to run after the old woman. "Inspector, stay here and wake up the people in the house. I'll give chase..." he yelled. Then shouting, "Fire! Fire!", he jumped to his feet and went tearing off among the vines. Detective Inui followed him, while Deputy Inspector Tachibana, Inspector Isokawa and Detective Yamamoto stayed behind to rescue courageously the people in the house.

Passing under the vines, the old woman tumbled down the slope and soon was on the road leading to the village. She was no longer bent double and hobbling as she had been on the mountain path, but still she was no match for the speed of the two men chasing her. The embankment surrounding the reservoir was soon in front of their eyes. The old woman put all her remaining energy into climbing it.

By this time, the fire had already spread to the annex, and it was lit up as if in broad daylight. The killer's silhouette, her head concealed by a scarf, and a loose peasant dress covering her body, loomed at the top of the embankment. But the very next moment, like a dead tree being felled, she suddenly collapsed down on the other side. Kosuke Kindaichi and Detective Inui arrived almost immediately, climbed to the top too and found her buried face down in the deep mud of the dried-up reservoir. She had already stopped moving.

An hour later, work was started on recovering the body. The mud was so thick, however, that it was nigh impossible to reach it, and in the end there was no alternative but to wait for the young men from the village to return from their hunt. By then, the mansion had been reduced to ashes. With the drought of recent days, the fire had spread with tremendous speed and, as the firemen were also taking part in the search, there was a dearth of men to put it out. The only positive thing was that there had been no casualties, and the blaze had been confined to Yukari's house. On the other hand, its inhabitants had left in such a hurry that they had no time to take anything with them; they had been so busy saving the old and infirm grandmother that they had not even thought about their belongings.

As soon as the fire had been doused, they set about removing the body from the reservoir.

Kanao was among those who rushed to the scene. As soon as Kosuke Kindaichi saw him, he turned pale.

"Kanao, you'd better go over there. We only need three or four people here."

"Why, Kindaichi-san?"

"Because it's more important to make sure it doesn't catch again, and we're short of manpower over there…"

"I'm staying here. Just send someone else. I want to be the first to see who killed Yasuko, Fumiko and Satoko."

Kosuke Kindaichi watched Kanao's face silently as he breathed a slight sigh before concluding:

"Very well… Have it your way."

His lips twitched as if he wanted to add something, but he lowered his eyes and walked behind Inspector Isokawa, who had overheard their conversation. When he saw the profound look of anguish on Kosuke Kindaichi's face, he drew a sharp breath and clenched his fists, his nails digging into the palms of his hands. The inspector had no desire to see a scene like this ever again in his life.

Bonfires had been lit at the top of the embankment. Beside them, a platform had been hastily erected with a pulley to hoist the body up.

Using the rope, Kanao took charge of tying the body up. He was lying flat out in the mud, his legs being held by Shohei and Goro.

"Are you all right, Kanao?"

"Yes, just don't let go of my legs!"

Kanao stretched his large frame even further, plunged the rope into the mud, tied it around the body's waist and, after checking the knot, shouted:

"All right, Shohei, Goro, help me up."

"Wait, I'll give you a hand," shouted Deputy Inspector Tachibana, running down the embankment and taking hold of Kanao by the legs. "Come on! One, two, three!"

When Kanao found himself standing back on the embankment, his face was dripping with sweat.

"Right, let's hoist it up."

A cry of acknowledgement then issued from the top. The pulley began to turn, and the body gradually emerged from the mud.

"Keep it coming! A little more!"

Soon, with a squelching sound, the body finally rose from the mud and was hoisted about six feet into the air, bent double.

"Wait!" shouted Shohei, keeping one hand on the rope. "Hey, Kanao! Our two sisters were killed because of her, so the first thing we have to do is see her face. Goro, go and get us a wet towel!"

Caked as it was in mud, the body was indeed unrecognizable in its present state. Kanao stared intently at the mud-covered face as he waited for Goro to arrive with a wet towel.

"What's the matter, Kanao? Why are you shaking?"

"Just pass me the towel, Goro," said Shohei, his teeth chattering.

No sooner had he cleaned the mud off a part of the face than Kanao gave out a piercing cry.

"Ah, Mother!… Mother!…"

Inspector Isokawa was roused from his dream.

"Were you having a nightmare, Inspector?" asked Kosuke Kindaichi anxiously, sitting up in the bed beside him.

They found themselves at Doctor Honda's house, where, after taking a bath, they had both fallen into a deep slumber and the inspector had dreamt about the events of the previous day.

"I don't think I'll ever be able to forget that scream when Kanao recognized his mother," said the inspector with a sigh.

"Nor I," replied Kosuke Kindaichi, nodding solemnly. But then he smiled to lighten the mood. "And yet, Inspector, you slept well. It's nine o'clock, you know. Shall we get up?"

As they were tidying up their room, Doctor Honda's daughter-in-law appeared on the veranda.

"Ah, you're awake? Please, don't worry about putting the futons away. Kindaichi-san, you have a visitor. A Joji Yoshida from Kobe.

He's just arrived. He says he's found what you were looking for and has come to deliver it to you."

"Ah, excellent!"

Inspector Isokawa looked quizzically at the happy expression on the detective's face.

"Who is this Joji Yoshida?" he asked.

"He's the eldest son of Junkichi Yoshida's brother, Ryokichi. Now, Inspector, let's try to lift each other's spirits…"

One Last Surprise

It was eight o'clock on the evening of 17 August 1955. A number of people, all gathered in the back room at Doctor Honda's surgery, were sitting with bated breath, waiting to learn the truth about this series of murders that had just taken place. Among the police officers present were Inspector Isokawa, Deputy Inspector Tachibana and two of the detectives, Inui and Kato. Of those involved in the case, there were Kahei Nire and his youngest sister, Sakie, Harue Bessho and her daughter, Chieko, and, as an observer, Koreya Kusakabe. The young singer, her mother and the manager, having lost everything in the fire, were dressed in lightweight summer kimonos lent to them by Mrs Honda. And of course, also present were Kosuke Kindaichi and old Doctor Honda, whose son was still at the Turtle Spring.

In the tatami room, beer, fruit juice, as well as a dish of peaches had been laid out, but so far nobody had touched any of them. Instead, they were all waiting impatiently for explanations.

Old Doctor Honda spoke up:

"My son told me, Inspector, that Mrs Aoike ingested an insecticide before jumping into the marsh."

"Yes, it's true," he replied. "She'd planned it all along."

"She seemed like such a nice woman…"

"Kindaichi-san," old Kahei cut in, "my son tells me that you already knew that Rika was the murderer. At what point did you realize?"

Looking somewhat embarrassed, Kosuke Kindaichi scratched his dishevelled bird's nest of hair and said, "In cases like this, there's always a moment when you have a vague suspicion about someone. The problem is knowing when to confirm it. In this instance, I began to suspect the owner of the Turtle Spring just after Yasuko's death."

"But Kindaichi," Inspector Isokawa intervened, "you may well call it a 'vague suspicion', but you must have had good reason for it, surely?"

"In a sense, yes."

"Then let me put it another way. What was it exactly that we missed?"

"Oh, I wouldn't quite put it like that, Inspector," he said with a chuckle. "My first clue was something that Tatsuzo mentioned. He said that on evening of the 12th, the day before Yasuko's murder, as he was heading home at around seven o'clock, he passed by the bench waterfall before stopping to have a drink at the winery. He then passed the waterfall again at around half-past eight and noticed the barrel and the funnel that hadn't been there before. Afterwards, he remembered that on his way to the winery, he'd seen somebody with what could have been a funnel running off into the vineyards not far from the crossroads."

"Yes, I remember him saying all that."

"Let's now try to put ourselves in the murderer's shoes. That night, she stole a barrel and a funnel from the winery in preparation for the crime, and when she arrived at the crossroads, she saw someone. She then fled into the vineyards, and I'm sure that at that moment she would have realized that it was Tatsuzo who was coming. But why did the murderer leave the barrel and the funnel at the bench waterfall with the risk of having them taken away by Tatsuzo? She must have thought that he would head straight down from the winery towards Sakura; hence she didn't know that the road between the winery and Sakura had been blocked by a landslide. This rockfall was clearly visible from the village road, which runs past the temple at Sakura. So, the murderer couldn't have been a resident of the hamlet. With Sakura at the far end of the village, all that remained was Mr Tatara's cabin and the Turtle Spring resort."

The group listened on in complete silence, and Doctor Honda nodded automatically.

"It's true," he said. "But did you have any particular reason to suspect Mrs Aoike?"

"I did, as it so happens. It was because of Satoko's behaviour."

"Satoko's behaviour?!"

"Satoko, as you know, had never shown her face uncovered in public before. But from the day after the first incident, she dared to throw away her headscarf and gloves. It struck me that for a girl of that age to make such a serious decision, there had to be a very serious reason. This made me think of the murder the night before."

"Kindaichi-san," said Deputy Inspector Tachibana, coughing, "are you saying that Satoko *knew* that it was her mother who killed Yasuko?"

"I believe so, yes… She must have worked it out for herself. Perhaps she realized that her mother was bitter about how she, her poor girl, had suffered as a result of her looks and that she had intended to take revenge by killing Yasuko, whose beauty made her jealous. So, she decided to stop worrying about her looks. By showing that she could live happily just as she was, she probably intended to send a message to her mother not to do any other terrible things… For the poor girl, this was about the only thing she could do."

"But, Kindaichi," said Inspector Isokawa, leaning in. "That evening, Satoko and O-Miki bumped into Yasuko and the old woman. Do you suppose that Satoko realized at that moment that the old woman was really her mother?"

"I don't believe so, Inspector. Otherwise, she wouldn't have gone all the way to the old ruins."

"Then, when did she realize?"

"I think not knowing about the landslide was Rika's fatal error. Because of this, Tatsuzo made off with the barrel and the funnel, so she had to go and fetch more from the winery after killing Yasuko. This cost her precious time. Especially as Yasuko's disappearance was soon discovered and Satoko returned home earlier than expected. So, she would already have been in the annex by the time her mother came in on her bicycle through the back gate, probably still wearing her bizarre disguise. Satoko might not have understood what it all meant at that point, but when she found out what had happened in the morning, she must have made up her mind to get rid of her gloves and headscarf. These were the two things that made me suspect Rika quite quickly, but I still couldn't tell what her motive was. She hadn't killed Yasuko because she wanted Fumiko for a daughter-in-law, after all. Then, while I was pondering this, the two other crimes took place in quick succession... I really am very sorry about that."

He remained silent, his head bowed.

Deputy Inspector Tachibana, who was standing next to him, spoke up.

"It isn't your fault, Kindaichi-san... But why do you think she did it? I suppose that, if Yasuko, Fumiko and Yukari were all children of Ikuzo Onda, that would make them all daughters of the man who'd killed Rika's husband. And then *they* were all very beautiful, whereas her own daughter had been so disadvantaged by nature. Deep down she must have envied them. And to make matters worse, the Yuras and Nires were trying to get her son to marry their daughters. Maybe that was what finally pushed her over the edge."

He spoke very insistently, trying to cheer the detective up, who still looked troubled.

"Well, you say that, Deputy Inspector, but—"

Just then, Detective Yamamoto arrived.

"I'm sorry I'm late, Kindaichi-san. Mr Yura gave me this for you."

Tachibana looked suspiciously at Yamamoto as he handed Kosuke Kindaichi an envelope.

"What is that, Yamamoto?"

"Kindaichi-san sent me with a letter for Mr Yura, so I'm bringing him the answer."

Kosuke Kindaichi read the letter and immediately placed it back in the envelope.

"I'll explain about the letter later, Deputy Inspector. In fact, Doctor Honda…"

"Yes?"

"It's a pity that Mrs Yura can't be present at this little meeting, as I have something here that I'd like to show her, as well as to Sakie and Harue, who, fortunately, are present. I'd have liked for the three of them to have a look at it before we discussed the matter together. Since we seem to have put the cart before the horse, you see, I'm not sure that the deputy inspector has fully grasped Rika's motives… Doctor Honda?"

"Yes?"

"I'd like you to take a look at these documents together with Sakie and Harue."

"What would you like us to look at?"

"Photographs. There are exactly three of them."

He reached into the paper envelope, extracted postcard-sized photographs and handed one to each of them.

"If you would, please take a close look at these three photographs. He hasn't grown a moustache yet, but imagine if he did…"

The three of them peered curiously at the photos handed to them.

Suddenly, Sakie let out a hoarse cry, while the blood quickly drained from Harue's face.

"What's the matter, Sakie?"

"What is it, dear?" asked Kahei. "Do you know the person in the photo?"

He and Koreya Kusakabe leant in close to the two women to try to see the photographs, but what they saw took their breath away. The two of them were so startled that neither could reply.

After a few moments, old Doctor Honda broke the silence, his voice trembling in astonishment.

"Kindaichi-san, where did you find this? Why, this is a photo of Ikuzo Onda."

Ikuzo Onda! An explosion of dynamite would probably not have produced a greater shock. Kahei snatched the photograph from Sakie's hands, while, fascinated by all this, Koreya Kusakabe and Yukari Ozora peered over Harue's shoulder.

Stunned by this revelation, Inspector Isokawa and the other police officers rose to their feet to look at the photographs. It was as if Ikuzo Onda had appeared before them in the flesh.

The three photographs were portraits, and so the face was especially clear. One showed Onda in Western clothes, another in a ceremonial robes, and the last in a lightweight summer kimono. He had no moustache, and his face, adorned with little spectacles, was well chiselled. Despite some minor burn marks to the photographs, it was clear that he had been a handsome man.

"K… Kindaichi!"

"Inspector, wait a moment. We have to check with everyone. Sakie, do you know who this person is?"

"Why, yes, it's him," she said, bursting into tears.

"And you, Harue? What do you think?"

"It's Chieko's father. There's no mistake about it." She did not shed any tears, but her eyes misted over and her lip trembled.

"Kindaichi!… Kindaichi!" The two veins on the inspector's forehead looked as though they were about to burst. "Where on earth did these come from?!"

"From Joji Yoshida, of course. Junkichi's nephew. He brought them to me earlier from Kobe, where they were hidden away in a newspaper archive."

"You're saying that Onda's photos were printed in a newspaper?"

Deputy Inspector Tachibana still looked sceptical.

"Yes, only not as photos of Ikuzo Onda, but as Shiro Aoyagi, the famous silent-film narrator from Kobe in the early twenties…"

Kosuke Kindaichi Speculates

Moments of shock or sudden excitement are usually followed by feelings of emptiness or relief, and this is exactly the kind of atmosphere that now prevailed in the back room of Doctor Honda's surgery.

Shiro Aoyagi, the famous silent-film commentator, was also Genjiro, from the Turtle Spring. Genjiro had been killed at the age of twenty-eight, but in these photographs he seemed older. In all the dignity of his profession, and with a moustache, he might well have passed for thirty-four or thirty-five.

So, Ikuzo Onda was Genjiro. It was, thanks to these three photographs, an undeniable reality. Twenty-three years ago, the man had played two roles at once. So, it was only natural that when Genjiro vanished from this world, so too did Ikuzo Onda.

In the now quiet room, all that could be heard was the hum of an electric fan and the sobbing of Harue and Sakie.

"What a story! What a story!" young Doctor Honda, who had just returned, kept repeating.

Deputy Inspector Tachibana, for his part, doffed his cap and paid tribute to Kosuke Kindaichi's perceptiveness.

"But now that we know that Ikuzo Onda and Genjiro were one and the same person," he said, "do you have any idea who the murderer was back in 1932?"

"It could only have been Rika…" said Inspector Isokawa, his voice trailing off.

"Ah, yes, of course! But then, did Mr Tatara know this?" asked Kahei, edging closer.

"He must have done… Hence the *temari* song," said the famous detective.

"How do you mean exactly?"

"Well, what was the line? 'And, sure enough, having hunted high and low, some girls he found, But he talked and talked and talked too much, And so to sleep he had to go, Put to sleep with chieftain's death he was…'?"

"Then, Kindaichi-san, you believe that Mr Tatara was killed?"

"I really must apologize, Deputy Inspector Tachibana. It seems that all I've done is raise unnecessary questions and thrown the investigation off course. To be specific, it was none other than I who first fell into Rika's trap."

"Her trap…?"

"Now, wait just a minute, Deputy Inspector…" It was old Doctor Honda who addressed the group. "If we all ask a hundred and one questions, there'll be no end to this. Inspector, don't you think it would be much more logical if Kindaichi-san began by explaining the 1932 case first?"

The doctor's proposal met with no objection.

"Well, I'd be only too happy to, but you have to understand that at this point all I can do is speculate…"

Having received the general approval, he continued:

"I'm going to offer up some ideas, but, please, don't make me do all the talking. You can all speak up, too. Let's call it an exchange of ideas."

This, too, received the group's consent.

"We-well then…" said Kosuke Kindaichi, stammering slightly. "The first time that the man called Ikuzo Onda appeared in Onikobe was at the end of 1931, which, if you think about the timing in terms of the film industry, was an important year. It was just as the talkies were beginning to take off, and those people who'd worked as silent-film narrators were starting to worry about their future prospects. Mr Kusakabe, you must remember this well, surely?"

"Oh, absolutely," he replied, casting his mind back. "I remember that it was in 1933 that those narrators had their last gasp, so the two years before that must have been a real period of turmoil."

"Exactly! That's why Genjiro, or should I say Shiro Aoyagi, probably felt uneasy about his future and felt compelled to jump ship. So, for whatever reason, he decided to try his hand as a tinsel broker. It's one thing that he decided to start off back in his home town, but I wonder: what do you make of the fact, Doctor Honda, Mr Nire, that he decided to conceal his identity?"

"Perhaps it was only to be expected," replied the old doctor. "After all, the villagers here would never have trusted somebody from the Turtle Spring… What do you say, Mr Nire?"

"I agree, Doctor. The villagers never change…"

"Yes, for all his good looks," the doctor continued, "he'd never have got anywhere if people knew he was connected to the Turtle Spring. That's just how the countryside is, Kindaichi-san. Even more so before the war."

"Still though," Detective Inui chimed in, "no matter how he might have tried to hide his roots, I do find it incredible that not a single person in the village recognized him."

"But that's just it, Inui," said Inspector Isokawa. "The incredible really did happen. Now that I think about it, I can see how it would have been possible. Genjiro left the village as soon as he finished primary school, and, until he came back fourteen years later, everybody in the village had forgotten he existed. What's more, the little boy who had once been so quiet and unassuming had now become a gentleman with a silver tongue, so nobody would even suspect that the boy and the man were one and the same. In fact, when the doctor here saw this photograph earlier, he immediately said that it was Ikuzo Onda. Even he didn't realize that the man was really the second son of the Aoike family…" The inspector's face was filled with deep emotion. "I'm sorry for interrupting, Kindaichi. Please, continue."

"Thank you, Inspector. Well, one way or another, Genjiro came back to the village under the pseudonym Ikuzo Onda, and after that he must have cosied up to the richest family in the village: the Yuras. At any rate, it doesn't really matter how he did this. Whatever the case, both Mr and Mrs Yura fell for Genjiro's patter lock, stock and barrel. I should say, however, for Yukari's sake, that I don't believe Genjiro intended to cheat them from the very outset. As the inspector and others have suggested, I really do think that in the beginning he wanted to introduce the business as a lucrative sideline for the farming community here. The fact that he used a false name, as Doctor Honda and Mr Nire have just pointed out, is sooner indicative of some inferiority complex, and this in turn could have led to his relationships with Atsuko and Sakie…"

"What do you mean by that, Kindaichi-san?" asked Kahei, taken aback. "How could Genjiro's inferiority complex lead to relationships with Atsuko and Sakie?"

"I believe what Kindaichi-san is trying to say," Doctor Honda cut in, seeing the detective's hesitation, "is that ever since childhood, Genjiro had been at the bottom of the social pile and had a deep-rooted sense of inferiority. But, when he arrived in the village as Ikuzo Onda, the Yuras, not knowing who he really was, made such a fuss of him. And so, all it took was a little bit of seduction for Atsuko to come running. She belonged to the most powerful family in the village. Then, having won her over, he set his sights on the daughter of another powerful family— the Nires—and tried his luck with her… In other words, what

Kindaichi-san is trying to say is that Genjiro's relationships with Atsuko and Sakie were born of a desire for revenge… Have I understood you correctly, Kindaichi-san?"

"Forgive me, Doctor, but saying so is very harsh on poor Sakie here…"

"But, Kindaichi-san, there's no need to sugar-coat it. What better time to set the record straight? So please, you mustn't be afraid to tell us all the unvarnished truth."

Sakie did indeed press her handkerchief to her eyes, but she did not look offended; rather, she looked as though a burden had been lifted from her shoulders.

"So, it wasn't just revenge against these two families, but against the entire village? And these two girls happened to be the ones into whom that desire for vengeance was channelled?"

"No," replied Kosuke Kindaichi, "it wasn't only about revenge. Of course, sex played a large part in this, too. Take this newspaper piece about Shiro Aoyagi, for instance: it suggests he was quite the Don Juan and had a never-ending string of women. So, while he might well have had a lot of love to give, deep down in his heart…"

"Deep down in his heart," Doctor Honda carried on, "there was also a strong desire to make toys of Atsuko and Sakie, who both came from the most powerful families in the village. At least, that's a possibility. There was a lot of discrimination in the past, after all…"

"But if that's so," said Koreya Kusakabe, "then what about Harue here? Was she also a victim of his desire for revenge?"

"No," said Kosuke Kindaichi. "In fact, I think that his love for Harue was the only thing about him that was real. And I believe this fact was the cause of everything that happened back in 1932. What do you think, Inspector?"

"Well, when you put it that way…" he mumbled somewhat distractedly. "What exactly makes you say that?"

"I'd like to hear your opinion first, Inspector. Would you mind telling us?" said Kosuke Kindaichi.

"Oh, well, um… You see, Mr Kusakabe," said the inspector, trying to recover an air of authority, "Rika's story was that Genjiro planned to leave her and the children at the Turtle Spring, while he headed off to Manchuria on his own to set himself up there. However, by Harue's own admission, Onda had already promised to elope with her to Manchuria. Is that right, Harue?"

"Yes, Inspector."

Harue's cheeks flushed as the topic of conversation turned to her, while Yukari's eyes were gleaming brightly.

"When you compare their stories, it seems clear that Genjiro was planning to leave Rika and Kanao at the Turtle Spring and run off to Manchuria with Harue. There must have come a point when Rika got wind of this… At least, that's how I understand it, Kindaichi."

"I see…"

"But then," said young Doctor Honda, "are you saying that Genjiro continued to play these two roles even after he brought his wife and child back here?"

"Well, that's precisely what I'd like to ask Harue about. Do you have any ideas on this point?"

"Listening to you speak," she said, "I'm reminded of a number of things… For instance, he shaved off his moustache about a month before the tragedy took place… He made up some excuse about it not being the done thing to have a moustache in Manchuria…"

"Yes," added Kahei. "Onda was killed in the cottage belonging to Mr Tatara. When it was still standing, that cottage was only a short distance from the Turtle Spring. So, if Genjiro did want to play both roles, there'd be nothing to stop him. Onda only came to the village once in a blue moon, and Genjiro was supposedly busy with his preparations for Manchuria, so there'd have been any number of excuses for him to get away for a night or two at a time. Don't you think, Kindaichi-san?"

"Exactly."

"Now that I think about it, Onda never went in the direction of Sakura. At the time, I thought he was avoiding us, but perhaps he didn't want to get too close to the spot where he was born."

Many things seemed to be falling into place, and old Doctor Honda now frowned as he recalled the tragedy.

"So, then, Kindaichi-san," he said, taking a deep breath. "Genjiro was pretending to be Onda, and Rika found him while he was at Mr Tatara's cottage?"

"That's certainly what seems to have happened. Genjiro probably had no intention of committing fraud in the beginning, but the panic in the United States must have rattled him. And, to make matters worse, silent-film narrators were on the way out. So, partly out of desperation, he'd decided to leave his wife and child in his home town and run off with his mistress to make a new life for himself out in Manchuria. At the time, it would have been safe to make Onda disappear, but in order to make a fresh start, he'd have to scrape together a little extra money."

"And that's when Rika caught him out?" suggested Kahei.

"No, Mr Nire, it's just a hypothesis, but my guess would be that the village chieftain warned her."

Several people in the room gasped.

"Yes, yes! That must be it!" exclaimed Kahei. "Mr Tatara was the one renting the little cottage to Ikuzo Onda, so he must have got to know his secret."

Kahei paused, mulling over the implications of this.

"Precisely," said Kosuke Kindaichi. "Here, I'd like to remind everybody that the tragedy was far from being a premeditated crime. The fact that the murder weapon was an axe that just happened to be lying there suggests this. I'd like to say in Rika's defence, however, that she was pregnant at the time. And besides, she'd suddenly found herself in the unenviable position of living in a strange part of the country with her mother-in-law, which must have been very distressing for her. Of course, it seems likely that she was by nature quite a volatile person. Besides, she'd probably been troubled by her husband's philandering for some time, and so this must have been the last straw. Finding out would doubtless have sent her into a blind rage, so there's probably room for a little compassion here. Ah, of course, Harue…" he said, flustered. "I'm not blaming you for this in any way. What I'm trying to say is that the tragedy that took place was probably a crime of passion. And that's why I don't believe that Rika, after killing her husband in such a fit of passion, would have been capable of deceiving the investigating team, no matter how clever she may have been."

"I see what you mean, Kindaichi," said the inspector, nodding automatically. "So, you're saying that it was the village chieftain who arranged it so that we wouldn't be able to recognize the victim's face, and that he took advantage of Genjiro's double life to pull the wool over our eyes?"

"Of course!" Deputy Inspector Tachibana interjected. "He knew the secret and was using it to blackmail Rika."

"Blackmail?!" exclaimed old Doctor Honda. "Inspector, is there any truth to this?"

Here, Inspector Isokawa explained to the doctor the secret of Mr Tatara's living expenses, the origins of which were such a mystery.

The doctor was astonished.

"But, Inspector, I may not have liked Mr Tatara all that much, but, even though he had his faults, as the scion of a family of village chieftains, he was a terribly proud man. I don't believe for a second that he would ever have taken advantage of another person's weakness and blackmailed them. Don't you agree, Mr Nire?"

"It's just as the good doctor says," said Kahei. "Even if his living expenses did ultimately come from the Turtle Spring, the village chieftain wouldn't have been blackmailing Rika. It's more likely that she would have offered it to him. Given his nature, I think it would have been very hard for him to accept favours from somewhere like the Turtle Spring. But it seems he did."

"In the end, though, it amounts to almost the same thing," the doctor commented.

"Yes, I suppose you're right," said Inspector Isokawa, nodding again. "Well then, now that we've put the 1932 case to bed, why don't we now turn to these recent events and let Kindaichi-san tell us what he thinks?"

There were no objections.

"Please, Kindaichi-san," said young Doctor Honda, offering him a beer.

"Oh, er, thank you," he said. "Well, once again I'd like to know your opinions, so let's have a discussion. Deputy Inspector?..."

"Yes?"

"Now that you know that Onda and Genjiro were one and the same person, I'd like you to reconsider Rika's motives based on that fact."

"Thank you for the second chance, Kindaichi-san," he said, scratching his head. "I appreciate it... Here's what I think. If there had been no trace left of Ikuzo Onda, then none of these recent events would have taken place. But, fortunately or not, the man left behind three children, each one to a different woman. Moreover, he also left his lawful wife with child. Then, the following year, all four women gave birth, all of them having girls. This was, I think, the ultimate cause of these events."

"He's right!" said old Doctor Honda, nodding. "You suggested earlier that Rika's motive was that her daughter wasn't as beautiful as the others, but there was more to it than that, wasn't there? Though Rika's own legitimate daughter wasn't beautiful, the other daughters born to the women who had stolen her husband away from her all turned out to be great beauties. This must have been awfully hard for Rika to bear... Do you suppose this was one of her motives, Kindaichi-san?"

"Not just one of her motives, Doctor Honda, but the cause of everything... I do believe that, given her fragile psychological state, this would have been almost unavoidable for her."

"Well, when you put it in those terms, Kindaichi, it makes Rika seem like quite a pitiful woman," said Inspector Isokawa.

"Yes, that is what I believe."

Kosuke Kindaichi's sombre tone calmed everyone down a little, but Tachibana could not afford to dwell on such sentimentality right now and said:

"But if that's true, then Rika must have known that Yasuko, Fumiko and Yukari were Genjiro's daughters..."

"Precisely, Deputy Inspector. Mr Tatara knew that all three girls had been fathered by Ikuzo Onda. And what's more, Mr Tatara and Rika had long been bound together by their shared secret. So, even though we can't be certain when exactly he divulged all this, I think he must have done so out of concern for Rika. And because of Kanao, especially."

Kahei began to tremble violently.

"Mr Tachibana," he said, "you said earlier that we were trying to force our daughters on Kanao, whereas in reality it was far more serious than that. We were trying to force his half-sisters on him…"

"Yes, that's right," said old Doctor Honda, heaving a sigh. "And, to make matters worse, Rika couldn't say anything about it. To say something would have meant revealing what had really happened back in 1932, which would have been tantamount to slipping a noose around her neck."

"So, she'd been backed into a corner," young Doctor Honda muttered.

Suddenly, there was a burst of sobbing in the corner of the room.

Sakie was dabbing her eyes with her handkerchief. Her maternal grief was probably setting in again as she contemplated the tragedy that would have ensued if her daughter had unknowingly married Kanao.

"So, there was Rika's psychology on the one hand, but then it was the two marriage proposals, as well as Yukari's phenomenal success, that really lit the fuse to this whole affair," said Kosuke Kindaichi.

"Yukari's success?" said Harue, looking both startled and frightened.

"Well, yes, Mrs Bessho. After all, when she was young, Rika also performed in the *yose* theatre. I think that's why her admiration for those who had achieved success in the arts was stronger than most. Her husband must have been the same. But then, her daughter being the way she was… And for the daughter born to Genjiro's mistress to inherit all his talent… Surely that must have been awfully hard for her to stomach as well."

"Why, yes! Yes, of course," exclaimed Koreya Kusakabe, startling them all. "It all makes sense."

"This is all very interesting, Kindaichi-san," said Deputy Inspector Tachibana, sitting up, "but now that we understand Rika's motivation, could you tell us a little more about the murders?"

"Of course, Deputy Inspector, but once again, let's discuss it as a group. I'll set the ball rolling, shall I?" he said, slaking his thirst with a sip of beer. "We've no way of knowing exactly when it was that Rika finally made up her mind to do all this, but it could have been when Yukari had her splendid mansion built in the village. Alternatively, it could have been when she received the offers of marriage from the Yuras and the Nires... They both happened around the same time, in any case, and I suspect they are what triggered things."

"Yes, come to think of it, those events did coincide, more or less," said Kahei, blinking.

"It occurs to me that Rika must have always been at least a little suspicious of Mr Tatara. After all, he held her fate in the palm of his hand. Even if what Doctor Honda and Mr Nire say is true, and Mr Tatara wasn't a bad man, it's still understandable that Rika would feel insecure. Hence, she would have been constantly wary of him, keeping a close eye on everything he said and did. This is why I suspect Rika would also have known about the article he'd published in *Folk Traditions*. Just imagine her surprise when she discovered that the three girls mentioned in the *temari* song belonged to the same families that her husband's illegitimate children belonged to. Perhaps it was from that moment on that Rika, even subconsciously, began hatching her plan."

"It's certainly feasible," said Inspector Isokawa. "Thus, the first thing to do would be to kill the village chieftain, hide his body and then shift the blame for the murders onto him."

"Of course... And I was the very first to fall into the trap that Rika had laid."

"What do you mean by that, Kindaichi-san?" asked Kahei.

"Just that a short while ago, you and the doctor were totally against the notion that Mr Tatara would have resorted to blackmail. And yet, despite that, when we found out that these murders were being carried out in accordance with the *temari* song, everybody—myself included—immediately suspected the village chieftain of being the murderer. Not least because of that article he submitted to *Folk Traditions*. In other words, Mr Tatara was not the sort of man who'd blackmail somebody, but he *was* the sort of man who could very well have been responsible for the string of *temari*-song murders…" Here, Kosuke Kindaichi seemed to realize something. "We could go on speculating like this for ever, so perhaps we'd better move on to something more concrete."

"By all means," said Deputy Inspector Tachibana.

"Well, for starters, Mr Tatara moved to the cabin on the bank of the marsh in May of last year. I suspect that this was also at Rika's suggestion, so that she could keep a closer eye on him. And as a result, last summer she took what I believe could be called a preparatory step for the murders…,"

"And what was that, Kindaichi-san?" asked old Doctor Honda, looking startled.

"Well, last summer, O-Rin sent a letter to Mr Tatara, in which she asked whether they should make another go of it. I think it's likely that this letter was delivered while he was out, and that Rika came across it by chance and decided to hide it. I doubt it ever occurred to her that she could perhaps use it later, but it just so happened that O-Rin had been Mr Tatara's wife at the time of the tragedy back in 1932. That's probably why Rika didn't like the notion of her coming back to the village to be at Mr Tatara's side. And so, having hidden that letter, she would have had no choice but to hide the notice of O-Rin's death last spring when it arrived—again, probably when Mr Tatara was out."

"Because if Mr Tatara turned up at the funeral and found out that somebody had concealed the previous letter, it would cause problems."

"Exactly."

"And then," said Deputy Inspector Tachibana, "having kept the letter that she had intercepted last year, she put it back into the envelope, resealed it and, with a look of innocence, left it at the cabin for Mr Tatara to think that it had just been delivered."

"That's right… Most people don't think to check the postmark when they receive a letter, do they?"

As he said this, Kosuke Kindaichi recalled the joy with which Mr Tatara had responded to the letter.

"But, Kindaichi-san, what do you suppose became of the reply that you wrote on Mr Tatara's behalf?"

"I was just wondering about that myself, as it so happens. On the day I wrote it for him, I went back to the Turtle Spring and mentioned the whole episode to O-Miki. I told her that O-Rin was coming back and that I'd written the reply for Mr Tatara myself… Rika must have heard about this from O-Miki, headed straight for the cabin and made off with the letter on some pretext. There are any number of things she could have said, after all. 'I'm just about to pop into the village, so why don't I post it for you?' It wouldn't have been difficult for her to do this."

"But, Kindaichi-san," said young Doctor Honda, leaning in. "Why did Rika have to drag O-Rin up again? Just to muddy the waters with another shady character?"

"Yes, and at the same time to make everybody think that it was Mr Tatara playing two roles."

"Of course... She'd been inspired by the events twenty-odd years ago!" Old Doctor Honda shook his head in near disbelief.

"Another thing is the fact that she had your number, Kindaichi-san," said Kahei. "Didn't she? Even I knew who you were, so she, not least because of a past like hers, would have known exactly who you were right from the very start."

"Yes, you're quite correct, Mr Nire. The proof of that came when Rika, disguised as O-Rin, was heading to the village on the night of the 10th."

"Speaking of the 10th... That was the night when the memorial service was being held at the Yuras' house, and Rika had gone there to help. So, did she rush from the Yuras' house to the Sennin Pass and lie in wait for you, Kindaichi-san?"

Kahei's question produced an indescribable look of horror on the famous detective's face. There was a brief pause, and then, having just recalled the list with ten points that Kosuke Kindaichi had once written down for him, Deputy Inspector Tachibana extracted it from his pocket.

"Kindaichi-san, the eighth point in your list asks whether it was possible that Mr Tatara, after sitting opposite O-Rin for more than two hours, could have failed to clock that it wasn't her, and if so why? Are you able to explain this?..."

"Deputy Inspector," he replied, grinning broadly to reveal his white teeth, "at the very end of that list I also mentioned the salamander, didn't I? That terrible creature holds the key to your question."

"How so?"

"It was in fact Junkichi Yoshida's widow in Kobe who told me. Apparently, Mr Tatara's vision had been deteriorating in recent years, to the point where he suffered from night-blindness."

A cry of surprise went up in the room. To lose one's sight must surely have been a bitter experience for a man like Mr Tatara.

"So, you see, Tachibana: knowing this, we can reasonably assume that it would have been impossible for Mr Tatara to blackmail anybody—he would surely have felt too vulnerable to attempt such a thing. He must have contented himself with the meagre stipend that Rika gave him and didn't dare ask for anything more. And every summer, Mrs Yoshida would receive a letter complaining about his eyes, while at the same time Mr Tatara went about the village, hiding the fact."

"And only Rika knew about it!"

Deputy Inspector Tachibana's sudden exclamation made everybody turn and look at him.

"All right, Kindaichi," said Inspector Isokawa with a sigh. "So, Mr Tatara wanted to rekindle his relationship with O-Rin and was trying to 'boost his energy' with the salamander?"

Nobody laughed at the chieftain's tragic efforts. When they recalled the ghastly scene that must have been enacted between an old man and Rika dressed as the old woman on the banks of the marsh in the middle of a heavy thunderstorm, they could not help but gasp with horror. That scene had been the beginning of the *temari*-song murders.

"How do you suppose Rika disposed of the body, then?" the inspector asked Kosuke Kindaichi.

"Well, that's just it. She's too slight to have carried the body any distance, so at first I assumed she must have thrown it into the marsh. But then I noticed all the wheelbarrows around here. It would be possible to transport a body some distance using one of those, so, 'man-eating marsh' or not, I'd search for the body elsewhere. As for where, exactly, I'm reliant on all your ideas, since you're much more familiar with the village than I."

"With your permission, Kindaichi-san, there's one thing I'd like to ask before we move on to that. I understand that Mr Tatara had trouble with his sight. But what I can't work out," said Kahei, still blinking, "is how Yasuko could have been taken in so easily."

"Ah, that… Deputy Inspector, do you have with you the letter that lured Yasuko out?"

"Yes, here it is, Kindaichi-san."

"Would you be so good as to show it to everyone?"

What he produced was a letter that had been written on a scrap of paper with a very shaky brush. The content of the letter was as follows:

If you want to know the dark secret of your father's death, meet me at nine o'clock this evening behind the temple at Sakura, where I shall reveal this to you.

Hoan Tatara

"At first, Mr Nire, when I saw the letter, I naturally assumed that the father mentioned was Utaro. But when I heard from Doctor Honda here that there was no dark secret surrounding Utaro's last moments, and then, the very next evening, when you told me that Yasuko's real father was in fact Ikuzo Onda, it suddenly struck me that the letter must have been referring to Onda. This made me suspect that the letter must have originally had more to it. That is why I asked Detective Yamamoto earlier to take the letter to Toshio, the man who discovered it, and ask him outright."

"Ah, so that was what all that was about!" exclaimed Deputy Inspector Tachibana. "So, what did he say?"

"Just as I expected, there was more to it. Toshio had thrown it away, but fortunately he remembers what it said. Here, Deputy Inspector, I think you'd better read this."

The deputy inspector glanced down at the letter, groaned and then read it out for everybody to hear.

Yasuko,

I am sure you already suspect this, but you are not Utaro's daughter. Your real father was a man called Ikuzo Onda, who disappeared in 1932. Your mother had an affair with this man, and you were born of that union. Though your father is said to be missing, the truth of the matter is that he is dead. Therefore: …

Tachibana paused. "So, Toshio wanted to protect his family from shame and hid the most important part of the letter…"

"But in that case," said Inspector Isokawa, shaking his head, "wouldn't that imply that the Yuras already knew that Utaro wasn't Yasuko's real father? Given that the girl was so easily lured out with this?"

"Well, Inspector," said old Doctor Honda, "it isn't my place to reveal the secrets of other families, but I will say this. Utaro was so enraged by this secret that in the end it was the death of him. When he told me about it, I must admit I had my doubts. But then, when his widow took up with Mr Nire for a while… Are the police and Kindaichi-san aware of this, Mr Nire?"

"They are, Doctor. I confessed this to them only the other day."

"But if all this is true, then it must have been Rika who wrote the letter!"

"Bravo, Doctor. In fact, you were the one who first hit upon the truth of that letter!" said Kosuke Kindaichi.

"I was?"

"Yes, when I asked you whether Mr Tatara could ever have written the letter with his right hand, you said that it would have been simpler just to write it with his left. Rika must have written it with her left hand. Just try it, and you'll see yourself how your writing shakes just like this."

"I see…"

Everybody looked at those uneven characters once again.

"Well, Kindaichi-san," said Kahei. "That just about explains it for Yasuko. But what about our poor Fumiko? What pretext do you suppose Rika used to lure her out?"

"That was after Yasuko's wake, Mr Nire, wasn't it? I suspect she must have mentioned something to do with Kanao. Maybe something about their proposed marriage? Or perhaps told her that Kanao was waiting for her at the winery?"

"Yes, I see. She really was in love with Kanao… But then, was it Rika who told her to bring the balance and the *mayudama*?"

"She must have done. Fumiko would have thought it odd, but she probably took it as a sign that things were progressing."

"What about the shadow of the old woman on the storehouse wall at the Yuras' house? That was the same night, wasn't it?" continued Kahei.

"Rika must have staged it," said the famous detective, chuckling. "On the one hand, everybody knew that she was in the Yura residence at the time, so nobody would think to suspect her. On the other, she most likely wanted to maintain a general atmosphere of fear in the village. Besides, all it took to frighten a jittery girl like that was a torch and a shadow puppet."

"I see," said Inspector Isokawa, nodding. "Then, what about Satoko?"

"Well, I'd like to ask Yukari about that," said Kosuke Kindaichi, turning to the singer.

"Kindaichi-san!" cried Yukari, clutching her handkerchief with a terrified look in her eyes. "I think Satoko took my place…"

"Chieko!" exclaimed Harue, startled. "What do you mean?"

Yukari suddenly burst into tears, and everybody looked at each other in shock. Having waited for her sobs to subside, Kosuke Kindaichi spoke in a hoarse voice:

"Tell me, please, Yukari. Do you have any particular reason for thinking that?"

"Yes," she said, wiping away her tears. "It was on the night of Fumiko's wake. Satoko and I went outside to get some air. We'd both left our bags in the main room. When we came back not much later, I returned to my seat and opened my handbag to find a sealed envelope with a note inside. Thinking it was odd, I showed it to Satoko. When she saw it, she became flustered and said, 'Oh, it's my mistake. It was for me. Our handbags look so similar that I must have put it in the wrong one.' And with that, she snatched it out of my hand and put it away. The handbags were almost matching ones that I'd brought as gifts from Tokyo. I didn't even think to question what she said…"

"It must have been a letter telling you to come to the crossroads, mustn't it?"

"Yes," said Yukari, glancing tearfully at the letter that had lured Yasuko away. "It must have been a letter just like that. I'd almost begun to open the envelope, but Satoko…"

"What would you have done, Yukari, if you'd opened the letter and found a note telling you that Ikuzo Onda was your father?"

"I wouldn't have been able to resist going. Even if I knew it could be a trap…"

"You wanted to know who your father was so very badly?"

"Yes, I'd have given my life to know who he was. I don't know how many times I've thought this, ever since I was a little girl."

The group waited for Yukari once again to master her sobbing. Eventually, old Doctor Honda lamented:

"I suppose it's only natural. Yasuko must have thought the very same."

Everybody nodded in silence, as Yukari choked back yet more tears.

"Given that Satoko knew her own mother was responsible for these terrible murders," she said, "she must have known what lay in store and went to take my place, knowing that she'd die. That's just the kind of person she was."

"How do you mean?"

"She was a very kind-hearted person with a strong sense of self-sacrifice. When we were at school together after the war, she was the only person who sympathized with my situation. We always looked out for one another."

Yukari burst into tears again, but nobody tried to stop her. Those who had been through the hardships of life knew that it was better to let the child cry as much as possible.

It was Deputy Inspector Tachibana who broke the silence a few moments later.

"I understand all this, Kindaichi-san, but why did Rika have to strip Satoko naked?"

"Why do you think?"

"Well, on the night in question, Satoko was wearing her mourning clothes, whereas Yukari was wearing an evening gown. So, in order for Satoko to take Yukari's place, she would have had to change into a dress. That must be why she quickly sneaked back into the Turtle Spring and changed her outfit before making her way to the crossroads. After killing her, Rika must have been shocked to discover that it was actually Satoko. But since she didn't want there to be the slightest hint that Satoko had taken Yukari's place, she had to get rid of the dress. What do you think, Kindaichi-san?"

"I'd agree with that theory."

"But then, whatever happened to Satoko's mourning clothes?"

"They'll most likely be hidden at the bottom of a chest of drawers in the Turtle Spring. Rika probably intended to fetch the mourning clothes and put them on Satoko's body, but she must have run out of time."

"Thank you, Kindaichi-san," said the deputy inspector, bowing solemnly.

A profound silence then descended over the group. Nobody said a word, for they were all lost in their own thoughts. There were still lingering doubts and questions, but each of those gathered there seemed afraid to break the heavy silence. It had been a terrible ordeal, and the horrible memory of it would remain with them. However, Satoko's final act of self-sacrifice had warmed everybody's heart just a little.

It was Deputy Inspector Tachibana who again broke the silence.

"Kindaichi-san, there is one last thing that I'd like to ask you…"

"Oh yes? And what would that be, Deputy Inspector?"

"When exactly did you realize that Ikuzo Onda and Genjiro Aoike were the same man?"

The question was a good one. All of them, even a still-tearful Yukari Ozora, turned to look at the detective.

He paused for a moment before speaking.

"You see, Deputy Inspector, as I listened to all your accounts, including that of the inspector here, I began to form an image in my head of this man known as Ikuzo Onda. He was a handsome man with gold-rimmed spectacles and a moustache, a fine orator, a decent enough sort who did not originally intend to commit fraud, even if that's how it turned out. And yet, where his relationships with women were concerned, he was rather

311

unscrupulous. That was the impression I had of the man. But when I came to this village, I also learnt that the victim, Genjiro, had used his voice professionally, that he had, moreover, been a tremendously popular silent-film narrator, and that he had two beautiful children… For, were it not for her birthmark, Satoko would also have been a great beauty, don't you think?"

"Oh, absolutely, Kindaichi-san," readily agreed Kazuko, the young doctor's wife who had just joined them. "That's why everybody felt so much sorrier for her."

"It struck me that the father of those two must have been a handsome enough man, and the more I thought about it, the more the image of Ikuzo Onda and that of Shiro Aoyagi drew closer and closer. I knew that many of those old film-industry people had a reputation for being lady-killers, and I could read between the lines of what Rika said that she'd had a bit of trouble with him in that regard. I believe the inspector here had a similar impression."

"That's right enough, I did," he said, bowing his head.

"However, there was one thing that was stubbornly keeping these two images apart. And that was that the villagers themselves didn't suspect that Onda, Aoyagi and Genjiro could all be the same person. However, my reluctance to make that connection between the two images was finally dispelled when Mr Nire told me, on the evening of the fifteenth, that before Genjiro's death, nobody in the village had any idea that he'd become such a star in Kobe. Later, I asked Mrs Bessho about Ikuzo Onda's physical characteristics, and found that they seemed to match those of the victim in the 1932 case. So, I decided to go to Kobe."

"So, you went there with the intent of looking for photographs of Shiro Aoyagi rather than for a copy of *Folk Traditions*?"

"Yes. If I'd only needed a copy of the magazine, I could easily have just telephoned the Yoshida household. Still, I was lucky that there were photographs of Shiro Aoyagi…"

He bowed his head, after which there was another pregnant pause. The heavy silence was broken by Inspector Isokawa's raucous laughter.

"Doctor Honda!" he said, sounding almost delirious. "What idiots we've been! From the very start, you were so certain that the corpse was Genjiro's, while I continued to suspect that it was Onda's. We were both so stubborn. Why did it never occur to us that they could have been the same person?"

"What a thing to say, Inspector!" said the old doctor, his wide eyes glaring. "But if I had brains good enough to work that one out, then I wouldn't be a doctor out here in the countryside…"

"No, I suppose you'd have gone to Tokyo a long time ago and opened the Honda Detective Agency!"

Kahei began to laugh, and even Sakie, Harue and Yukari and the policemen got caught up in the general mirth.

It had just gone midnight, and the long-absent rain had begun to fall gently once again…

Epilogue

Thanks to Mr Kosuke Kindaichi, the Onikobe *temari*-song case, which had shaken not only Okayama Prefecture but the whole country, was solved. At the same time, it cast light on the murder that had taken place there in 1932, a case that I shall never forget. I therefore intend to record here what happened afterwards.

On the afternoon of 18 August 1955, we found the body of one Kazuyoshi Tatara, known commonly as Hoan. Kahei Nire, of the weighers' family, informed me that he was later buried in the village cemetery.

A few days earlier, on 7 August, an old woman called Kin Murasaki had died, and two days later, at around three o'clock, she had been buried in the grave of her ancestors. In this region, it is customary to bury the dead. As ever, Rika had been one of the first to rush to the funeral. Consequently, she knew the location of the grave and knew that if she dug up the freshly disturbed earth, nobody would notice. Moreover, the cemetery was near the "man-eating marsh", only a hundred yards or so from Mr Tatara's cabin. As Kindaichi-san had suggested, Rika must have transported Mr Tatara's body by wheelbarrow.

The Murasaki family had gone to the cemetery on the 15th, during the O-Bon festival, and noticed that the grave appeared somewhat disturbed. However, since the storm on the evening of the 10th had caused damage everywhere, they were not overly concerned by this. As there were no traces of upturned earth, Kindaichi-san deduced that Rika must have buried Mr Tatara's body before the storm broke; that is, before nine o'clock in the evening. This providential downpour for Rika had compacted the earth that she had turned over and made the wheelbarrow tracks disappear. The last unexplained point was the candle that had been found at the cabin. It seems likely that Rika's idea had been to make it look as though Mr Tatara was still alive during the storm.

In the end, his naked body was discovered inside the coffin, in Mrs Murasaki's arms. Mr Tatara was not a very large man, but still, the coffin was too small for two people, and so when it was exhumed, the lid was found to be ajar. Over time, the bodies would have putrefied, and the two skeletons would probably have become intertwined. Mr Tatara, who had had eight wives during his life, now found himself in death in yet another woman's embrace! This would doubtless have incurred the wrath of the deceased woman's family…

Be that as it may, Mr Tatara's corpse was found perfectly intact. We immediately noticed a mark around his neck, and so it transpired that he had not been poisoned, but in fact strangled with a cord of some type. The subsequent autopsy revealed, however, that he had already ingested a large dose of lobeline, the powerful alkaloid, and so, if he had not been strangled, he would eventually have died of poisoning. It seems likely that, when he began to suffer, Rika strangled him to death, fearing that the situation would drag on. It was a terribly cruel end for this prodigal son who had spent his life in idleness and dissipation.

That same day, Deputy Inspector Tachibana's team discovered Satoko's mourning kimono hidden in a chest of drawers at the Turtle Spring resort. It was the one she had worn for the wake, and as there were no muddy marks or bloodstains on it, we concluded that Satoko must indeed have gone home to change before proceeding to her rendezvous with death. The

316

maid, O-Miki, was now asked to confirm that the girl had been wearing an outfit that could pass for an evening dress, but they searched in vain.

Satoko's dress and Mr Tatara's clothes were, regrettably, never recovered. It is believed that Rika had time to dispose of them by burning them.

The person who suffered the greatest shock of all in this affair was undoubtedly Kanao. This handsome young man was beloved by the whole village. By killing five people, his mother, whatever her motives, has plunged him into a despair from which he will no doubt find it very difficult to escape.

At the time of writing this record, his future is yet to be decided. However, I should like to note that Koreya Kusakabe, who so admired the young man's beautiful voice, has proposed to take him under his wing and turn him into a professional singer.

I will not soon forget the words spoken by Yukari Ozora, when Kosuke Kindaichi brought her into the presence of her half-brother, Kanao, on the afternoon of 24 August:

"My brother, for I dare to call you that from now on, I want you to know that ever since I was old enough to understand, I've suffered from the fact of being the daughter of a cheat and a criminal. You can't imagine how many times I've wanted to die. But I didn't. I managed to endure the persecution by gritting my teeth. If I can do this, then somebody as brave as you will be able to do it as well. Please, be strong. You have to hang in there."

No doubt due in part to Yukari's encouragement, Kanao decided to leave the Turtle Spring to close relatives and move to Tokyo.

After winding up this affair, I took another holiday—a real one this time, with Kosuke Kindaichi. For three weeks, we relaxed in

317

the Kyoto and Osaka regions, in Yamato and Nara. We parted on 20 September, in front of Kyoto station.

Before leaving, one headed to the west and the other to the east, I thanked Kindaichi-san and told him as I shook his hand: "I'm getting old these days, but if there's still enough time left to me, I hope with all my heart I'll have the chance to work with you again—so long as it isn't on something like this! This one was truly awful, and I won't forget it in a hurry."

Without saying a word, he looked me straight in the eye. Then he took a step towards me and whispered in my ear:

"Forgive me, Inspector, but you were in love with Rika, weren't you?"

By the time I came to my senses, he was already on a train that had begun to move off.

Tsunejiro Isokawa
21 September 1955

Seishi Yokomizo

A classic Japanese
murder mystery

THE INUGAMI CURSE

PUSHKIN VERTIGO